FICTION   Smith, Lawrence R.,
SMI   1945-

           Annie's soup
           kitchen.

DISCARDED

DATE			

BAKER & TAYLOR

LITERATURE OF THE AMERICAN WEST

William Kittredge, *General Editor*

ANNIE'S SOUP KITCHEN

ALSO BY
Lawrence R. Smith

The Plain Talk of the Dead
(Hanover, 1992)

The King of the Storeroom
Trans. from the Italian
of Antonio Porta
(Hanover, 1992)

The Map of Who We Are
(Norman, 1997)

No Trace of the Gardener
Trans., with Michelle Yeh,
from the Chinese of Yang Hu
(New Haven, 1998)

ANNIE'S SOUP KITCHEN

A NOVEL

LAWRENCE R. SMITH

UNIVERSITY OF OKLAHOMA PRESS • NORMAN

This book is a work of fiction. Names, characters, places,
and incidents are either the product of the author's imagination
or are used fictitiously, and any resemblance to actual events, locales,
or persons, living or dead, is entirely coincidental.

Annie's Soup Kitchen: A Novel is Volume 13 in
the Literature of the American West series.

Library of Congress Cataloging-in-Publication Data

Smith, Lawrence R., 1945–
Annie's soup kitchen: a novel / Lawrence R. Smith
p.   cm. — (Literature of the American West; v. 13)
ISBN 0-8061-3529-8 (hc: alk. paper)
1. California, Southern—Fiction.   2. Environmentalists—Fiction.
3. Soup kitchens—Fiction.   4. Aged women—Fiction.   5. Floods—Fiction.
I. Title.   II. Series.

PS3569.M537575 A8 2003
813'.54—dc21
2002035892

The paper in this book meets the guidelines for permanence
and durability of the Committee on Production Guidelines for
Book Longevity of the Council on Library Resources, Inc. ∞

1   2   3   4   5   6   7   8   9   10

for Deedee

ACKNOWLEDGMENTS

I would like to thank Gerald Vizenor for his continuing guidance and encouragement; Jim Harrison and Jack Hicks for their valuable insights; Victoria Shoemaker for her high energy and good faith; Karen Wieder and Alice Stanton at the University of Oklahoma Press for assisting me in so many different ways; and Deanne Yorita, my partner, who also happens to be an extraordinary editor. Without her, this book would not exist.

ANNIE'S SOUP KITCHEN

CHAPTER ONE

WATERSHED

Hawks rise from the scorched canyons of east Orange County, vector toward the Pacific's mantle of shattered glass. Red-tails spinning overhead in wild lopsided circles, fix their eyes not on mice, small birds, rats, or squirrels but on piles of gravel and asphalt, big-bladed plows, pavement grinders, trenchers, and earthmovers, all at rest below in the yard of the Lemon City DPW. Not much to catch the eye here, except a blonde-bearded man in full green apron standing on the ramp that fronts a trailer turned cook shack. A slow freight trundles along one edge of the enclosure: broken pavement skirted by high chain link and barbed wire. Consecrated to Annie O'Rourke's legendary Soup Kitchen, humanity's last chance for healing, birds seldom plunder here. The alpha hawk sizes up the aproned man. Seeing he is larger than a rabbit, more than a winged predator could seize and carry off, the messenger dances toward an open blue window and the horizon that provides its hazy sill.

Every Friday in that temple of Annie's devotions Grady Roberts, the man in the green apron, performs the ritual of preparing dishes. But at this moment he's standing on the ramp, a temporary escape. The Kitchen's chatter and unspoken tension charge him with such frantic energy, his body threatens to break free and run away from him. Clear of the stove's dizzying heat, he leans into the small morning breeze. A few more deep breaths and he is ready once more to go inside and make barbecued chicken or chicken cacciatore, mashed potatoes, meatballs or Italian sausage, carrots and cauliflower with cheese sauce, ratatouille, pasta sauced with tomatoes and whatever protein can be safely recovered from the freezers and food bin. He is ready to survey the stash of reject produce pulled from the shelves of grocery stores, now stacked on the floor and countertops of Annie's Soup Kitchen. Bags of spinach and collard greens with yellowed leaves, cauliflower with black spots, tomatoes torn or barely holding under the skin, bruised and wrinkled zucchini, battered peppers, and everything else, from corn to fennel buns, that someone thought unfit to sell or eat. "First, procure the best ingredients": a maxim attributed to Apicius. But what happens when you can't? If food as devastated as this can be redeemed, cooked, and offered up to men, women, and children, then there will be a great healing.

Healing was the dream that lured the entire crew back week after week to perform those changes: energized vegetable narration, the free fall into edibility of pure goodwill. Of course, denials of the Kitchen's transformational power occurred—like the washout MBA who ignited sleeping bag, beard, and hair with a crack pipe, incinerated himself in his hideaway under a bridge on the Santa Ana city line. Yet there were remarkably few casualties, until the Shadow Plague became widely recognized.

And you can bet more than spaghetti was being conjured there. Things happened at Annie's Soup Kitchen that eluded the sharpest eye or even the most flexible fiction. Objects would come into being, then dissolve, without raising even casual interest. Leakage between dimensions occurred at every moment but was seldom perceived, except by the Magnificent Seven. In Annie's special landscape of broken pavement and ravaged souls, there were places where ordinary folks could simply disappear. There were corners of space and jointures of light and steel you could photograph one day and never see again.

Annie's eyes were sharp from the moment of her birth. In peat country, she had been conditioned by childhood encounters with the good people—those small creatures who either made an apprentice of you or turned your brains inside out. Leaving that world when she and her sister fled Ulster for New York after the Easter Rebellion, she carried great power in her heart. Since her father was killed in the fighting and her family was on the English blacklist, she always claimed to come from Tyrone of the Bushes, unwilling to admit she'd been raised in a suburb of Belfast. Maybe the claim was God's own truth. Conceived in the land of stark changes, she might have been simultaneously delivered in each town and county, stretching the translucent pane of her transmigrating spirit over every newborn creature in the land. Ninety-five years later, after a long career as a nurse, the old trickster managed to create the world from scratch each day. She dreamed it into the animals, minerals, and vegetables that would stumble into her Kitchen's permanently temporary location in the warehouse district of Lemon City. To calculate such complex variables would require the skill of Navajo Bill, a retired Rockwell engineer who'd once worked on the Apollo project and now chauffeured Annie. He slouched through daily chores at the Kitchen: washing dishes, mopping the floor, thanking other volunteers for letting him be of service. However, since we are still triangulating vectors, that particular crossfiction will have to wait.

The ancient nurse pushed through the trailer's north door, threw hands over head, and trudged to the table where volunteers took their customary lunch break, sampling food they were about to serve. "I am honest to my God, but I can't understand what these men expect of me! You know I told them they could have one T-shirt and one pair of undershorts, the purple things that were given us by the people at the clothes store. But a man out there, big with the red face, he put on three T-shirts, each over the top of another. And when I caught him at it, I pulled them off, all three, and the one that was his own to boot. I would have pulled his drawers down and given him a good spank if I were a day younger than I am. But the truth of it is I'm old, looking like the last rose of summer and standing alone. The scripture tells us to feed the hungry and clothe the poor, and I ask no questions of them, as you know, but I can't . . ."

Annie sat down hard at the formica table pushed to the wall at one end of the cook shack. Beset with palsy, her yellow-gray hair permed into a helmet-shaped halo, everything about her vibrated. She swept a knuckle across her brow and glowered at one face after another, taking note of who was there for the first time that morning. The volunteers were terrified by her fits of temper. She'd recently had some near-death episodes—once being admitted to an emergency room with a pulse of thirty-five. Since her congestive heart failure was inoperable, everyone was sure one of her tirades would carry her off. But most often these fits led only to exhaustion and a hypoglycemic attack, as happened on this occasion. She seldom ate breakfast; a granddaughter had convinced her she needed to weight watch and lower her cholesterol. Just one or two encounters with the men, or the volunteers, and she had drained the last of her blood sugar. You could tell she had fallen into one of her spells by the turns her language would take.

"Did I point a finger and drive the demons out? Because the refrigeration, you see, the space around the food in the freezer. It's too much in there. We'll have to look into it—for the Kingdom of God has come to us right here and now, in this place and time. No, no, my dear, it's Friday and I couldn't eat flesh on Friday. Couldn't do it at all, though I can't eat fish for the life of me, either."

Grady rushed forward with a plate of mashed potatoes and creamed vegetables hot from the stove. He knew she was on the verge of passing out when her face began to twitch and her eyes turned glassy. "Annie, please eat some of this. You need it. Don't worry about the men. We'll take care of all that for you. Wanda is out there locking up the clothes bin right now. Everything's fine. Here's a fork for you. Please eat now."

Sally, a middle-aged high school girl with a taste for Martha Stewart good things, pushed a piece of her homemade apple pie before Annie. Betty sat down beside the Kitchen saint and tentatively lifted a forkful of potatoes to the shaking woman's lips. But Annie's ancient irises snapped into focus and her eyes went suddenly clear as she scrutinized the Friday lieutenant. "And what are you setting to do with me? No hand but mine has put food in my mouth since my dear mother first brought me to mass back in Tyrone of the Bushes. God bless the good woman's soul. And will you give me that fork!"

The volunteers laughed as Betty jumped up, moved to safety four paces from the table. Annie ate several bites of the potato, a taste of creamed cauliflower and carrots, then laid eyes on the apple pie. After she exclaimed on their excellence, the relieved volunteers got ready to transfer the dishes they'd prepared for the multitudes to the serving tables outside.

"Grady, you're a wonderful man to cook all of this food for us, an angel of mercy. My God, we're so thankful to have you here." Annie dropped her fork and bowed her head. Realizing she had begun, against all custom, to eat without first saying grace, she mumbled one quietly to herself, took a deep breath, straightened her back, and readdressed the mashed potatoes. After a few bites more she dropped the fork again, put both hands on the table, and tried to struggle up. "Is it time for me to pray yet? Is it almost one o'clock now?"

Betty and Marlene moved toward the table but maintained a safe distance. As always, Betty appointed herself spokesperson.

When Annie wasn't around, Betty Blankenship battered the sweet music of the Friday crew with her hollering about the leaking sink, dirty bins, irresponsible volunteers on other days of the week, and the moral and genetic failures of the poor who were being served. She'd lean down by one of the sinks, go to one knee with a melodramatic sigh, and curse the semifunctional garbage disposal. She'd sniff at a bowl of pasta salad from the back of a refrigerator shelf, curl her upper lip, and deliver her usual pronouncement: "It's good enough for *them*." Out of the corner of her eye she'd catch Grady's grimace and be pleased she'd irritated the one person who posed a challenge to her authority. After he'd dumped the contents of the bowl into a trash can, she'd call to him from the other side of the trailer, making sure he knew she'd caught him in the act. "And don't you make that food too spicy, Grady. You know they're all alcoholics with bad stomachs. They just can't take it." The Friday lieutenant would rush back and forth, flatten her A's and roll her R's in the full belief that directing one day of the Kitchen's activities would some-how make her as saintly and Irish as Annie. But these routines were never undertaken in the presence of the master.

"Oh, Annie dear, you're in no condition to go out there in the hot sun and pray. Sister Claire can do it for you. She'll do a fine job." Betty clapped her hands together to gesture piety.

"She will, Annie. Why don't you let her do it and just rest your-self?" Marlene, whose smiling face was as shy as her voice, looked over her shoulder for a seconding opinion from the nun. Both Sis-ter Claire and Grady, with no taste for futile argumentation, had already turned their eyes elsewhere. Furthermore, Sister Claire was not up to the task. Whenever she listened to Annie deliver her usual premensal prayer at one o'clock, she would always exclaim, "Good gracious, it's a regular High Mass. She's got everything covered, including all the souls in purgatory!"

Annie, still struggling to get up, cried out for assistance. "For the love of mercy, would someone come over here and help me? If I can't pray with the men, then what good am I? If I can't do this lit-tle thing, then it's surely time for the Lord to take me home."

And, as she did every day she wasn't bedridden, Annie prayed.

"We're all ready now?" The great-hearted nurse gripped the rail-ing that divided the cook shack ramp from the elevated area where an L of four long tables had been set up. From her mount, Saint

Annie looked over the line of men, women, and children. To the slothful and irreverent she shouted orders to stand, remove hats, and be humble before the Lord. She drew in a long breath, crossed herself with broad gestures. "In the name of the Father, and of the Son, and of the Holy Spirit. Amen. Bless us, O Lord, and these Thy gifts, which are Thy bounty we are about to receive through Jesus Christ Our Lord. Amen. Eternal rest grant to the souls in purgatory. May the eternal light shine upon them, may they rest in peace. Amen. I ask God in His mercy to bless each one of you, to help you, to guide you, and grant with God's help you'll soon be able to take care of yourselves."

Over fifty men, women, and children bowed their heads before the palpable power of Annie's prayer, except for a couple of smirkers who peeked up through their eyebrows, and another unbeliever who watched the car of a latecomer pass through the gate. But Annie wasn't finished yet.

"Most Sacred Heart of Jesus, we place our trust in You. We thank You, Father, for this day and the food that You're giving to us. In the name of the Father, and of the Son, and of the Holy Spirit. Amen. God bless each one of you. And we're having a great dinner."

The volunteers had been rushing out trays and pots of hot food to the tables, setting them down on a scroungy assortment of oven mitts and pot holders. They tilted their heads in deference to Annie's prayer, but the banging and chatter inside the kitchen went on at full volume, in denial of the sacred.

Annie scrutinized the front of the line. "Women, children, and workers first. We need our workers now. Last time you all left and didn't clean trays or bathrooms. I won't have it. I want the workers up in the front of the line."

The men looked contemplatively toward the horizon, or shuffled, nudging one another and chuckling. Perry stepped forward and volunteered. "I'll scrub the bathrooms, Annie."

"My God, you're a good man. And what about the rest of you? If you won't come forward, I'll lock the lot of you in here till the work is done."

Several more men stepped forward, offering to sweep and wash, and the rest breathed easy, until the man—an enormous configuration of pregnant darkness with dreadlocked prominences leaping from his skull—made his way up the stairs to the head of Annie's chow line, carrying his future strapped across his back in an overstuffed knapsack. The volunteers called him the General, because he wore five-star clusters on the lapels of his military tunic. As he proceeded toward the spread of food, silent Walkman earphones muffling the clatter around him, looseleaf Koran held up under his nose, his snort and drone, snort and drone was a chant that served as protection from the contamination that surrounded him day and night.

"Hmmmm. Bad smells, white boy smells. Praise Allah that He protects me by taking the worms from my food before it touches my tongue. His hand lets only the purest of creation enter my mouth."

As he took another step toward the food tables, the General's knee-high rubber boots, filled with sudsy water, sloshed and spilled over on the man behind him in line. Laughter from the others, curses from the victim, who hoped the General was too spaced out to hear him and retaliate.

Still droning, a sound like an extended belch. "Hmmmm. Agh! Hmmmm. Agh! That white boy Pastaman, serving up his jive white boy spaghetti. Better not get his fingers in it again, or I'll bite him good. Arf! The boy looks to me like Captain Sharple—even with his skinny-assed pathetic beard, I still recognize the cocksucker. It don't fool me. I'll give *him* some marching orders now. Hmmmm. Agh! Hmmmm. Like back at Itaewon, when old Cap'n Sharps got a mickey in the strip bar. Magic marker on his rosy-assed cheeks and lips. I let him know what black on your face means. Redneck sonofabitch.

"Hey, Pastaman, you ever been in the army?"

Grady, having caught most of the careening monologue, looked up, tried to decide how honest to be. "No."

"That's too bad, because I was. Tell me where you live. Maybe I'll show up and the two of us can play war. How would you like that?"

"Well, Grady, it seems the General has taken a liking to you." Stationed a couple of positions away, Sweet Pea giggled. She had waitressed twenty-six years at the Disneyland Hotel. In sleeveless blouse and jeans, her flirtatious laughter—receding gums and drooping eyelids notwithstanding—was always on automatic pilot. Even after raising nine children and a handful of grandchildren, she knew how to stay naughty. "You're not going to believe this, but they made us buy our own serving trays. I can't tell you how many I lost putting them on top of the car so I could get out my keys, then forgetting and driving away. Hope this doesn't offend anybody, but Walt Disney was the cheapest old booger who ever lived." After all those years of loyal service, one day she shook her blonde ringlets, dumped a full pot of decaf on the rug, and retired on $59 a month. Sweet Pea now played the stock market, chattered as she peeled and gouged the stuff she retrieved from the produce refuse boxes. She was one of four volunteers devoted to fruit and vegetable repair. And on the serving line, she dished leftover soup and salads from an upscale caterer who needed a tax deduction.

Grady was hoping the General would move down the food line and forget about him. Sweet Pea's joking remark was the last thing he needed. Dropping his eyes and stirring his spaghetti, he planned a path of flight if the General's overtures turned into a full confrontation. But the huge warrior was not going to make it easy. "Yowsa! Yowsa!" Looking up in surprise, then turning away from the General's sardonic smile, the cook put three large scoops of spaghetti and meat sauce on the warrior's styrofoam plate. The sound of crashing pans in the kitchen made the volunteer jump.

As the General moved to the next station in the serving line, manned by Ethel Springfield, he became less intimidating. After she fearlessly dished mashed potatoes and creamed vegetables onto his plate, he turned intimate and conversational. "Did you know I invented my own kind of martial arts? It makes all the women movie stars in Hollywood look at me. I'm ready for this opportunity; it makes me feel well accepted." The General bowed his head with a shy smile as he reached for his plate and moved down to Sweet Pea's station. The retired waitress dealt the caterer's castoff rice and pasta salads with a heavy hand. Most of the Soup Kitchen veterans passed them by, having gotten sick on them at one time or another, but the General took everything he was offered.

"How ya doing today, General?" Sweet Pea handed him a styrofoam bowl of Manhattan clam chowder. "You're looking good."

He moved to the next station, where Wanda, the volunteer who made sandwiches for takeaway bag dinners, served a variety of sweets. She eyed the huge mound of food on his tray. "Do you want dessert? Do you have room on there?"

"Yes. Yes."

"Cake or fruit cocktail?"

"Yes."

Wanda rolled her eyes, pursed her mouth, put a piece of cake and a cup of fruit cocktail on the General's tray. He grabbed a sack dinner from a box, sloshed down the ramp to a picnic table covered with bread, rolls, and margarine, loaded up, returned to his place under the large canopy that arched over picnic tables designated for eating. Chanting, leaking suds, he fell back into his continuous *alta voce* meditation, a careening interior monologue he shared with everyone and from which he never took a break.

~

An angel of the Lord came to Annie in a dream one night, gave her instructions on how to build the ark and tabernacle, the vehicle of the third covenant of our salvation.

"He is going to test the people mightily with a terrible plague, because they have filled the earth with violence, greed, and venality. So make yourself a commensal ark to save the righteous, and those lucky enough to be in the right place at the right time. Let there be fifteen picnic tables and thirty matching benches. Let the planks for the tables and benches be cut from Douglas fir and let them be joined together by skilled craftsmen, stained the color of dried blood. Raise upright frames of steel to hold a canopy of woven plastic thread. This tabernacle will be thirty cubits long, thirty cubits wide, and twenty cubits high at the peak. Let there be a white windscreen of woven plastic thread attached to the south side of the tabernacle. See that you make all of these things according to the pattern He has set before you."

Annie was eager to ask more about her mission, but the angel quickly metamorphosed into a bedroom dresser. The next day the chosen nurse set out to fulfill her divine instructions.

~

Under the canopy, sitting on a wooden picnic bench, performing, talking to everyone and no one, the General continued. "That's Angelique—you know, the one with the big boobies? She said she admired my style. You know, '*J'aime ton style*,' and all that. It's what she said. And I don't have to tell you what that means. But then I said, 'Baby, my contract won't carry me more than one thousand a week. Yeah, I just send in the vouchers and they redeem them. I know that's not enough for you, Baby. And they got a lifetime limit of forty million on me.' She understood because she's a Republican. You know, the Lincoln kind. Like 'Yowsa! Yowsa!' I know I got big hair and a stovepipe hat, but I ain't gonna die for no white man. You dig? I know Denzel too. In the service, together there at Khe Sanh. Didn't know which way to duck. Hands over ears, mouth open, bag full of Thai stick. It was sizzling rice everywhere you looked. And me a trained killer. But don't ask me to kill no Arabs now. They're my brothers and Allah protects the righteous. And don't call me no

Hare Krishna neither. Don't even have to move my hands to blow your raggedy white asses down the street."

A few minutes earlier, after the General had seated himself beside Roderigo at table two, loosing his torrent of circular speech, the Mexican thug assumed one of his two facial expressions: stunned confusion. His other was surliness, although sometimes he'd blend the two to achieve various nuances. But this time, as a forkful of spaghetti made a long pause halfway to his open mouth, the mask of the surly hoodlum had virtually disappeared. When the spell broke, he dropped fork to plate, swung his legs over the bench, grabbed his food tray, and bailed out, scurrying to table six.

As he sat down across from Jimmy Griffin, also known as Dracula since the four incisors between his two prominent canine teeth were missing, the refugee complained. "That motherfucker gone. Busted out his brains. Don't want no soap all over my food. *Cabrón*, big motherfucking *cabrón. Zafado!*"

Dracula leaned over, whispering a confidence. "Yeah, I know, but I think he's got some money. I don't know how he got it, but it's there in that field pack."

Roderigo threw back his shoulders, shook his curly silver mane, thrust forth the matching chest hair, revealed by a half-buttoned sport shirt, and yelled—at this moment 100 percent surly. "If he got money, he don't come around here, asshole!"

Fixing his eyes nervously on the back of the General's camouflage T-shirt, as the giant rocked, rolled, and chanted, Dracula was preparing to spring off the bench and run. "Just take it easy, man. Keep it down. I'm just telling you what I heard, man."

The nameless young woman seated at table seven, who had appeared at Annie's for the first time that day, let her eyes fix on Roderigo, raised one shoulder as if to free herself from an unwanted grasp. Her violent argument with a number of demonic presences resumed. "Oh yeah, sure you wanted me to call you then. But I was gone and you'd only blame me anyhow. That's right! Just leave me alone or I'll do it. Then they'll have to kill the Jews all over again." She began to laugh, then whimper, taking another spoonful of clam chowder. Library Lady sat next to her, protectively watching the young woman's tormented face. The other end of the table was packed with day laborers, their Spanish jabs and jokes leaving them little opportunity to notice the young woman wrestle her pack of furies.

Sitting on the edge of picnic table ten, one foot on a bench, tray balanced on his knee, Phil Tabangbang laughed largely at Madalene's habitual sarcasm, made sure his big teeth and long black hair caught the sunshine. But he was watching the new arrival, the demon-tormented girl, wondering what force other than bad parents could have left such a young person so totally bewildered. Madalene, whose working girl days were long over, whose only companion now was a yipping lap dog, its leash tied to the bench by her side, must have noticed his lack of attention. She slipped in an oblique comment about the size of Asian cocks. But since Phil could look and listen at the same time, he dropped his loaded tray on the table, pulled back his fist, and almost swept Madalene off her seat. The dog was shrieking, and everyone but the General and the possessed girl turned to watch the fight develop. However, Phil knew how easily assault charges stuck to a husky guy with a record like his, so he walked to his bicycle, pulled it away from the fence, mounted up, and rode out the gate.

Skulford Elephant sat next to John DeLorean at table fourteen. Both had watched the incident and were amused that Madalene waited until Phil was out of earshot, then unleashed a torrent of insults regarding his race, masculinity, and the fecal composition of various bodily parts. Skulford grabbed the edge of the picnic table and elevated his chin. "The earth's seven chakras need protection from defilement. Madalene has piddled on all the chakras, but most especially the first."

DeLorean laughed and shook his head, tugged at an earlobe. "Yeah, but you know more about that stuff than I do, Skulford. I just follow baseball. Can you imagine what the Dodgers would do if they could clean up the General and put him into the outfield? Yeah, have him bat cleanup! You can't tell me he wouldn't be a real slugger."

Skulford was not listening. He hummed as he fine-penned details into a new homemade baseball card. His fingertips could feel the stock tremble as it prepared to enter the world of his stacked deck. Earlier that morning, he'd tested Grady Roberts with some of these extraordinary creations.

"Guess. Go on, just tell me who it is."

The volunteer in the green apron leaned elbows on the railing, nudged glasses down, peeked over them as the card maker waved one of his works through the air. The little man who called himself Skulford Elephant possessed a pulsing energy that refused to let his misfingered hand choose a place in space and linger there. After vainly trying to follow the hand-held picture's eccentric path, Grady demanded that Skulford hold it still, then glanced away. Since the year of his sickness the cook had been unable to watch an object in rapid vibration without feeling nerves revolt, threaten to catapult him right out of his skin. "OK, what's the trick? That's Elvis, of course, but I'm sure you're going to say it's someone else."

Skulford used his proper hand to sweep back dark greasy hair, giggled, then held up another picture. It wasn't that he disliked Grady. In fact, he liked him very much. This was about trying to tease the teacher through the open door in the California air of a summering Friday. Grady had traveled a good deal but never through doors like this. He studied the quizmaster's eyes, not the card, so he never noticed how light wrapped around Skulford's morphing hand. As he gripped the railing to steady himself, the disoriented cook ran through a mental shopping list of drugs, wondered which combination had determined the itinerant's behavior. It was always hard at Annie's Soup Kitchen to distinguish substance abuse from garden variety schizophrenia. Often the two just blended together. Pathological or not, Skulford always seemed to be enjoying a joke no one else could get, and that hint of unshared knowledge irritated Grady.

He leaned forward and made an identification. "Chuck Berry." Hero of those drag-racing, rock 'n' roll days, the old duck walker was as easy a call as Elvis.

"That's right. How about this one?" Skulford shuddered, bounced his good hand through air with an image of the alpha Beatle in the full regalia of the Fab Four's Maharishi Mahesh Yogi period. Grady nailed it. Lennon had been the idol of his antiwar activist days in the late sixties. But these identifications were so effortless, he wondered momentarily if Mr. Elephant were testing reactions, using this visual trivia quiz to put together a psychological profile.

"OK, then, how about this?" Skulford's special hand looped his version of an Edward Curtis portrait through the sunlight. It looked familiar, as all Curtis photogravures do, but Grady could not find this particular warrior's name in his mnemonic file.

"Sorry, don't know that one."

"Perry Como."

The card maker's eyes surged from squinting to fullness, a blossoming burst of light—then shrank, growing dark and restless, searching for an escape route. He had to be looking for something other than the door in the air, because that had just closed. "No, no. Just kidding. It's White Cloud. And you know something? He could fly."

The General, still at his exclusive table, continued to make dinner conversation with the air. "Those agents keep calling me about my underwater martial arts. They offer me parts in action pictures and stuff. *Prelude to a Kiss*. There are probably two or three dozen movie stars asking me out now. That magazine says there's no place in Hollywood for Black men, but look at me. They're going to need two or three nuclear submarines just to try and figure out my moves. Paperback rights and subsidiaries. And that short-sheeted bed full of frogs! Drop and give me fifty more flying fucks, white boy. You know, the business end of all this is starting to get me down. I need a weekend out at my place in Palm Springs."

The chanting warrior reascended the ramp to the serving tables, asking for more food to be heaped on a plate he'd hardly touched. "Hmmmm. Hah! Hmmmm. Hah! Spaghetti, mashed potatoes. Don't want no more of that salad." As he returned to his spot at table two, the eaters all cut the General plenty of slack. They might complain in whispers about his chanting or gripe to Annie when he wasn't around, but they discreetly peeled off and shifted to other tables if he moved too close.

Annie stood above, holding the railing, exhorting the men to pitch in and clean up when they'd finished eating, take care of the service areas and bathrooms. She noticed a commotion at the tables surrounding the General's private one as he threw out his elbows, rocked back and forth on the bench, ate and chanted. Annie watched in fascination, muttered, "Lord, he's bothering the men again."

Taking courage from her leader's survey of the eating area, Betty decided to descend to the lower level and exert some authority of her own. She lurked by one of the plastic-lined fifty-five-gallon drums that served as trash cans. A young Mexican dumped his styrofoam plate and bowl into the can, clean except for the infamous rice and pasta salads, which had been given without his asking. He turned to walk away.

"Wait one minute! Where do you think you're going?" The man jumped back, shocked out of the quiet contemplation of his life as a day laborer. This woman's tone didn't match her smiling face and grandmotherly hair. "Dumping all that good food today. I bet that would make somebody a pretty good meal back where you come from."

The young man first tried to construct a retort in English but unable to do so, muttered several variations of "old witch" in Spanish. As he attempted again to walk away, Betty took another step, stayed at his side, and yelled. "Learn English! Come back here and look at me! Speak English! This is America!"

Pastaman, as Grady was known to the men, looked down on this scene from behind the serving tables atop the ramp, where he was scraping the last remnants of spaghetti and vegetables into a pan reserved for latecomers. Betty's bigotry made him so angry he'd go dizzy. He contemplated running down to the eating area and haranguing her about the Treaty of Guadalupe Hidalgo, the legal protection of Spanish as a legitimate language in the United States. But he kept silent. He had the same reaction when she'd shout out, on the serving line, that no potatoes should be wasted on Mexicans, since they only knew how to eat rice and beans. He wanted to remind her that it was the Incas who first cultivated potatoes, that she and the Irish ancestors owed their potatoes to the very people she was reviling.

Although seldom aggressive enough to defend them, Grady Roberts had a lot of ideas, notwithstanding occasional bouts of pseudodementia since his year of sickness. He was particularly proud of protein socialism, a concept hard to promote in an Orange County dominated by troglodyte conservatives. However, in spite of their suspicions concerning his politics, the other volunteers deferred to him, and nothing went into the cook pots or came out of them without his approval. Against all his protestations, Annie and the others called Grady "the gourmet chef." Having moonlighted as a restaurant cook many years before—caught in the financial crunch of a divorce—he knew the difference between cook and chef. But why argue with people who were just trying to be kind? Grady fancied himself a subversive positioned at a strategic point along the food chain. He was the worm in the apple, with dreams of transforming the entire world from just under that polished skin, all without tipping off the authorities.

After Betty's affront, Grady just grumbled to himself. He justified his usual reticence as good manners, but a deep fear of personal conflict was a more honest explanation. When Betty rushed into the cook shack and began to shout about men dumping out good food, it suddenly came to him. In all the years he'd worked at Annie's Soup Kitchen, Grady had never seen the woman eat a bite of any of those salads. Annie required all the volunteers to sit down and eat a little of everything before serving it to the men. She said it was union rules and that she wanted everyone to enjoy their meal. But it also kept people from getting careless about what they offered the folks who'd landed on the streets, or who had to make a choice between buying food or paying the rent. During this ritual, Betty always made excuses about not being hungry, or being on a diet, as she nibbled at a piece of raw carrot. Pastaman looked over the crowd—black, brown, and beige as well as white. It occurred to him that if Betty knew a single word of Spanish, or a word of any language other than English, she might begin to hear what the world thought of her.

Under the shelter of Annie's tabernacle, the General continued to eat and chant, providing good evidence that the veil of schizophrenia had given the man a precise understanding of the nature of metaphor. When the threads of creation gather together, and they do so on a regular basis, they look a lot like the coiled hair dripping with soap suds above his ferocious eyes. Earlier that morning some men complained because the General had installed himself in one of the laundry tubs where they washed food trays. He was completely clothed and taking a bath. Since Annie was busy in the clothes bin, there was a debate inside the cook shack as to what should be done. Ethel suggested calling the authorities, but everyone else knew Annie would never agree to that. She had memories of the Black and Tans, the British police in the Ireland of her childhood. They were the reason she had become an American in the first place. Police were of a "certain ilk," she'd say. And though polite when uniformed officers from the station down the street would arrive in her domain to search for a certain man, she'd mutter "The nerve of it!" when they climbed into their patrol car and drove out the gate.

Annie recognized the gates of metaphor too, and the reach of her vision traveled fast into the tunnel of primal connections. She knew the wet hair of the universe was hot-wired into the Mind of God, the electromagnetic nexus of all spirit and flesh. She knew every journey and every passing leads to the same place and time, which is always and everywhere at once. Annie would say, "May you be in heaven an hour before the devil knows you're dead," understanding that the hour before and the hour after are always happening. Her Irish sayings were pure metaphor. They simultaneously evoked and celebrated the knowledge that all watersheds on earth, all the gatherings of liquid and energy throughout the universe, come from the same drop. Annie's hands were often covered with rivulets of liquid darkness, but they possessed the power to deliver us from shadows gathering within, to allow plenary divinity to burn through.

A numbness at the back of the head pulls neck tendons into stiffness, misdirection. Neural corridors search for a message. They can hear the sound of darkness coming, the sound of the Shadow Plague gathering catastrophic cumulus that will pass over us all and leave nothing untouched. There are memories of pain and survival, of trips through the watershed of multiple betrayals, a story or hologram entitled *The Other Side*.

Sister Claire was in the trailer loading old loaves of bread into dark green garbage bags. She was preparing to drag them to her car and back to the convent, where the sisters distributed Annie's surplus bread among Latino janitors, kitchen workers, and groundskeepers. Lugging this stuff was part of her service, her penance. Maybe that push for self-denial came from guilt: her father died the night she was born. She told Grady her older sister was so angry she wouldn't speak to her until she was sixteen years old. Or maybe it was something she'd done as a navy nurse during World War II. Grady had seen a picture of her in uniform; there was no doubt she had been gorgeous, but he couldn't understand why a woman this good had anything to do penance for. To give up chocolate, her only vice? When she cut the men's hair on her makeshift barber's chair outside the cook shack, listened to their stories, maybe she took on their sins as she gathered up the pungent trimmings.

Annie edged up to the left-leaning nun, a liberation theologian, as she flipped a plastic bag of white bread to look for mold. There was a constellation of blue spots on the underside, so it went into the trash can.

"Can I talk English to you, Sister dear?"

Claire looked up from her bread and nodded. "Sure, but why are we whispering?"

"It's about the men. I'm worried about them. They need to have more work to do. Could we grow vegetables, do you think, in that place between the trailer and the railroad tracks? Peas and carrots and squash and tomatoes. I'm sure we could find someone to donate the tools and seeds. It would give the men something to do, don't you see?"

Sister Claire leaned over the sink and glanced out the window at the small plot of hardpan, separated from the railroad gravel bed by chain link and barbed wire. Annie put her hand on the nun's shoulder, lifted herself on tiptoe in an effort to see the proposed garden. "Do you think we can do it, Sister dear?"

The only evidence of life in that plot was a scruffy volunteer fan palm, the kind you sometimes see pushing up through a crack in the concrete of a street divider. It was two or three feet tall, fronds fringed with brown, stubbornly hanging on. Sister Claire turned to Annie, who was vibrating with expectancy and the neurological wear and tear of ninety-five years of activist compassion. It was hard to be a skeptic, looking into such a face.

"Annie, it isn't a question of whether we could do something out there or not but whether we want to put our energy into a project like that."

As Annie turned away and bit her lower lip, the nun caught her by the shoulder and smiled. "But I think we should look into the possibilities, don't you? Maybe the gardener at the mother house could come out and take a look at it."

Grady overheard the conversation between Annie and Sister Claire. Never having taken a good look at the space behind the trailer, it was hard for him to visualize the project. He slipped out to the food bin and pulled a large container of oregano from the spice shelf. Exiting the bin, he paused and scrutinized the hardpan. It seemed impenetrable. Then he looked at the fan palm. It vibrated slightly, gave off a burst of light that made him turn his eyes away. When Grady looked back, light dripped from the stringy fronds and onto the ground. Switching the oregano to his left hand, he returned to the cook shack.

Sister Claire had loaded up her bread, donuts, and bagels and was out in the lot trying to crank her old Ford. The car was not cooperating. Hearing her trouble, the men began to gather around her, more to sympathize than to help. Whiskey Ed, the electronics wizard and car healer, pushed through. He lifted the hood, called out instructions to Sister Claire. His frizzed wreath of white hair looked as if he'd already grabbed the battery cables by mistake. As the nun responded to instructions, grinding the starter engine one more time, a terrible screeching sent hands over ears throughout Annie's domain. But it was not Sister Claire's engine. It was the railroad track cleaning car, lumbering by, grinding metal against metal until sparks flew and teeth ground against one another for relief. Since the City Council of Lemon City didn't approve of Annie's Soup Kitchen, even in its distant exile to the warehouse district, there were rumors that the frequent rail-cleaning runs during serving time were an attempt to close her down. Or at least to make sure no one who worked or ate there was comfortable. If that were true, the folks on the city council underestimated Annie. When she'd previously fed the homeless in a public park, for almost ten years, she'd received death threats by mail and telephone, and even those didn't slow her down. After the grinder finally passed by, Annie took up her position on the ramp again, shouting to the men that they hadn't properly cleaned up. Then came the familiar threat: she'd close the gate and lock everyone in if they didn't satisfy her. The men scattered, retrieving their belongings and leaving quickly, in case Annie were in an ornery enough mood to convert parable into action.

Whiskey Ed alternately fiddled with the engine and peeked around the hood at a frustrated Sister Claire. When the flooded engine took, sending up a cloud of blue-gray smoke, Ed slammed down the hood, waved her on, and the bread angel made a large circular turn past a bulldozer, two ditchers, a steamroller, piles of gravel and tar, before heading out the gate past the retreating homeless, their kits in tow. She drove past dilapidated warehouses, the offices of the DPW, the police station, into the heat and smog of Lemon City's summer afternoon.

Long after the eating and cleaning were finished, after Annie's faithful had dispersed down the street on foot, by bicycle and car, a long-bearded stranger strode quickly toward her gate. A lone red-tailed hawk circled in the air above.

CHAPTER TWO

SHADOW PLAGUE

Although in your overflights you might miss her, a woman named California lies on her tender and explosive spine. She sings praise in the sun to the swimmers and crouchers, the spinners and fliers, as they dance over her skin, inscribing the darkness of her veins and meridians. Born in Big Bear Lake and the San Bernardino Mountains, the Santa Ana River— conduit back to the heart of the world—pulls us down sheer drops, over plateaus, and into valleys, leads us to a sacred gathering place. With a sun-bleached sign affixed to a telephone pole on the corner of Marston and Palm, the City Council of Lemon City has proclaimed the current incarnation of Annie's Soup Kitchen a "temporary location." Here time has found sanctuary, a place to rest and grow strong. The sign, and the covenant it signifies, promises to burn a hole in the darkness that cloaks our diurnal light.

Annie O'Rourke sat at the formica table—today draped with red and white plastic in feigned cotton check. The leader herself was covered in peach, a dress and string of costume jewelry pearls, both a sign of faith and hope. She sipped her coffee, set down the cup with a grimace, then stabbed a spoon into a bowl of mashed potatoes. Sweet Pea mimed silence and invisibility as she tiptoed back from the bathroom, slipping between Annie's chair and a freezer. When the chief told stories, not even Sweet Pea dared interrupt.

Annie ran through her customary prelude: a deeply drawn breath, the deliberate closing of eyes, clenching of fists, and a quiver into silence. Then the director of all Soup Kitchen activities blinked her eyelids open and spoke.

"I don't want you to think I'm complaining about the service here. You're all very good and we'll be keeping you on for another while." The volunteers who sat around the table, taking a break from prepping and cooking, could never tell where Annie's melodramatic preambles would take them, to praise or condemnation. Charitable souls who could not tolerate her tantrums, triggered by such things as the dangerous mishandling of large pots of boiled spaghetti or the overuse of aluminum foil, had dropped out along the way. "In fact, I'm going to give all of you a 100 percent raise. **But!**" The emphasis gave Sweet Pea such a start as she was sitting down, she almost missed the metal folding chair. Slapping palms to cheeks, she shook her Shirley Temple curls and cackled. Annie ignored the interruption, lowered her voice, proceeded with a sorrowful quaver. "Leaving an eye in cooked potatoes is terrible bad luck." Each of the Soup Kitchen volunteers wondered if he or she were guilty of the small gray mass Annie had removed from her bowl. "It comes from the starving time, the Great Potato Famine. The blight, you see," nodding her head at the abomination, "was a sick-looking thing like that." Over the top of her glasses, she marched her scrutiny around the table, fixing on each face for a painful moment.

Failing to hang on to a smile, Marlene drooped her shoulders. Wanda and Ethel, less willing to feel guilty or be put upon, sat taller in their chairs, stiffened their spines. Tumult intruded from outside the cook shack; unintelligible shouts flew back and forth between two parties in the area of the tabernacle, punctuated by lower voices attempting mediation.

After allowing her glance to drift momentarily out the door, Annie returned to her history lesson. "Did you ever notice that when I yawn I take my thumb and make the sign of the cross over my mouth?" She demonstrated, finishing with a kiss on the thumbnail. "It's because of the starving people. When they took their last breath, they opened their mouths and yawned. We must always bless ourselves to drive away that curse, for a plague like the Great Famine might come again. We must never, never, never let anyone go hungry." Forgetting that her spoon was once again in her right hand, Annie made a sign of the cross over her chest, dropped a bit of mashed potatoes on her optimistic dress.

~

Earlier that morning a hawk broke from one of those looping aerial rings over the Kitchen, steered southward, sighted Annie O'Rourke, nurse of the sad and joyful countenance. A few minutes before the arrival of Navajo Bill, she passed through the front door at 1525 Ross Street, formidable in house dress, hair net, and tarnished sneakers. Striking her staff of gnarled wood on the sidewalk, a sound rang out as if the ground itself were hollow. Small seeds fell from the air and scattered everywhere, first attracting doves, then sparrows and crows, mockingbirds, and a hummingbird that darted and hovered over the feast. The good woman sang her favorite Gaelic song, a lament for the loss of an enchanted forest. As she struck the staff once more, seeds rained over a sidewalk crowded with incompatible birds. When she struck the staff a third time, the circling hawk descended, joined the other birds in their peaceful pecking and Annie in her singing. As the two warriors hit a long shrill note together, the hawk rose in multicolored flame and was consumed by morning sun.

~

The Kitchen's spiritual leader would have gone on about the Great Potato Famine but was distracted by a hand rapping on the jamb of the open door. She waited for the supplicant to reveal herself fully: a slouched figure in black nylon windbreaker and matching loose nylon pants—Library Lady in her trademark outfit, the only set of clothes she owned, as far as anyone knew.

Annie nodded acknowledgment. "What in the world is going on out there with the men?"

"Oh, it's just that a new guy knocked over Trask's bike and they're yelling at each other." The woman looked over her shoulder, ran fingers over a wild mass of black and gray hair, impenetrable to brush or comb. "No, it doesn't look serious. The guys are getting everybody calmed down. But the reason I came up is I wanted to ask if you had a phone call for me."

Annie's head vibrated slightly as she sized up Library Lady, wondering once again how she had become a Soup Kitchen regular. "What is your name, my dear?"

"You know me—I'm Evelyn Stubbs. Did anyone call? I'm expecting someone to call any day now."

The bringer together of souls directed her shouting throughout the trailer. "Has anyone taken a call for . . . What was your name again, dear?"

"Evelyn Stubbs."

"For Evelyn Stubbs! For Evelyn Stubbs! My goodness, what is it now, young man?"

Perry, who had pushed Library Lady out of the doorway, was emitting a sound between a groan and a teenager's cracking voice. His thick glasses were dramatically askew and the skin of his face had folded over itself in terror. "Call the ambulance! The General stopped breathing. I think he's dead!"

Annie was already up and moving with surprising speed out the door and down the steps toward the tabernacle. The men had formed a human amphitheater around the General's body, which was lying stiffly on one of the picnic benches. There was humane concern among the spectators, but there was also a lingering fear of the huge form and of the complications that might result from approaching it.

"Clear back from him! Give him air to breathe!" Annie reached down and touched the General's forehead, dreadlocks above still dripping with soap suds from his daily shampoo. "My God, he's cold as a fish!" She shouted toward the cook shack, asking if 911 had been called, and Grady shouted back in the affirmative. Annie tried to lift an arm, because she wanted to chafe his hand, but it was stiff and remained folded across the warrior's chest. "My God, it may be too late. And where were all of you when this terrible thing happened?"

Perry stepped forward. "We didn't see nothing, Annie. We thought he was taking a nap. It was Jimmy noticed he wasn't breathing. I don't know how."

Distant sirens, the Kitchen's restless clients looking at the man all feared and some hated: it was dissonant choral music in that noon-time sunshine until John DeLorean stepped forward and asked if he should attempt CPR. The ancient nurse whispered that she thought rigor mortis had set in and it was too late for such measures. Kneeling with great effort by the bench, Annie took the crucifix from around her neck, laid it over the giant's dark hands, crossed herself, and began her own version of the last rites. She knew the Lord would accept this substitute, since no priest was present to administer the official version. When the fire rescue truck came through the gate, DeLorean helped her to her feet and both stood back while the paramedics began their assessment.

The woman with short dark hair asked how long he'd been in that state while her male partner applied a stethoscope to various points on the General's chest and neck. Before anyone could answer, the paramedic with the stethoscope sent the other one leaping to the open case. "Can't get a heartbeat or pulse. Prep 1 cc of epinephrine while I start a heart massage."

Approaching with a loaded syringe, the woman watched her partner rip the camouflage shirt away from the General's chest. As the man straddled the torso, began his first thrust against the sternum, the General bolted to a sitting position and roared. Annie fell back into DeLorean's arms and a number of the spectators relieved their bladders in response to the terrifying miracle.

"Get off me, you crazy motherfucker! The liquid light's all around, and it's gonna poison you! Trying to kill me? Better think about my powers, fool. My martial arts. These hands are wings, dripping from flight through the other world. Hey you! Get back from me with that needle, lady, or I'm gonna have to kill you too with these black wings." He was up. Turning, pivoting again, the General spread his feet and bent his knees, hands open and poised before him. The crowd scattered and the paramedics retreated to their truck. As an ambulance entered the gate, the female paramedic signaled the attendants to stop and hold their distance. Two squad cars arrived from the police station at the end of the block. There was a fifteen-minute discussion between the General and various authorities. Or rather the police and paramedics urged the black giant to go quietly to a hospital for testing and observation while he countered with his tortuous nonstop monologue. After the General impressed upon them that he had not asked for help, was only taking a magic nap, and had every intention of staying for lunch, they all wrote up their paperwork and departed.

As Sweet Pea surveyed the silent faces reassembled around the table inside the cook shack, she felt an urgent need for conversation. "Annie, you were talking about the Potato Famine. Do you really remember the way people looked when they died of starvation?"

"Bless us, merciful heavens, I don't recall what in the world I was talking about before all this happened just now. As I am true to my God. The Potato Famine? My dear, I'm old, but not that old. The starving time was a long, long while ago. I can't remember when it was. There were so many things today, I can't get my senses right. Bless me, Lord, and bless us all."

Grabbing Grady Roberts by the arm, Sweet Pea fixed him with her sly smile, tried to shake him out of his ongoing state of astonishment. "You're a teacher. Tell us when the Potato Famine was."

The volunteer cook, who spent his other days as a professor at a local university, took a sip of orange Gatorade, eased back in the steel folding chair. "I don't recall the exact dates, but it was some-time in the 1840s. There were Potato Famine Irish in my family too. And a lot of scientists say that since we're so dependent on just a few strains of vegetables . . . you're right, Annie, it really could hap-pen again. That's why those people in the Southwest are trying to preserve and grow all the old, traditional seeds."

Grady had already overshot the attention span of the retired waitress. She was looking out the cook shack's open door, giggling at the shenanigans of the men who had regathered around the donut box. She noticed the General standing, knapsack on back, looking toward the police station through the chain-link fence. As Sweet Pea's mind escaped out the door, the teacher-cook's brief dissertation provoked Betty into a thunderous slamming and rattling of pans in one of the lower cupboards.

After a thoughtful pause, the great nurse continued her narrative. "Yes, the starving time was a long, long while ago, back over a century. I can't remember it, but my grandmother could. That's why she always had a bed on the porch and a bowl of hot porridge for men who were passing on the road through our village."

Sweet Pea's attention snapped back to the kitchen table. Seeds didn't interest her, but the apocalypse was one of her favorite subjects, and she always perked up when there was talk of dis-aster. "You know, Annie, I was reading in the *Enquirer* about plagues and volcanoes and all these terrible storms. Like *El Niño*. You know, those really famous psychics are predicting that it's just going to get worse and worse. Dont you think it's punish-ment for all the immorality in the world? Just like Get 'em in Somorra."

There was silence around the table. Sweet Pea looked from face to face. "You know what I'm talking about. Get 'em in Somorra. It's right there in the Bible. Fire and brimstone."

Setting down his glass of Gatorade, the cook finally decided to venture in. "You mean Sodom and Gomorrah?"

She lifted slightly off her seat, knocked a piece of expired chocolate cake over the table's edge. "Yeah, that's it. What did I say anyway?"

Sister Claire lowered her head to hide a smile, then looked up, straightened the apron that covered her starched white blouse. "Don't talk to me about storms. I'm scared to death of them. When I was a little girl my mother would take us all to the basement during thunderstorms. We'd get on our knees and shout the rosary together. I can't stand the sound of thunder or the sight of lightning, even to this day. Once I was on the rim of the Grand Canyon, standing there and chatting with a sister who was visiting from Boston. She was holding an umbrella and the lightning struck her. I looked down and saw her lying on the rock, smoke rising from her habit. Then I ran away."

Grady laughed, then stopped himself, searched Sister Claire's eyes to see if she were joking. Nun or not, she was partial to wicked, irreverent humor.

Hand over her mouth in horror, Marlene gasped. "Didn't you try to help her?"

"Well, I ran to the ranger station and they went back to look."

The eyes of the veteran Disneyland waitress registered terror, but her mouth twisted into a smile. This story was better than anything she'd read in the *National Enquirer* lately. "Did the nun from Boston die?"

Sister Claire folded her hands on her lap and looked out the window. "No, but she was never quite right after that. Of course, she was never quite right before the lightning either."

Annie stared across the table at Sister Claire—bride of Christ, detox and emergency room nurse, dishwasher, Soup Kitchen hairdresser and beautician all rolled into one. "Sister dear, bless us all. It was a miracle the nun survived. And it was a miracle the man outside came back to life. When the Lord works His mercies, He always does it in mysterious ways."

Leaning against the counter, Betty crossed her arms as aggressively as she could. She hated meditations on mercy and redemption but couldn't resist an opportunity to talk about herself. "Well, you know He's saved my old sack of bones a few times." She laughed without spirit. Grady, Wanda, and Marlene stared at the remains on their plates.

Only Sweet Pea showed a desire to pursue the new subject of conversation. "Which operation we talking about now, Betty?"

The Friday lieutenant made a casual gesture with one hand. "You all remember how after my lung cancer operation they had that drainage tube going into my chest? Pinned it right onto my skin with a big safety pin. Remember when you all came to visit me? Of course, not Grady. He wasn't here yet."

Annie closed her eyes and slowly shook her head in sympathy. Sweet Pea got up from the table and walked to the other end of the kitchen. Wanda looked up from her plate, squared her farmer's shoulders, and smiled ferociously, rejecting Betty's bravado. "Well, I know it didn't feel too good, but at least you came out of it alive. My Bobby never had the same chance."

With this evocation of personal anguish, the eyes of the volunteers wandered evasively, all except Ethel's. Since her pharmacist husband had died a drawn-out death from colon cancer, she refused to let anyone trump her in matters of suffering and grief. "What did your boy die of, Wanda?" Betty coughed, began to speak again, but Ethel wouldn't have it. She simply raised her voice and went on. "It was cancer, wasn't it?"

Wanda inflated her big chest. "Yeah, a brain tumor that the HMO people said was a sinus infection. Treated him with antibiotics for almost nine months. He died about a week after they finally figured out what it was."

Groaning out loud, Grady thought of his own mother, who had spent years being treated for anemia by an idiot family practitioner. By the time they discovered the colon cancer, it had metastasized into her liver. The doctor had never even given her a simple hemacult test.

Annie O'Rourke once again looked out the open door, strained her impaired hearing to pick up the voices of men laughing, bragging, and arguing outside. By and large, the guys Annie administered to were a pretty decent crew. From time to time they might commit random acts of anger and violence: shaving off an eyebrow when a buddy passed out, stealing his kit, or using a switchblade to cut off a fingertip or two. But who, after all, was completely whole in this megalopolis on the fiery Pacific rim? And how could anyone be held responsible? The strangely chemical air these people breathed had the same effect as the heady drink prepared for airmen of Imperial Japan before they took off in their balsawood planes. And if trees can communicate in the forest, warning one another of invasions by disease, insects, or humans, why couldn't Annie call together the forces of nature in Lemon City, serve the poor and homeless a dose of something so powerful they could be healed from the Plague that had infected so many—and redeem the rest of the planet with them?

You'd have to say the flies and crawlers were a part of Annie's project too. As we watch them spin and turn, it is clear we cannot safely exclude a single miracle of creation from our general assessment. Since the godhead can choose any species as the vehicle of salvation, why couldn't the Second Coming arrive in the life of a moth, or a single tree? There are more stories in this world than all the flies and crawlers that inhabit it, and yet they all must be told, "out of particulars making them general, rolling up the sum by defective means." To do so requires fire words, infinitely expandable and as dimensionally flexible as a Möbius strip.

As she heard the voices from the tabernacle mix with the ones shuttling back and forth around the table inside the trailer, Annie observed the intricate dance the two strains made together. There was a harmony in the great nurse's head, and she felt an urgency to tease the rough material that surrounded her into the rhythm of its measures. It was her dance, but it was the dance of all creatures and creation as well. Glory be to God. Amen. She put her hands on the

table, struggled up out of her chair, and walked to the door. Annie
knew the magnitude of her undertaking, but the blue sky lifting
itself to the gates of heaven, the California light that seemed to make
anything possible, reassured her. Then again she was ninety-five,
and even a woman with her extraordinary powers knew that time,
which is either nonexistent or in short supply, taunted her with
impossible limits. God knew she was ready to meet Him, except for
the embarrassing moments of terror that came late at night or in
the dark of the morning. But she hoped He'd show her enough
mercy to let her finish her work. Not just the installation of the
showers, which was almost complete, or the big dream of a shelter
with forty beds, but the restoration of the broken watershed that
cradled the sporadic Santa Ana River. Compromised by the trickle
of pesticide-laced runoff and "accidental sewage spills," such a cleans-
ing would let water and light chase unobstructed and untainted
down the mountainside, over the plain, and into the Catalina sunset.
Annie knew that touching just one damaged nerve in the ganglion
that forms when watersheds are taken together, in what cartogra-
phers call a continent, would send a healing pulse through the fabric
of the entire world. She tilted her head back, squinted into the lumi-
nous sky, and adjusted her metal-rimmed glasses. There was a hawk
or vulture circling above. Annie crossed herself.

Taking no pleasure in being called a saint, Annie wouldn't stand
for even humorous comparisons between herself and the Lord's
chosen. She knew about limits, the likelihood from moment to
moment that her healing powers might weaken, or stop working
altogether. Doubts had become even stronger as the strength of her
adversaries had increased. When news came of the loss of Janine
Hartung—and Annie clearly saw, for the first time, the face of the
Shadow Plague—she was trembling with fear. They'd found the
poor woman, one of her original volunteers from the old feeding
days at the public park, wandering in South Coast Plaza, in the
northern hallway leading to Nordstrom's. Janine was unresponsive

to questioning by the authorities and unrecognizable even to her family—beyond identification, if it weren't for the driver's license in her wallet. During a two-hour shopping trip, she had somehow walked away from herself. Now Annie searched the eyes of everyone she spoke to. Dilated pupils, irises with flattened color were sure signs. If she had not talked to the angel, she would never have been able to calculate the numbers who had fallen to the Shadow Plague. But every walk through a crowd reminded her that the legion of the lost was growing and the power of the beast was increasing. The nature of the disease, its vector of penetration and infection, remained unknown even to this nurse of nurses, the leader of the Magnificent Seven.

"Will one of you please check the stove and ovens? I smell something burning." Betty was yelling again. In the midst of pouring a fifteen-gallon stock pot of boiled carrots and broccoli into a colander in the sink, steam rose and engulfed Grady's torso, obscuring his glasses. He mumbled obscenities to himself, muting them more out of respect for Sister Claire than anyone else. He knew about Betty's deadly sense of timing: she would always shout commands when they were difficult or impossible to follow. After drying his glasses on his T-shirt, he nosed around the top of the eight-burner institutional stove. It was new, the fruit of Annie's latest fund-raising triumph. He found a slight boil over from the soup pot, threw the switch for the evacuation fan in the hood.

In the Kitchen that Annie made, Grady navigated a free-form collision of people, fruit, diseases, vegetables, ideas, animals of various sorts—and stories. There was the time he stumbled over a box of artichokes with his frostbite-damaged foot, the seventeen-year-old legacy of exile in the Midwest. Even without untying the shoe, he knew the blackened big toe and its protruding neighbor were bruised, maybe bleeding. The cook looked down at the artichokes, the tips of the outer leaves hard and curled like the claws of a bird of prey, and exclaimed. "Why do people give us junk like this?" Picking up the box with the intention of throwing it into the dumpster, Grady was intercepted by Sister Gianetta, a tiny woman all nose and eyes, face more like a parrot than a hawk.

"Grady, don't throw those away! There's no such thing as a bad artichoke. It's a crown of thorns, but it nourishes us, gives us everything we need. No matter how bad it looks, somehow the heart is always good."

Better angel at his elbow, Grady eased the box back to the floor. "Thorns? More like a crown of rotten thistles, I'd say."

Sister Gianetta stooped and selected the best of the lot, continued her narration from floor level. "My mother's brother lived in Salinas. When I was a little girl he'd bring a burlap sack full of young, tender artichokes up to San Francisco when he visited. Mother made *carciofi alla Giudea*: snipped the leaves, pulled out the cores, and deep fried them in olive oil. She changed them into delicious flowers! If my mother had continued to eat them, she never would have gotten cancer. There's roughage, plenty of fiber inside."

Grady was trying to move away from the nun's story, back to the cutting board where he was dicing onions. "But you don't eat the fiber when you eat artichokes, just the soft part."

Sister Gianetta smiled tolerantly. She had tucked four away in a plastic bag to take back to the convent. "Of course you do. You scrape if off with your teeth."

It was 12:45 P.M. Snack and gossip finished, there was talk of pulling food from the ovens, transporting it to the serving area outside in anticipation of Annie's prayer, the beginning of another commensal encounter. The volunteers who still lingered at the inside table jumped up and began preparations, all but Annie and Ethel. The nurse had spiritually imploded toward a point deep within herself, meditating there on the philosophical nature of disease. Ethel, whose spirit floated free in the air before her empty eyes, moved from the heat of an August afternoon into a vision of cold December leaking through her living room curtains. In the harshly lit edges of five years before, she had not yet lost the sleepy comfort of knowing her husband was alive and working at the pharmacy to take care of her needs. Jane sat beside her on the couch, weeping into a cup of coffee.

"That American Legion guy gave me the flag they put over the coffin, all wrapped up neat in a triangle." Ethel's friend narrated atonally, then paused, but would not look up.

Annie's most stoic volunteer, in those earlier days relatively free from arthritis, pulled her right leg up onto the leather couch, turned to face the grieving woman. "Well, I know it's hard for you now, Jane, but there is no greater honor than to die in the service of your country."

The woman jerked up her head, showed teeth but no smile, her eyes hard and angry. "He died of a heart attack, Ethel, because he wouldn't watch his diet like the doctor told him to. How do you figure that's dying for his country? There's no glory in Ed's death, flag or not. And there's not enough insurance money for me to keep up the mortgage payments for more than a couple of years."

Frantic gestures had no effect on Ethel. Regardless of situation, her face showed just one emotion: determination. "If Ed had a flag draped over his coffin, he died for his country. It doesn't matter when he served. I'm proud of him and you should be too. Listen, let me heat up your coffee."

Looking through the curtains into the heartless light, Jane lifted a hand in refusal. Having risen and taken a few steps toward the kitchen, Ethel returned to the couch, leaned a hip against the back of it. She and Jane had met in 1944, working at the San Diego USO. At that time Jane had been the optimist; Ethel was the one who was certain her husband didn't possess the strength to make it back alive from the Pacific Campaign.

"You know something? You may be right." Jane snorted a small laugh. "Maybe Ed did die for his country. A lot of him never left Iwo Jima. He came back, all right, but his eyes were wrong, and he never laughed the old way again. Sometimes he'd cry late at night and give me little pieces of stories. Like when his boots got ruined squatting in a water-filled hole on the beach where he'd set up his radio post. He'd asked a Marine if he knew where to get a new pair of boots. The guy pointed him to a pile of them, laughed, and said, 'Take your pick.' But when he got there, he found each one had a foot and ankle inside."

The stoic volunteer hardened the lines on her face. "War means killing. It's always ugly, but it's got to happen if you're going to defend your country from people who mean you harm. That's what heroes do, doesn't matter what time in history we're talking about. A soldier can be the best and purest thing there is. You may not agree with me, but I think it's more beautiful to see a soldier obeying orders, standing his ground, and watching the bullet come than to see a live one running away. There's no question we all have to die. It's the way it happens that counts."

Sitting down again, closer to her friend, Ethel put a hand on her knee. Jane looked down at the hand, hesitated, folded her arms with a shiver. "Ed watched for a bullet like that for the rest of his life. Or whatever you want to call the time he spent in the house with me after he came back. He only showed it to me once, but I found it again when I went through his pants after they took him to the mortuary. It was a bronze-colored Japanese cartridge. He told me they meant it for him, but he decided not to take it. Sometimes he'd pull it out and stare at it when he didn't think I was watching. But you know, even though it was clean and polished, and didn't look like it had ever been fired, I think that bullet killed him all the same."

Ethel snapped back to summer in the cook shack as three of Annie's regular clients—Whiskey Ed, Perry, and Skulford Elephant—carried boxes of frozen cheese Danish into the kitchen and let them drop by the freezers. Because Annie was outside by the clothes bin, Betty felt free to shout at the carriers, curse the timing of the delivery, and vociferously celebrate the burdens that came with her authority. Hating ingratitude for any charitable contribution, Ethel looked away, slipped out the door to take up her position behind the serving table.

The teacher-cook wrestled a huge pan of macaroni with meat sauce out of its electrical warmer. As he lugged it through the door toward the serving table, a man in sleeveless T-shirt—its logo a motorcycle and death's head—leaned over and spoke confidentially. "Hey, buddy, can I have a word with you?"

"Yeah. Hang on a second until I put this down." After dropping the pan, Grady returned and sized up the man, big enough to be a professional wrestler. "So what can I do for you?"

"Do you think you or somebody here could front me a few dollars for gas?"

Grady grabbed another hot dish in the kitchen and charged through the door. "Nope, we don't do that here. Just food, plenty of good food. If I were you, I'd go ahead and get in line. You don't want to be at the tail end. A lot of the good stuff might be gone by the time we get around to you."

Having returned to her prayer station, Annie grasped the rail, steadying the fragile cook shack more than it steadied her. After she took the assembled men, women, and children on her ritual descent into purgatory, pleading with the Lord to bless the lost souls who wandered there, a hawk that had circled all morning above Annie's Soup Kitchen tilted its wings, took a sharp turn, paused in midair, then dove into the brush by the railroad tracks. Annie was still blessing her congregation when she observed the fatal attack. She stopped praying, hunched shoulders, let a terrible shudder pass through her gray and blonde hair. Losing all words, she could only cross herself and cross herself again.

CHAPTER THREE

CONJURING

Whiskey Ed aimed the blunt nose of his van in the direction of the Santa Ana city line. Rocking as he rolled, the electronics wizard hummed a few bars of Ellington's "Jump for Joy," found himself entirely overwhelmed by the spirit of the song. Leaping straight to the chorus, his voice cracked on every ecstatic note. Annie O'Rourke rode shotgun on the Watershed Express, slapped time on her knees as they moved through late night Lemon City streets toward the most heavily populated bridge in Orange County. Dubbed Troll City by police and local residents, la Ciudad de los Duendes by Spanish-speaking folks, there was often moon dancing there, as you might expect, and solemn enumerations of the stars, whether those heavenly bodies were visible or completely blocked by fog. When you live outside, or in this case underside, the body's thermal regulator steps up and substitutes for society's more mundane configurations of shelter and insulation. It has to do with metabolism, a fire about which the old Irish nurse was knowledgeable—and expert in stoking. Not just through food, although she always took care of that, providing breakfast, lunch, and dinner to all souls who entered her compound. In November of every year she also gave out sleeping bags and metallic "space blankets," hoping her men would hang on to them through the cold months. Regardless of those outcomes, she knew there would be heat under that bridge. We're not talking about the visible kind, like the gentleman who incinerated himself with a crack pipe, but the communal warmth necessary for survival in any beehive, anthill, or city of lost mortals. Closing in on Troll City, Annie and Whiskey Ed laughed at the impossible sounds coming from beneath the van's hood. It was a new music, irresistible as the Duke's: rattle and bop, ping, pang, and clunk, a celebration of historical coming together, the first time the Magnificent Seven would gather as a group.

Skulford Elephant and the General waited under the bridge, watching for Ed's signal: headlights flashed on and off three times. Skulford, being hip to the secret affinities of various species, made Elephant his surname and yet elected to continue as a snake man too. He walked up to the van traveling light—only the clothes on his back and a pack of cards—but the General had his overpacked knapsack in tow, including a large umbrella stuffed down one side, black handle jutting out the top.

"General." Whiskey Ed cleared his voice. "We got a serious space problem here. Just look at all the equipment in the back. And beyond that, we haven't had any rain for over five months. You could easily lose that umbrella. Maybe the whole kit. How about leaving it right here at home tonight?"

The General squeezed past the gear stowed in the van, pushing his knapsack in front of him. Back pressed against the tentative rear door, his weight testing the rope that held it closed, he glowered back at Whiskey Ed. With no functional interior lights, it was as dark inside the van as it was outside, but his sizzling eyes generated their own illumination. "My medicine bag's on the rocky road to darkness. Got it filled with no look feathers, no hands martial arts. Hmmmm. Hah! So drive this Cadillac, white boy. It's all cool back here—takes no extra space when you're inside and outside at the same time."

Skulford was less enthusiastic than the General. He climbed through the side doors of the van eyeing their exposed internal structure of metal struts and insulation—a reminder that all solidity is illusory—and tried to pull them closed. Crouching behind Annie's seat, he waited as Ed disembarked, circled the van, and refastened the doors from the outside. It felt something like a trap, but then so does the tunnel of a long dream. As Whiskey Ed returned to his captain's seat, Skulford raised his unstable hand, signed that he was ready to risk the ride.

Back to Lemon City for three more stops, music was temporarily on hold, if you don't count the General's droning chant. Neither was there any conversation in the van for five minutes. Annie was always quiet around the General. The sheer mass and strength of the warrior, coupled with his careering speech, whether she could catch the gist of the latter or not, inspired both fear and admiration in her. Whiskey Ed, on the other hand, had no fear of bodily harm. He had been on a mission to destroy his corporeal envelope for such a long time, any outside help was welcome. What was keeping the driver quiet on this occasion was not fear but love of suspense. However, his manic passion for the new project finally broke through.

"Isn't anybody going to ask me why we're all here together?" The General's droning continued its dust devil whirl. Ed cleared his throat, slapped a hand on the steering wheel, shifted into lecture mode. "I'm sure you're wondering . . ."

Skulford wasn't wondering at all, and he let that be known by emitting an unpleasant animal noise.

Ed looked over his shoulder but could see only a fragile middle finger awash in sickly luminescence. Skulford was demonstrative about not being a people person. Looping his thin voice over the seat, he wanted to make sure no one misconstrued his presence on this mysterious trip as enthusiasm. "Look, I'm here, but don't think I've signed on for anything yet. If you want to talk, start by telling me how you got my number." Then, in an act of relative bravado, he reared up over the back of the seat, showed himself in the street's dim light, pulled back his greasy hair with both hands, slipped a

rubber band over the ponytail. It was his ninja look, something no
one at the Kitchen had ever seen before.

Whiskey Ed's eager words, running slightly ahead of his voice,
caught for a moment as they transited his throat. Then the flood:
how he collected obsolete electronic gadgets—cheap or free—to keep
an eye on the waveform universe. Scopes connected to the computer
in his head, not the kind you buy in stores. How he caught every one
of them on his ultra-low-frequency pickup, just zeroed right in.
Annie, a tremendous spike on the low end oscilloscope every time
she stepped out the trailer door. How by isolation and elimination
he got the General first, then Evelyn, Perry, and the hard to track
Skulford. Roderigo was still difficult for him to believe, but oscillo-
scopes don't lie.

When the Watershed Express jerked to a stop in front of Roderigo's
house, a tiny stucco with caged windows and doors, Annie turned
and looked over her shoulder at the droning General. She squinted,
could barely see his closed eyes, squeezed tight with concentration.
Noticing Skulford's pale face looming in the half light, she drew
back her head, startled. "Oh, young man, it's you again."

Since he knew he was on the great nurse's shit list, Skulford was
intrigued that he'd been included at all. When she'd discovered his
alchemical experiment tucked behind the trailer, Annie was in such
a fury, she hollered at everyone inside and outside the Kitchen for
the next two hours. First, that someone would have the nerve to lift
one of her wheeled yellow mop buckets with attached wringer (she
reminded everyone how expensive they were), then to find it filled
with water and fermented garbage! Annie was a Lysol zealot, all spit
and polish, so she chased Skulford out the gate with a dry mop.
How could the little man tell Annie he was doing vital research and
development at her Soup Kitchen? Spiriting food and plastic refuse
out of the dumpster, he'd ground it up and let it ferment in a secret
niche behind the cook shack. This was urgent conjuring he'd undertaken. Skulford had it on good information that sunspots were a

cosmic plot to enslave humans and animals by interfering with normal brain patterns. And where was such damage more evident than in Southern California? Furthermore, Skulford knew the heart of the world was being poisoned by veins laden with toxic runoff, everything from herbicides and pesticides to discarded motor oil and dog feces. It was common knowledge—mentioned frequently right in the *L.A. Times*. That such information should be dispersed so openly made him suspicious, but that's another story entirely. Polluting the rivers and ocean produced the same results as a human mainlining bad drugs. A sure suicide, sooner or later. That's why he was trying to create an antitoxin for the watershed, one that could be injected into the river's vein in order to save the body. Dross to gold, industrial poison to environmental salvation.

"Go! Go! Go!" Roderigo propelled his chunky body at such speed out the caged door of his house and down the sidewalk to the van, he couldn't stop. After bouncing off the vehicle, then finding the door handles limp and unresponsive to his grasp, he sent up a panicked torrent of Spanish profanity. Ed moved around to let him in but apparently not quickly enough.

"Man, we got to get the fuck out of here! Get this dump moving!"

Annie turned and scowled as the overaged punk scrambled in. "You listen to me right now! You have no right to use such language in front of us. And would you tell me what it is you are so afraid of?"

"My oldest kid's friends. I know they're hiding out around here. Maybe across the street."

"Now what kind of friends are those?" The nurse was being unusually restrained with Roderigo. She had already eighty-sixed him from the Soup Kitchen several times, typically following a violent physical confrontation—always one-sided and applied with mop, broom, or bag of old carrots. Counting on her mercy, he'd sneak back in a few days, walk around with the gingerly step of Oliver Hardy and a huge parodic smile, and she'd let him stay. Three weeks earlier, the ninety-five-year-old visionary had pinned him against the cyclone fence, her ferocity frightening both Roderigo and the volunteers who looked on. This time it concerned his youngest child, a stubby kid with the same surly swagger, different only in that he was smaller and his curly hair light brown instead of silver gray. It was a school day and the boy was there having lunch with his father. Parent-approved truancy was high on the list of nearly unforgivable sins in the Annie O'Rourke orthodoxy. As she yelled and sprayed saliva into Roderigo's face, she reminded him that even a shoe clerk needed an education, and did he want his son to turn out like him? Roderigo shrugged his shoulders, as if to say, "What's so bad about that?" After Wanda interceded, throwing her hefty body between them, Annie backed off, fed both father and son, and sent them on their way saying she never wanted to see the boy on a school day again.

Roderigo fidgeted in the back of Whiskey Ed's van, trying to see out. Since there were no side windows, he was having difficulty. "Get this mother going, man! I think that's their car over there. Look in your mirror! Can you see it? A black BMW?"

The electronics wizard stomped a saddle shoe on the accelerator and forced his groaning vehicle through its gears. Three blocks down the street he took a right turn on two wheels. After careening another hundred yards, the engine sputtered and stopped. Roderigo cursed and pounded the back of the seat as they coasted, threw himself on the floor in anticipation of a spray of bullets. The General's voice rose up from the rear and drowned out the newcomer's whining. "Who's gonna shoot you, Silver Man? There's cloud all over this buggy. Ain't none of us here."

When the car in question drove by in completely normal fashion, Roderigo was relieved, and for a moment a picture of pure stunned confusion. However, surliness quickly returned, directed at Ed as the car healer disembarked and raised the hood to make repairs.

"Hey man, if you got magic, why don't you get yourself a better ride? Grand Cherokee or Explorer, something like that." He gave a formal hello to Annie, apologized for the excitement, then noticed the General had resumed chanting. Roderigo was about to comment when Mr. Elephant stuck his head out the open window, pressed his own skepticism about Ed's gathering of experts.

"But so what if we're all wired? You found out, now what's the plan? You haven't told me what we're supposed to do."

Ed laughed, savoring the collective urge for enlightenment as he wiggled a distributor wire. For a man of such unimpressive external attributes, usually inspiring contempt or worse from both sexes, the temptation to prolong the tease was too much to resist. "Why don't you guys settle down and wait until we're all together? I'm not going to go through this more than once."

Perry was picked up without event from his hideout in the back of an empty warehouse. Library Lady awaited the Express in front of the Riverside Senior Apartments. She may not have known the plan, but she knew who she was dealing with when she climbed in back. Evelyn could see the undulating colors that surround all objects, including humans, in the amplifying dance of her *chi*. Optic sensitivity to the electromagnetic radiation around this extraordinary crew made the van a feasting presence full of light. Lucky she was wearing sunglasses.

$\sim$

"I've done the engineering, crunched the numbers, but that in itself ain't gonna get us there." Whiskey Ed grabbed a fistful of his frizzed white hair with one hand, scratched an expanse of forehead with the other. "Now do you see why we need to do this together?"

The great nurse stood in darkness—hands on hips, feet planted like the Colossus—and surveyed the lights that rose into the night sky, outlining the equipment of the sewage treatment plant, warning low-flying planes, hawks, and angels. Annie wore a short-sleeved red dress, sporty but hardly appropriate camouflage for a guerrilla raid.

She lifted her arms and exhaled a formidable sigh. "But it's against the law, Edward. For the love of mercy, you're asking us all to break the law and it worries me terribly."

The rest of the Magnificent Seven waited in the dark for their leader's decision. Still in the back of Whiskey Ed's three-toned van, the General was chanting a cloud of invisibility that would obscure even Annie's most flamboyant outfit. He didn't need to join the debate, would groove with whatever decision the visionary feeder might make.

Having finished his flashlight presentation, Ed refolded the plans to the treatment plant. "So you're just going to let these guys keep sending their 'accidental spills' into the river and let the canning company pollute both air and water with illegal solvents?" Although you couldn't see him roll his protruding eyes, his awkward body language echoed frustration in silhouette. "Annie, *they're* the ones who are breaking the law! Why should they stop? The little fines they get every once in a while cost much less than cleaning up."

Roderigo, hands stuffed in jean pockets, managed to thrust even more silver chest hair out a half-buttoned shirt. His gold St. Christopher shot a sharp glint at a klieg light on the plant's superstructure. "Why don't we just get some dynamite and blow the place up?"

"Shut up, Rod. You're not helping. Listen, Annie, I'm pleading with you." Ed held the flashlight under his chin, illuminating eyes and harrowed face. They reflected alcohol abuse, certainly, but also compassion for a material world sinking into catastrophe. He shut off the light, bent his head down toward the philanthropist-nurse, the closest he would ever come to a gesture of supplication. Lowering his voice, he dared to speak the unspeakable. "You know what's happening with the Plague. Don't try to fool me. By the time all these people get taken to court, it's going to be over. We've got to do something quick. Right now, tonight."

Library Lady stood by the open manhole to the storm sewer, waving the lucky chocolate Easter egg—only five months out of date—she'd picked up the previous day at Annie's Soup Kitchen. As she danced, blocking out a choreography of the elements, it occurred to Evelyn that her black nylon warmup suit was reminiscent of the pajamas once favored by Vietnamese guerrillas. And yet she was a pacifist. Knowing that the plant's security guards were armed, she still hoped no bullets would be involved in this night's adventure. The world required serious changes. This project demanded that she dance shit into elegance—not metaphorical shit, but the powerful stream of untreated sewage her colleague had just released from the processing plant.

Perry channeled and accelerated the rapid liquid pulse with his language barrage, an amalgamation of all the twenty-plus tongues he knew, syntactically stripped down to pure linguistic power. For anyone taking the time to listen, he would happily explain that world history took its most tragic turn at the Tower of Babel. It wasn't because the primal language had fractured. That had to happen, sooner or later. It was just that those confused humans never lingered to recombine their utterances into an Esperanto that would lend strength and coherence to global culture. He'd witnessed such magic week after week on the old *Star Trek* series. If the people of Babel had only taken the right turn, we'd have been better off than we ever were before.

Perry and Library Lady secured the supply end of the plan. The other five marauders sang in Whiskey Ed's van as they sped down the road paralleling a storm sewer that beelined to the river. The General set up a prodigious bass, Annie covered soprano with her quavering rendition of "Amazing Grace," Roderigo slapped thighs and cheeks to set up a tricky salsa counterrhythm, and Skulford's paper and comb bebop riffs slipped in and around Annie's pauses. It was an unusual choice for the snake man. Where did it come from? Nobody had ever seen him run such an instrument through his hair. Ed thumped his left saddle shoe, threw in an occasional "Get down!" but the task that most concerned him was keeping his mechanically unreliable vehicle on the road. He hoped they'd arrive at the C & R Canning Company in time to get everything set up before the shit arrived.

Ed almost tipped the van as he ricocheted a front tire off the curb. Bouncing to a stop, he shouted for Skulford and Roderigo to pull up the manhole cover while he untied the rear doors of the van and hauled out an inflatable raft. The electronics genius crawled into the storm sewer, inflated the raft with a pressurized canister, but had no idea how to keep it in place to block the onward movement of the effluent. He wasn't even sure the rubberized fabric could withstand the kind of hydraulic force that was about to hit it. After scrambling out, he peered back into the sewer and shivered. "It's coming! Listen, you can hear the rumbling. Now you guys got to help me out quick. Somebody figure how to get the shit from here to the cannery."

Annie tilted her head back and looked at the stars. "Where's the cannery, Edward?"

Roderigo was kneeling by the manhole, his head thrust inside. His voice seemed to echo from a neighboring hill. "You crazy motherfucker! The caca is almost here and you got no idea?"

Skulford sat down hard on the ground. "Hey listen, Mr. Engineer, that stuff is going to take the rubber raft and blow it all the way to Huntington Beach. There's only one way it's going to work: we've got to put a bend in the sewer."

Whiskey Ed lunged at Skulford Elephant, wanting to shake him into action, but his fingers burned as he neared the little man. He turned to ask for Annie's help, but she had gone back to the van: head in the window, pleading with the General. She was sure the giant was the only one with enough physical strength to resolve the crisis.

Waving his hand, Skulford directed Ed and Roderigo to run to the building, make sure the loading dock door was open. He looked over his shoulder toward the proposed point of entry, positioned himself directly in the flow channel. "Has anybody checked to see if people are still inside the cannery?" This rhetorical question went unheard, since Ed and Roderigo were already gone and Annie was leaning against the van with one hand, crossing herself with the other, as the General continued to drone.

"Hey, General! Can you handle the guards and night shift?" Skulford had assumed a lotus position and was beginning to emit the cool blue light of high voltage discharge.

Droning put on pause, a voice bellowed out of the van. "How do you think I got out of Da Nang alive, white boy?"

The roar from the sewer ceased momentarily, then a geyser of human waste shot straight up, looped over the seated Skulford, ran through a neat but invisible channel to the cannery, leaped through the aluminum door Ed had just raised.

Annie fell back against the fence. She had the wide open eyes of epiphany, as if she were seeing the miracle of Lourdes rather than a small man sitting peacefully under a rainbow of fast-moving shit. She laughed, put her hand over her mouth, shook her head, then laughed again. The nurse had seen who Skulford was but was not yet ready to talk about it.

When Whiskey Ed and Roderigo returned, she held a finger to her lips, stopped them before they spoke to the new director of night operations. The three of them watched the phenomenon as she whispered to them, asking if Evelyn and Perry would know when to shut off the sewage and send water through to purge the storm sewer. Ed dropped his arms to his sides and borrowed Roderigo's trademark look of stunned confusion. He had forgotten another detail.

The surly Latino monkeywrencher flapped his arms, kicked his boots in the dust. "You pick us up, but you don't know shit about shit! Man, what we need now is a cell phone."

Annie put her hands on her hips and stretched her lips sideways into a rigid line. Even in the low light, Roderigo recognized the gesture and it made him nervous. But the great nurse was not satisfied with a silent reprimand. "And do you think we could be doing all the things we've done tonight and still be needing a telephone?"

Before she could finish speaking, the liquid arching over Skulford's head turned clear, translucent in the blue glow. It ran that way for several minutes, then ceased altogether. The light around the yogi dulled and he returned to his normal appearance: general greasiness with a light coating of dust. He stood, turned around twice, brushed himself off, directed an evasive smile at Annie.

Ed and Roderigo descended into the sewer to deflate and extract the rubber raft. As Annie and Skulford peered into the dank hole, rattling English profanities counterpointed the more melodic Spanish execrations. Roderigo popped up first, tugging the half-deflated raft behind him. Whiskey Ed followed, grimy and disheveled. Pushing the rubber dinghy with one hand and holding his flashlight in the other, he lost his footing and banged a shin on the iron ring of the manhole. He rolled in the dust, cursing all creation so thoroughly Annie was forced to choose between crossing herself and putting her hands over her ears. The resulting gesture, a combination of both, looked like a child playing with an imaginary antique telephone.

Ed finally got to his feet and hollered. "It's all my fault. I know, I know. It's my fault!" Waving his flashlight at the silver-haired punk, he continued yelling. "What the hell ever made me think you belong with us, Roderigo? My equipment had to be out of whack that day. Never failed me before, but there's always a first time."

Scratching his matted chest hair, the aging delinquent cocked an eyebrow and laughed. "You asshole, what kind of stuff you been showing me? You open the door on the dock, I mean you open it with your hand." Roderigo spit emphatically, inspiring everyone to worry about their shoes in the darkness. "Think that's some big deal? You wanna see something? You wanna see me without my beard?"

"You don't have a beard."

Roderigo was kicking dust again. "Oh yeah? You think you see so damn good, but you don't know shit."

Eyes rolling heavenward, Annie walked away from the confrontation, Skulford in tow. After a dozen steps, she turned back and shouted. "Will the two of you be staying to squabble like fools until the policemen come to talk to us? There is no power in the world except by the grace of God. Let the rock split and the water flow."

~

Absent the General's chanting, only the music of the van's engine serenaded the monkeywrenchers as they traveled back to the sewage treatment plant. When Library Lady climbed in, cheerfully describing the success at their end of the project, she immediately noticed a different configuration of light within the van. "Where's Skulford?"

A flashlight search inside and outside the vehicle revealed no sign of the expedition's hero. Ed was prepared to set up a search party, but Annie urged him to return to Lemon City and drop everyone off. She knew Skulford would find his way back.

The General, arms hugging knees as his shoulders pressed against the rear doors, began to chuckle. When he shifted to a full laugh, its low rolling thunder stopped all further conversation. No one had ever heard a laugh like that before.

"Yowsa! Y'all gonna like my atomic grits. Whip you up some and it'll go good with that down home chicken shack stuff: chitlins, collards, and beans. Gonna be quiet where we're all going to. Gentle, like water in a glass. Listen! A bunch of bones and joints don't mean you got no human being." The General stopped and snickered quietly at what appeared to be a private joke, then burst into a sound so loud and violent he choked on his own saliva. After a long spell of coughing, he caught his breath and continued. "Fossils. Live ones, like Hydra. You think I just read Edith Hamilton, but I know a whole lot more about that drill. I'm still coming home from Nam, and taking my sweet time. You know, sometimes animals is gods and sometimes gods is animals. And they do sneak up on you. We're not all here, are we? Nope. Shoup. Nope. Shoup, shoup. Proud Annie keep on burning. Yeah."

CHAPTER FOUR

GENERAL LOCOMOTION

There are self-created hells in this world—or maybe *purgatories* is a more accurate word, because hope always lingers that the creator can escape his or her chosen torment. The spiral road leads station by station up the purgatorial mountain, signs posted indicating a time of day or calendar date. Freudian therapists attempt to chart these archaeological nightmares, but shrinks tend to be clumsy amateurs, incapable of sifting through thousands of tons of dirt to discover the key artifact that will bring an entire monument to light.

This particular morning and early afternoon at Annie's Soup Kitchen seemed unique to Grady. He realized that the fragmentary moments logged between the various hours had become the stations of his suffering. And yet a mystery remained. His morose anger, his disgust with his life as a teacher, the bitter hopelessness with which he viewed his half-written novel: how was he able to take these raw materials and construct such exquisite compartments of pain—gorgeous Etruscan rooms, brilliantly furnished and decorated, except for the fact that they were built underground and peopled by the dead?

Station 1:15

Bas relief Corinthian columns fabricated from wood, leafed in gold to hide the softness at their hearts.

"So how much do we need?" Grady glanced at the cluster of hungry faces at the bottom of the ramp, counted three men, a woman, and the child on her hip. He threw a slotted spoon on the serving table and walked to the door of the trailer. "Five enough?"

Ethel looked farther, beyond the gate. "No, wait. There's three more coming down the street."

They'd only been serving fifteen minutes and everything, even the caterer's infamous rice and pasta salads, had been cleaned out. Gathering the last of the empty bowls and pans, Wanda was trying to assess the situation. "Why don't you go ahead and make enough for ten." Then she spoke to the anxious gathering below. "Don't worry, folks, get your trays and come on up. The cook's going to make you something. We won't let you starve."

As he entered the kitchen, Grady ignored Betty on her knees, cleaning out the vegetable trays at the bottom of one of the refrigerators. She was indulging in a loud and dramatic sniffle, hoping someone would comfort her or that Grady would apologize. Ten minutes earlier they had collided in the worst confrontation in the history of their long and unpleasant relationship at Annie's Soup Kitchen.

Station 1:05

Psychic motion, otherwise known as remembrance, piles all the little forgotten tombs of our lives one upon another in stories, then constantly rearranges them into labyrinths that dwarf the catacombs.

Grady glanced up from his serving tray in time to see pure astonishment covered by field dirt, topped with a greasy baseball cap. The day laborer had just declined a helping from the tray of warmed over fishcakes, but the hostility surging from behind the table had taken him by surprise. It was Betty, reaming out the ninth or tenth hapless customer that morning. "No thank you! That's what we say in this country. No thank you!"

The teacher-cook dropped his spoon into the remains of the tax write-off rice pilaf, turned to his right, and glared at Betty. "Why are you always badgering these guys?"

As was her habit, Betty smiled as she yelled, nodding to emphasize her words. This gave her the appearance of a huge silver-haired tree rat. "I'm teaching them some manners, that's what I'm doing. They need to learn to be thankful for what they're getting, and polite about it too."

Marlene, two places down the serving line, had stopped dishing potatoes and succotash so she could read Betty's head gestures from the rear.

Not satisfied with the Friday lieutenant's explanation, Grady put the first station in the serving line on hold. Nobody was going anywhere until he chose to pick up his spoon and begin loading rice again. He crossed his arms, took another shot at Betty. "You know, normally I wouldn't say anything to you about the way you behave, especially now, with everybody standing around listening. Except that you only yell at brown faces. The other guys can be as rude as hell, throw an insult into your teeth like Newt always does, and you don't say a word. Either pass out your etiquette lessons to everybody equally or keep your mouth shut."

He picked up his spoon and the line of men and women began to move again. Most pretended to have somehow missed the argument, but Skulford Elephant gave the cook a nose pull and wink. Betty sniffled, served fish to several more customers, then disappeared into the Kitchen. Marlene moved left to fill the gap, looked hard at Grady. He had lowered his head, feeling glum and a bit guilty, but his fellow volunteer whispered encouragement. "You were absolutely right to say what you did. I saw the whole thing. She only yells at Mexicans, and that's not fair."

Station 10:05

Dazzle lurks in the midst of suffering, blossoming through the cracks in our pain. A decorative splendor to distract us from impossible tasks: hoisting the slabs of stone we've quarried from our hearts, carrying them up the mountain on our backs. No matter how dark, there is no place in the cosmos where holy mysteries do not remain in effect.

As Grady walked toward the cook shack Friday morning, after parking his car next to Annie's locked clothes bin, there were all the signs this would shape up to be an interesting day. First he spotted a long, lozenge-shaped tan object, vaguely sexual and unsavory, on top of the front bumper of Whiskey Ed's van. It was hard to believe any feature could stand out on a vehicle that was white with gray splotches of primer on one side, entirely gray on the other, covered by an ocher rust patina above. Other anomalies: the heavy steel chain draped across the drooping rear bumper, a rope binding the rear doors together, four mismatched wheels, all innocent of hubcaps. Approaching the van, Grady identified the new addition: three quarters of a baguette, apparently glued in place. He smiled and shook his head in admiration of the electronics wizard—a Soup Kitchen Duchamp—and his flair for the absurd. This bit of filigree on Ed's magic wheels might be understood as a novel method of storing emergency rations, but more likely it was his reminder to the community at large that the miracle of transubstantiation is everywhere around us—a leap from word to flesh to bread and then to flesh again.

Fastening apron strings behind his back as he plodded across the blacktop, Grady bumped his worn white athletic shoes up the stairs to the trailer. Leaning over the railing above, Perry awaited.

"Pastaman! Aaahhh, happening, dude! What about today?" Perry's blur of scruffy hair—including a walrus moustache the color of a wet retriever—his thick glasses, usually in the process of slipping to the end of his nose, and his inability to make eye contact combined to render his appearance as unfocused as his speech. Grady had been working at the Soup Kitchen for over three years, and to his knowledge Perry had never missed a meal, but at the end of the day the cook could never be entirely sure whether or not he'd seen the man.

Grady responded with a laugh and an ironic two-handed tug on his green apron. "How about spaghetti with meat sauce for a change?"

"Hey, that's bellatissima!" Unaware that his linguistic improvisation made the cook wince, Perry charged ahead. "You know, I don't have a single drop of Italian blood in me—I'm Jewish and Arapaho—but I just love your pasta with meat sauce. And the language too. Can you teach me a few words? I mostly talk *español*, like people around here do—that and a few other languages—but I want to work this Italian thing."

The cook adjusted his own glasses, trying to bring Perry into focus. Even so, all he could see before him were small explosions of light. Perry's voice was entirely divorced from the world of body and blood. Once again, sensory overload for the volunteer. As more phrases of mangled Italian danced in the light, Grady mumbled "Later" and retreated into the cook shack.

Station 1:19

Can there be light without darkness? Borders define both beauty and art: the deft pull of Hieronymus Bosch's brush, leaving a raised edge of light yellow ocher paint to soar above the deep aquamarine beneath, the shaman holding up her hands to enclose the sun or moon.

"Sweet Pea! Please get me a couple of big institutional cans of pork and beans from the bin, would you?" Grady wiped his hands on his ocher-stained apron, pulled a large pot out of the cupboard, and slammed it on the stove. After retrieving a plastic cutting board from the drain rack, he was ready to slice semifrozen hot dogs into small circles. He often complained he was burned out teaching college students, having done it for almost thirty years, but on days like this volunteer work didn't seem to be much of an improvement.

Three hours before, after he'd pulled eight packages of frozen ground beef for spaghetti sauce, Betty had remarked that cooking fresh food that day would be a waste of time and resources. She'd insisted the food Wanda had picked up from the caterer and some leftovers from the refrigerators would be more than enough. After Grady ground his teeth, grunted a response, and put the tubes of beef back into the freezer, Betty walked to the answering machine, punched the button, walked away, and let muffled voices offering food and help drift unheeded into the morning air. When Ethel asked if someone shouldn't be writing down the messages, she offered a curt reply. "We don't happen to need any more food right now, and we certainly don't want any more volunteers." Before the machine turned itself off, a voice unheard by anyone requested an interview for television station KXON with Annie O'Rourke.

The miscalculations of Annie's Friday lieutenant never caused her any remorse. When the allotted food came up short, she'd laugh and say it was better than having trash cans filled with discards. As he rushed to heat up a lousy, last-minute meal for the tail end of the line, Grady brooded over her callous arrogance. The pan on the stove began to sizzle, then spat a large drop of oil on Grady's cheek. He dropped the knife, put his cold fingers on the burn. "Damn it! What the hell am I doing in this crazy place anyway?"

Standing at the counter behind him, Sister Claire continued scrubbing, sponging, rinsing dishes and pans as if nothing were happening around her. Occasionally she'd look up from her work, peer through the window above the sink, let her eyes linger on the railroad tracks that dominated the panorama. They carried her farther and farther away from all earthly vocations: hospital, Annie's Soup Kitchen, attending the corruptible and dying.

Wanda walked across the trailer, put an arm around Grady's shoulders. "Hey, take it easy. It's all right. I'll put some extra goodies in the bag lunches I'm making for them."

Still kneeling before the refrigerator, Betty looked over her shoulder and attempted to reassert her authority. "I wouldn't waste too much time on latecomers if I were you, Wanda."

Grady covered the twenty feet between the stove and the refrigerator in four huge strides, causing Betty to lose balance and fall against the milk containers on the lower shelf. She raised one hand, as if to fend off a blow.

The cook bent over her, allowing no space for movement or escape. His arms were rigid, struggling to keep the attached hands from mischief. "What is this? Are you the victim now? Listen, Betty, you always say the junk we have in the refrigerators is more than enough for them. Or that it's good enough for them. You know something? It isn't enough and it isn't good enough. How very damned generous of you, deciding what's good enough for *them*! I've never seen you eat any of it."

Betty held the refrigerator door with one hand, pushed her accuser's chest, and pulled herself to her feet. "Grady Roberts, you have no right talking to me that way."

He closed in on her again, as the rest of the volunteers gathered at the other end of the trailer and watched. "I have every damn right. I'm here because I believe we have an obligation to feed the poor. Just like Annie says—it's a prime directive of the New Testament. What I want to know is, why are you here?"

Her eyes swept over the cluster of volunteers in a silent but urgent call for help. They held their ground and Sister Claire continued to wash dishes. There would be no intercessions today.

The tears that covered Betty's face were beginning to drip from her chin, but she was not ready to surrender. The volume of her voice increased, then began to crack. "I've been working with Annie from the beginning, long before you ever showed up. Back when we were dragging huge pots of chicken soup over to the park. Do you think you can talk to me like this just because she isn't here today?"

"OK, I grant that you've been doing this a long time. Just tell me why you're here. If you have so much contempt for the people we serve, why bother coming at all?"

"That's it! Don't anyone try to stop me, I'm leaving right now!" No one in the cook shack moved as Betty pulled the apron over her head, threw it on the floor, walked down the ramp to the parking lot. She fired up her chartreuse Honda, spun surface gravel in a number of directions, and drove out the gate.

Station 1:25

The number and variety of dances the world has produced in these past millennia equals the need to fill the rooms of our pain with distracting motion.

After heating the hot dogs and beans, loading up styrofoam plates, and serving the last people, Grady sat on the steps, a distressed apron thrown over his shoulder. He leaned against the railing, feeling as funky as its institutional gray paint, but then lifted his gaze, let the California sun and sky take him by surprise. The cook's mind slipped a gear and a room full of laughter came back to him. He remembered Betty that morning, at the top of her form, calling him "Sunshine." It was an epithet she had recently become fond of using to address customers, riffraff in her estimation, as they passed through the serving line. "Would you like some potatoes, Sunshine?" That she should direct it at him stung hard, so Grady broke with habit and jabbed back.

"Oh, am I 'Sunshine' now? I must be radiating even more than usual."

Sweet Pea, overhearing at the far sink, guffawed. Then the cook cranked it up. "What do you think, Sweet Pea? Am I radiating sunshine even more than usual?" He began to sing: "Good morning, Grady Sunshine/How did you wake so soon?/You scared away the little stars/And shined away the moon." He was prancing, a finger poked in the part of his cheek that would be a dimple if he were

Shirley Temple. The Disney retiree joined in, picked up the same routine, danced with him side by side, shaking her blonde locks, leering, showing everyone the most sinister Shirley Temple of all. The volunteers looked on, and a couple of people lingering at the door cheered and applauded, calling for more.

Banging hard at something next to the microwave in the corner, Betty turned and offered her critique. "That's pretty impressive, you two. I didn't know you could dance, Mr. Grady." Moments later she disappeared into her usual refuge: the bin where bread and paper products were stored. She did not reappear until serving time.

Station 1:30

Grady got up from his place on the step and headed back into the trailer to face Sister Claire, found her still working the dishes. She was the protein socialist's ideal of moral commitment and service to the poor; her life set a standard he had no hope of achieving. The nun had previously shown great respect for him, but he wasn't sure how she'd feel after witnessing the antics and snarling in which he'd indulged himself earlier that day. Grady pulled a dish towel from the cupboard and picked up a wet baking tray from the drainer.

"Sister, I'm sorry about the stuff that happened with Betty."

The nun glanced at Grady, then returned her attention to the dishes. "You're a good man and you know I think highly of you. I'm not sure what you want me to say."

"Nothing. I guess I'm trying to find some way of not feeling so bad about what I did. I can't say I'm proud of how I acted."

She stopped washing, slouched against the counter, crossed ankles, and faced Grady. Her stern expression eased into the trademark half smile that announced she had something mischievous to deliver. "Do you know what I said to Betty when she first looked me up at the mother house years ago? As I was coming down the stairs, she hollered out in this brassy voice, 'You're my cousin!' I took one look at her and said, 'What makes you think so?'" Sister Claire raised a rubber glove to her mouth, muffling a laugh.

Grady checked around the trailer to see who might be listening in, but everyone appeared busy and out of earshot. "I'm not offering this as a mitigating circumstance, but I've been out of whack ever since I had this crazy dream last night. Did you ever see that old low budget horror movie, *Night of the Living Dead*? Last night was something like that—full of zombies. They'd lose arms, legs, all kinds of body parts, but keep moving around and talking like nothing had happened. When I woke up I felt scared and physically sick, even though I knew it was a stupid, low budget kind of dream. Can't explain it, but I still don't feel right."

Sister Claire looked down as she brushed her shoe over the muddy linoleum. "Sounds to me like some praying might be in order. I've had terrible dreams too, and they scared the willies out of me. Talking to the Lord is the best way I know to deal with it. Ask Him to help you get back to being yourself. Or just keep working hard at something else until the effects wear off. I guess either one will do."

"Thanks for the advice, but I think I'll go home before I get into any more trouble around here. I made the mistake of talking to my wife, Marcia, about the dream this morning. Maybe taking home a couple of these apple fritters will smooth the edges a little bit. Anyway, see you next Friday."

The cook shouted his good-byes to the volunteers inside the trailer, made his ritual promise to return the next week. Waving at the men who still loitered in the tabernacle, he walked past Annie's clothes bin. Skulford Elephant materialized behind him and touched his sleeve.

"No cards right now, Skulford. It's been a rough day."

The snake man's mouth contorted with anger. "There'll come a day when you'll wish you could see one of my cards again. Anyway, I was only going to ask you about your dream."

"Really? Boy, word sure travels fast around here."

"Words always travel fast, and they keep on changing. When they split into fibers and twist together, what you get is the Great Rope everything is hanging from. I've got something to tell you about that dream: a new life is choosing you. Pretty soon you're going to be able to see things that haven't even happened yet. If you don't give in to the new spirit that's entered you, you're going to die."

Skulford swept back his hair, shuffled a few steps in reverse, disappeared around the corner of the bin. As Grady pondered the meaning of the card maker's words—wondering if this were another psychological test, a riddle he'd been given to solve over the course of the next week—a stream of Annie's people caught his eye as they passed through her gate. There were men on bicycles, the long striding bearded man who always showed up last, Perry, Roderigo, and Dracula. Library Lady put on her helmet, straddled her motor scooter, and kick-started it. All the workers who had labored in the vineyard, regardless of how little or how much energy they had expended, traveled out, paying no attention whatsoever to the punishing angels on guard outside those portals—the Lemon City Police and the DPW. Last came the resurrected warrior. As he passed through the gate, the General stretched out his arms and clasped his hands, gave himself up to the perils of Palm Street on a summer afternoon.

"Hmmm. Agh. Hmmm. If I take these guys into battle, got to be one foot in front of the other. Step, tap, step, tap. First step is surely gonna take us a thousand miles." The General jigged a little as he marched past the DPW, did an eyes left at the Carter Custom Steel Fittings warehouse. It was time for another one of his splendid crossfictions. "Hmmm. Army marches on its stomach, but it needs steel gear too, sharp hooks and shiny buttons. Hmmm. Agh. Tappity tap. Tappity. Spit shined—and don't you be calling me no 'shine,' white boy, 'cause I'll lay a buzz on your ear that'll lift you up and plant you on your sorry-assed head. Flash buzz is what I'm talking about. Take a look at the studs on these gloves and sleeves. You know that's L.A. style."

He raised his face to the sky, smiled, then returned his gaze to the warehouse. "I could shinny up that palm, get on the roof, and slide behind the sign. Do recon. Palm tree's gonna take me right where I want to go. Must be a roof entrance up there too. Epaulets. Lots of stars. Patton, kiss my ass, you blind old fucker. How would you know if they used to call me 'Man of Steel,' those actresses? Can't say the starlets are wrong, no matter how hard you try. Once they work you over, front and back, with that oil and nipple massage, the fighting's gone and moved some other place they don't even tell you about. Easy to get lost out on patrol, and before you get new orders you're on the other side of the line. Best get my men outfitted right here and now, long as I've still got the vouchers in my pocket. Anything less than a million and you got to take your chances. This ain't no war game—just real steel and real mud. Could be a desert drop or years on some ocean you never heard of."

The General quick marched a few steps, stopped again, did another eyes left, set his mind in motion across the street and up to the front door of the steel fitting warehouse. Reluctant to take off his knapsack and retrieve his climbing equipment for an actual full assault, he sent a spirit probe through the double glass doors at the front of the building. Lifting past dream to full flight, the wandering warrior got his crossfiction up to speed.

"Walking in the door like I owned the place. Tappity tip tap. Slapping hands and dancing feet. Yowsa! Too many pictures in here, bad pictures with the wrong colors, and I bet they got one signed by John Wayne or Red Skelton. Hmmm. Agh. Hmmm. Condemn the unrighteous, comfort the weak. Clown-assed fools! No thank you, I'll just keep my pack on my back. At ease! And tell me, Miss Secretary, what's your name?"

"Charlene, sir. May I help you?" The hallucinating General imagined the kind of redhead who always sits behind a receptionist's desk. Sometimes his imagination—or the grand interface between the world and his hyperkinetic mind—was more pedestrian than you'd think. But for the General, the ordinary was a trick; in his crossfictional improvisations he'd drop in those clichés like false signposts or duck decoys, just so you'd let down your guard.

"You got to stand in a long line if you want to help me, Miss. But just go ahead and talk as much as you want, do hand signs like the girl with black shoes and little ankle straps. She wanted me, you know, but there's no time left for that jive anymore. You ever been in the army? Recognize me from recruiting posters?"

His imagined receptionist stood and walked to a file cabinet, putting a little more distance between them. "No, I don't believe I know you. Could you tell me your business so I can get the appropriate person to help you?"

"I can't tell nothing to a girl like you, Charlene. I think that's your name, but the dress is wrong. Let's not pretend we never met before. All those things you said about my patented hand jive. Baby, it's time to start all over if we're gonna get this war thing under way. I knew a woman like you: red hair, named Charlene, but with different fingernails. She drove a little black car with a license plate, funny letters and numbers to decode. At least one R and one 8. House in Santa Ana over near the bridge. You know, the one I staked out—I'm in recon, logistics and supply. How else you think I'd know? Husband named Dick, but you can't tell me why."

Charlene refocused, seized on the General's words, which had so far been entirely accurate. Somewhat calmed by the placid expression on his face, the signs of wisdom implicit in his high forehead and salt-and-pepper beard, she eased back to her desk. As she lowered herself into the chair, he described her two children, the toys they'd received for their birthdays, Scott's injury playing Little League baseball, and the Neighborhood Watch meeting on threats homeless in the area posed to children.

He stopped his wall-by-wall survey and stared at her mouth. The redhead tentatively raised one finger and gestured for the General to continue.

"You brush your teeth more than three times a day. Bite into thicker kinds of juices. You got to stand back and take stock, woman. Yeah. When Dick took you all out to the Grand Canyon, they screwed up the reservation and didn't let you stay at the hotel. Everybody cried, but you went out on the rim where that tree sits on a rock that looks like a diving board. You were sure gonna see some colors anyway, some colors and a lot of rock. Tap, tap, tappity, tap. Marching all over Grand Canyon. You saw that big old mother-fucker eagle fly right over you and around the top of that world, set off on a straight line for Phoenix. Put all the high tension lines and crazy-assed dune buggies—that tourist trash—behind him. Eagles need to take vacations too. Swooping down on the Greyhound Station, that old eagle sees Charlie Briscoe, a guy I knew in Fort Ord, getting on board the L.A. Express—you know, that Grand Canyon bird figured he'd made some kind of wrong turn. But there are big plans in this world, Eagle, and you can't make a wrong move even if you try. Understand, Charlene? Just watch my hands. Think about the kind of driving that's gonna be, for eagles or whoever, and Old Charlie didn't have but a couple of bucks over the fare. And he was surely not doing as good as me. Just quick hits, you know, in this staying alive game. No access to Hollywood, no condo in Palm Springs—but he passed through there and the Chocolate Mountains and the little desert bushes. Joshua trees, Jonah trees. It gets awful deep in the desert if you know where to look, riding and riding through air. Two motorized divisions. The whole world's out there: crawling, sliding, waking up to find out. When Charlie pulls into the Greyhound terminal at Seventh and Alameda, he remembers he don't have a dime, not even enough for a cheap burger. Once you land in L.A. you just look for any clue why you came there in the first place. So he says to this guy on the corner, with a piece of cardboard that says 'HUNGRY VETERAN,' a guy named Driftwood, 'Let's can the veteran jive and find us someplace to eat. You got any missions or soup kitchens around here?' It'd been a long time for Charlie since the old days in L.A. and San Diego, and he forgot all the names. You can stop me anytime, Charlene. Can't say I don't got the stuff, 'cause I talk way too sweet for some folks."

The receptionist smiled, eased the telephone receiver back on the hook. She appeared to be searching the wall behind the General for evidence.

"Fried baloney and potato salad, with a little cup of orange drink made him wonder about what he'd been thinking when he left Phoenix, because the beans and rice at the Brotherhood there was a lot better than this, when the cardboard veteran says, 'If you could get all the way to Lemon City, down in Orange County, you'd be on easy street, three meals a day at Annie's Soup Kitchen.' So he grabbed his kit and set out, walked a bit, got some rides, stopped in Downey because he thought Bobby Higgins might still be living there. And he was too. Charlie saw Bobby's name in the gas station phone book, and it took his mind all the way back to that first trip home to the World, Travis AFB and the chicks in Oakland. But then he recalled he owed Bobby money, and more than that too, if you think about what he did to Charlene. They both did it, but there's a difference who's doing the tap dance. Hmmm. That's what it was! I knew there was a name in this story like yours, Charlene." The General pointed to the band that held down his Bedouin-style camouflage headgear.

"He got down to Fullerton, slept in the rail yard, next day caught a ride to Lemon City, walked the rest of the way. He's waiting over there now, right by the Annie's Soup Kitchen sign, no more temporary than a granite telephone pole. You know what I mean about saying words that only seem to be different and making them go farther than anybody could ever think? He comes right to the corner of Marston and Palm. When I see him, I say, 'Howdy, but you're too late. You done missed the feed today. Come back tomorrow and bring your soap.'"

Grady was still staring at the General's receding figure as it swam into the bent light rays of the smoggy summer afternoon. The cook checked his own feet, tried to remember where he was going, what he'd intended to do, how much time had elapsed since what he assumed was his conscious mind had drifted away. He raised his eyes to search for the General at the corner of Marston and Palm, but the warrior had fused with the landscape and was now invisible to all but the most esoteric systems of waveform detection. Discovering himself standing next to his own car, Grady opened the door, lowered the windows, took a long drink from his water bottle. The contents were almost hot enough to make tea. Hallelujah! The hungry have gathered and they have dispersed, carrying enough in their stomachs to survive another day. There was a great hunger in Grady too, like the one that raged throughout the world. As he steered his car out Annie's gate toward the General's vanishing point, Grady saw the ambiguous horizon resolve into a row of teeth.

CHAPTER FIVE

VISUAL
MEDIATION

Dawn breaks, slips subtle aurora beneath grease-coated undercarriages, around the couplings of immobile freight cars. Below these empty hulks, tracks form the border between Annie's compound and the rest of the world. A fence topped with barbed wire, running along the back of the cook shack, strains pink and orange early light. On the trailer's roof a long-bearded stranger squats with his back to the action. Stocking cap pulled down over brows, he begins to stretch, twist arms and legs into a graceful human semaphore only birds and angels can decode. The Mysterious Stranger finishes his silent matins just as the sun pulls its full disk above the steel rails. He stands straight, hitches up the sleeves of his ragged brown jacket, points one index finger at the sun and the other where later that Friday a burning disk will plunge into the Pacific. The supplicant holds his scarecrow position until a red-tail circles into sight, drops from the sky with splayed claws, and takes up a gentle posture on the sunset arm.

The hawk turns its head, offers an implacable eye, a fixed circle of darkness without depth or limit. As the stranger moves through that black tunnel, he hears Sweet Pea calling from the other end, four and a half hours into the future.

"Grady, you want me to cut all this squash?" The retired waitress and vegetable repair specialist rested her peeler hand on hip and with the other wagged a limp zucchini.

The cook strolled over splattered linoleum and peeked into a produce box sitting on the counter behind her. What Grady saw was a box full of voicelessness. How could these zucchinis hope to join the battered but edible eggplants and peppers to sing an elegant ratatouille? All ritual requires a hedge when results fall short of redemption. Sometimes the magic doesn't work: bread stays bread and wine gets nowhere near the Sacred Heart. Once Annie traveled to Vegas with the idea of financing her dream shelter, certain her just cause and the prayers of Sister Claire were invincible. When the great nurse walked through the cook shack door the next Friday, everybody rushed up to ask what she'd won. Annie laughed, avoided eye contact with the eager volunteers.

"Darlings, it was for the pleasure of it. I had a jar of nickels I didn't know what to do with. We stayed at the Rio and had wonderful rooms. It was very grand."

As Grady searched through the sorry box of produce, he tried to explain vegetable triage to Sweet Pea. "It's no use bothering with the soft ones. Even if they're not moldy, when they get wrinkled like that they're so bitter, they'll ruin anything you cook them with." He searched for a model piece of squash, laid it on the investment queen's outstretched palm. She shook her blonde curls, tried to snag his eye with a naughty look, glanced back at the zucchini, giggled, and awaited the punch line. Pretending not to notice, he continued his deadpan instructions. "Try to find ones that are still a little crisp, like this one."

Betty stuck her head into the huddle. "We've got a lot of food here today. I wouldn't waste time on those vegetables. The men don't like that stuff anyway. Just meat and potatoes for them. And sweets, donuts and coffee with a lot of sugar in it." She turned on a heel, headed south to spread her supervisory sunshine to other volunteers, throwing up her hands and finishing her point as she walked away. "Sugar, sugar, sugar. That's what they want. All alcoholics love sugar."

"Before you go, Betty . . ." The teacher-cook tossed a moldy squash the length of the trailer. It slammed into a plastic trash can just as the boss woman passed. Sister Claire, who'd been watching the whole encounter, whistled approval for the three-point shot. Now that Grady had the Friday lieutenant's attention, he pressed a request he'd made many times before. "Would you mind talking to the people who put produce in the bin on the other days? Since it gets over one hundred degrees out there, how do they figure stuff is going to keep? The only things that keep well inside that bin are mold and fruit flies."

Sweet Pea cackled from her station at the far sink, where she was beginning to load a colander with edible pieces of squash. "Speaking of disease, Grady, did you see in the paper about that new disease where you lose your mind? Old people and young people too. And I'm not talking about Offenheimers either."

Everyone within earshot stopped work and turned toward the Disneyland veteran. Sister Claire rinsed a small iron skillet, held it aloft like a monstrance to bless Sweet Pea with soundness of mind. Grady surveyed the scene, trying to decide whether or not he was being set up. "No, I haven't read about the new disease. How do you know if you have it?"

At the other end of the trailer, Wanda turned off the machine she used to slice pressed ham for the bagged sandwiches. "Sounds like CRS syndrome to me. You know, can't remember shit."

Grady guffawed, but the rest of the crew was silent. Ethel moved her stern-faced presence to the center of the cook shack floor, gestured with her peeler. "This is no joke, Grady. I saw it in the morning paper too. They're calling the disease 'spontaneous amnesia' and they don't really know much about it right now. Except that an awful lot of people have come down with the symptoms."

Leaving off her folding of clean dish towels, Betty joined the new debate. "Yeah, I read about it too. But people who have this stuff do more than just forget everything. They just walk around, acting like they're drugged. And it's not chronic fatigue syndrome, either. The papers made a point of that. Doctors say they don't know where it comes from, but I have a pretty good idea. We have so many immigrants coming from Mexico and all those poor Asian countries, something like this was bound to happen sooner or later."

The cook dropped his chopping knife and groaned. "Since we're talking about aliens, why don't we get down to the real problem? I'm pretty sure it's the coyotes. We know they all come up from Mexico anyway. They not only eat cats and small kids, they drink bad Mexican water, come up here, and spread this terrible amnesia disease too. Sounds even worse than deer mice with hanta virus. I think we should sterilize all of Southern California, put out poison for everything that walks, crawls, or flies."

Betty stood her ground, enlarged her mirthless smile. "Well, Mr. Grady, I guess you have a smart answer for everything. But I'll bet you wouldn't think it was so darned funny if somebody you cared about got the disease. And let me give you one more little tidbit to put in your pipe and smoke. I've been a Democrat my whole life, but I've got to admit sometimes the Republicans are absolutely on target. When it comes to Barbara Coe and Save Our State, you can sign me right up. If we don't stop all these foreigners soon, it'll be the end of California as we know it."

He wiped wet hands on apron, squared off to respond to Betty, but Sweet Pea distracted him. "Hey Grady, you're a writer. I've got a question for you. I just bought Billy Graham's book on angels to give to my sister. I had to find something because she just sent me a book on Mother Teresa. Don't know why she did that—I'd rather have a book on movie stars. But would you tell me why hardback books are so expensive?"

Grady's eyes were following Betty's retreat as he processed Sweet Pea's question. When he gave the retired waitress his full attention, he noticed a mutilated zucchini dangling from one of her hands. In spite of that, he gave her a straight reply. "Do you have any idea how expensive it is to produce books?"

"OK, but why do they have to pass along the cost to us?" Everyone in the shack must have been listening, because they all burst into laughter. As Marlene walked past Sweet Pea and savored the comment, she fell back into her paroxysm of delight.

Sweet Pea was still holding her mangled vegetable in midair. "What! What's so funny?"

Grady returned to dicing onions. "I'll explain it to you some other time. But until then, maybe you'd better stick with the stock market."

Sister Gianetta stopped chopping parsley—she called the technique "Italian style." Her North Beach mother had taught her when she was fourteen, just before she joined the convent as a novitiate. That the nun had retired after serving sixty-nine years as a teacher and librarian in various parochial schools made Grady embarrassed to complain about being burned out. The tiny woman, inches on the downside of five feet, moved a step closer to the cook and spoke in a confidential tone. "You know, I read that book on angels by Billy Graham, and I didn't care for it much."

He looked down into Sister Gianetta's mischievous dark eyes. Although Grady judged that her remark was without intentional irony, he could not hold back his laughter.

"Why do you think that's funny? Have you read the book too?"

"No, Sister. But your dislike of Billy Graham's work doesn't come as a complete surprise, since his people don't consider Catholics real Christians."

Pastaman and the parsley expert still had their heads together when one of the tabernacle regulars appeared at the south entrance to the trailer. "Aaaahhhhhh." Perry prefaced many of his utterances with a long, nasal fanfare. "Ahhhhhh, if you give me a bucket of Lysol water and a mop, I'll clean out the bathrooms for you." He pushed his glasses back from their precarious position at the end of his nose, shuffled, and waited.

Grabbing a bucket, Betty added disinfectant and filled it to the top using the rinse hose from one of the sinks. During the whole process of preparation, she praised the man for his fine work ethic, asking him if he'd had his morning coffee and wondering if there was any-thing else she might do for him. Perry politely declined her offers, received the bucket and mop, and disappeared into the first bath-room. The rest of the volunteers forgot about him entirely, until he reappeared at the door fifteen minutes later, making a low whining noise and foaming at the mouth. Betty began to thank him, but once she set her eyes on his face, ceased in midsentence. He fidgeted at the door, dropped his bucket of filthy water, and took off.

Sister Claire brought a rubber-gloved hand to her lips. "What on earth happened to him? The poor fellow looks like he ate some kind of cleanser. Do you think we should go out there and find out if he's all right?"

The Friday lieutenant had recovered from the shock of the sight and waved her cousin off. "Oh, don't worry. If it was anything seri-ous, he'd be sure to let us know."

Ethel had a theory. "Maybe he mistook scouring powder for sugar and put it in his coffee. Do you think that might hurt him?"

The cook walked to the door, trying to discover where Perry had gone. He took off his glasses and wiped them on his apron. "Of course it would. That stuff is poison. Why do you think I'm always telling Sally to keep it away from the food? But I can't believe he'd swallow something as nasty as cleanser mixed with coffee. Maybe he just worked himself into a lather. He scrubs those serving tables like a demon, nose just off the surface. Perry's the only guy I know who has worse eyes than I do and doesn't carry a white stick."

Turning back to her dishes, Sister Claire stopped and stared out the window at the fan palm by the fence. "He does have terribly thick glasses, you know. That would explain why he's so careless about his grooming. I don't think he'd washed or cut his hair in years when I first sat him down to spruce him up."

The cook ran fingers over his cheek, remembering he'd forgotten to shave that morning. "Sister, you did a great job. I love the way you trimmed Perry's sideburns and moustache. He looks like a sixties cowboy now—Haight Ashbury, Jefferson Airplane style."

The liberation theologian eyed Grady's beard. "I could do wonders for you too. All you have to do is sit down next Friday and let me at it. I won't even make you put your name on the sign-up sheet."

Grady put his hands over his mouth and chin in mock horror. "I bet you're just like my wife. You'd Delilah my beard away, if you could."

She laughed but didn't contradict. "Perry is such a strange duck. He told me the funniest story the other day when I was cutting his hair. It was about a bet he made with DeLorean. He told DeLorean that if he were to go home, none of his family would recognize him. Of course, Perry was trying to get him to tell who he really was, whether he was the real one or someone else."

The mention of the auto magnate's name always made Sweet Pea perk up. She shouted from her squash repair station. "Well, if he's the actual millionaire he sure hasn't helped much with stock tips. I keep asking him and he only wants to talk about baseball."

"You keep asking him about Chrysler stock. I think you're confusing him with Lee Iacocca." Grady walked to the stove and unloaded a plastic cutting board piled with diced onions into a pot of sizzling ground beef.

"Let me finish my story, now." There were few things that made Sister Claire purse her lips, but an interruption was one of them. "I just wanted to tell you how DeLorean outfoxed Perry. Instead of talking about his family, or the things that had happened to him all these years after the trial, he said the question of mistaken identity reminded him of an old *Star Trek* episode, from the original television series. And, of course, Perry, who loves *Star Trek*, couldn't resist. Only after DeLorean had finished his version of the story and walked away did Perry realize he'd been had."

With her back to the door, and not having the proper line of sight anyway, there was no way Sister Claire could have witnessed DeLorean and a defoamed Perry sitting at table number six, under the canopy of the tabernacle, once again speaking about the question of identity.

"Aaaaahhhhhhh. You know, it's the damnedest thing, but when I start thinking about eating pussy, my mouth starts to foam up. Just can't help it. Happened to me again when I was cleaning the bathrooms." Perry smoothed his handlebar moustache with one finger, double checking to make sure no foam remained.

DeLorean tucked a bookmark into his paperback and laid it down on the picnic table. He was the only one, outside the Magnificent Seven, who was educated and insightful enough to appreciate the cowboy's linguistic achievements. More than that, Perry's conversation was a diversion for him. "Pussy eating sometimes gets a little sloppy, but then that's a problem you can deal with, considering all the possible things that are likely to go wrong in a man's life."

"Aaaaahhhhh, tell me about it, partner." Perry stretched his arms over his head, locked fingers, and cracked knuckles. "It's been a long time for me. Thinking about cunnilingus just makes me miss it all the more. Makes me even imagine being on the other end of it, if you know what I mean. You remember 'Return to Tomorrow,' Star Date 4768.3? Sargon puts Spock's conscious entity into Nurse Chapel's body for a while. And when Kirk looks at him at the end of the show, the old Vulcan never says a damned word about what it was like. Maybe he was going to have those woman feelings down there for the rest of his life. Like both male and female tinglings at the same time. What do you think?"

"Sure, why not?" The elegant silver-haired vagrant smiled largely. "If Tiresias could do it, why couldn't Spock?"

Perry stared out over the assembled tables in deep meditation. After some minutes, he took off his glasses and rubbed bloodshot eyes with the heels of his palms. "Last time I ate pussy was back in Texas, trying to get beside my wife again."

"Didn't know you were ever married." DeLorean set down the book he had picked up and begun to read again during the silent interlude.

"Yeah, way back. I tried to go home not so long ago, but it was a mistake. My mom and dad are dead, but my wife is still there in Amarillo. Went to our trailer, knocked on the door, and when she opened it I said, 'Howdy.' She hadn't seen me for ten or twelve years, but I was pretty sure she was putting me on when she claimed she didn't know who I was."

DeLorean raised one silver eyebrow and smirked.

"Aaaaahhhhhh, yep. Made me stand right there on the doorstep and prove who I was. I was getting mighty horny too. The old girl had put on a bit of weight on the lower end of the chassis, but she still had those magnificent tits peeking through the T-shirt. When I get to thinking about it, I sometimes wonder if I didn't have a little foam in the corner of my mouth at the time. But she stared at me, saying she had a husband who'd left a long while ago, but I didn't look anything like him. So I said, 'It's me, baby.' I threw her a profile, but she didn't budge. 'Maybe the hair and moustache are a little different, but what about my voice?'"

Perry cleared his throat, hummed a few bars of "The Streets of El Paso," rested chin on hand, and stared at the tabletop.

DeLorean pulled one leg up and over, straddling the picnic bench, giving the cowboy full attention as he unraveled his narrative. "So did she believe you?"

"Nope. She said it had been so long she'd forgot her husband's voice. And she declared mine didn't sound at all familiar. So then I thought about stories. You know how you always tell a woman a secret story so you can identify yourselves to each other in an emergency? Like a kidnapping or alien invasion or something? I knew we had a story, but I'd forgot what it was. So I started talking, figuring with luck I might hit on it. Man, I told her a couple of stories about the dog. Of course, the dog was dead by that time, so it didn't help. Then I told about the time I was so drunk I couldn't get out of the bathroom. Must have come up with a dozen or so of those little scenes, but she just stands there with her arms folded, shaking her head.

"So I say, 'Don't play with me, baby. You know it's me. I'm your lover man. I'm sorry I been gone so long, but I'll explain all that later. I'm back for you, baby.' I just kept chattering, but she wasn't buying. I was still on the step and she was still behind the screen door. Then I got this idea—why not cut right to the chase? So I say, 'Baby, there's one thing I know you'll never forget—the way I eat your big beautiful pussy. Just let me at it, and my tongue'll prove who I am, once and for all.'

"She stood there, arms still folded, for the longest time. I was thinking about how much I was going to hate crawling back to that Amarillo Greyhound station. But then she opened the door and said, 'OK, big boy, I'll give you a try.' Well, she unbuckled that old silver steer's head and down come the jeans and panties, right to the boots. But she don't slip them over the shit kickers, you see. She just lifts the whole affair over her head, bends her knees a little, and offers me deluxe burger with the works. Well, I'm at it as soon as my tongue hits the mark. She groaned and she bucked for a good while, and it was so wet I thought I was swimming upstream. Then she went rigid, shivering and shaking all that jelly, let out a real big whoop. I went back on my haunches, trying to catch my breath and dry off my face a bit.

"She drops her legs to the floor, pulls up the jeans and buckles. Walks over to the phone and puts her hand on the receiver, saying,

'I don't know who you are, buddy, but you sure as hell aren't my husband. I'm giving you thirty seconds to get out that door before I call 911.'"

~

The river is a beckoning woman. But how do you locate your aboriginal watershed? How can you find your way home? Ancestral spirits can fly much higher than eagles, hawks, or turkey vultures—even higher than ghost condors. They are the spirits who have become the probable narrators of our redemption, our only hope for survival in any form. Whiskey Ed listens to those spirits. Along with the wandering prophets dismissed as schizophrenic street people, he circulates at ground level, gathering final data. When the findings are chanted, there will be a great conjuring. A crossfictional scenario beyond imagination will come to light. This is precisely what Annie means when she says, "I think I'm making this up."

"Top o' the morning to you!" Navajo Bill took a step through the north door of the trailer, shouted his usual greeting, which signified that Annie was working her way up the ramp and would momentarily announce her presence through the other door. Navajo Bill assumed his usual slouching posture, removed sunglasses, accepted return good wishes from the crew. The man fascinated Grady, because he could never quite read his narrow eyes or embarrassed smile. A mathematical genius who appeared even farther out in space than Albert Einstein in a sweatshirt, he gave no clue to the inner workings of his mind. Of course, there were plausible guesses. Maybe the quizzical look came from the space program retiree wondering how he'd gotten so inextricably tied into Annie's daily comings and goings.

Annie burst through the south door, hugging the first body she could put her hands on—in this case Wanda. "Oh, hello, hello, hello. I'm on the Internet!" Her eyes danced out of control and her shoulders were drawn up in a joyful shrug, poised to launch her straight into heaven on sheer rapturous energy. "My dears, I love you all so much, you'll live forever. I'm on the Internet!"

As the volunteers suspended their tasks and gathered around their spiritual leader, Sweet Pea was the first to offer an assessment. "Well, Annie, it looks like you're in business now. You'll probably get rich."

The nurse's celebratory smile went suddenly sober. "Oh no, my dear, this is all for the men. It's not me but Annie's Soup Kitchen that's on the Internet."

Grady stepped forward, wiped hands on his apron, gave her a hug and a kiss on the cheek. "Do you have a Web page now?"

Annie grabbed the cook and pushed him away to arm's length. "My good man, I don't have the slightest idea what you're talking about. He was named Nod. I'll never forget the name, because it makes me think of my own head. He called me on the telephone and said, 'Annie, you're on the Internet.' And I pretended I wasn't so stupid, but I had no idea what he was talking about. I didn't even know what the word meant until I called my daughter and she told me."

Sister Claire stepped forward and touched her fellow nurse on the shoulder. "Congratulations, Annie. Do you think this will be a big help to you?"

Having exhausted her supply of blood sugar, Annie began to shake more than surge. "Sister dear, it already has. A couple came yesterday and gave me towels and underwear for the men. All the things I had no money to buy. It was just lovely. And it's because I'm on the Internet."

Ethel laughed with amazement, then caught herself and returned to the usual deadpan. As the self-appointed sheriff, her mission was to keep everyone honest, even her leader. "Did you give those underwear people the lecture, Annie?"

"I did. And it brought tears to their eyes, bless their souls."

The crew all laughed, including the visionary feeder, who looked as though she'd just robbed a bank and was enormously pleased with herself, hoping no one would make her put the money back.

Grady loved to encourage her when she was sly and rascally, in her full benevolent trickster mode. "But you know Annie only tells them the truth."

"That's so, my dear. I never lie to them. But there's another thing I must tell all of you. Some men from television are coming over today to talk to me. They'll be here at noon. I want all of you to do your usual business. You can just pretend they aren't even here."

Sweet Pea, who was not good at pretending, began to jump up and down. "We're all going to be on TV! What channel, Annie? What station?"

The ninety-five year old nurse walked to the table, sat down heavily, and looked through her purse for the note she had made on the details of the interview. Not being able to find it, she declared it unimportant, adding that it didn't matter what station the men were from as long as they were from television. That would surely be good news for Annie's Soup Kitchen.

When the white van with the long collapsible antenna on its roof drove into the compound just before noon, Betty was the first to get out and greet the television people. She assured them she was the person in charge and would be happy to provide background information, show them around the facility. The reporter and cameraman smiled at the Friday lieutenant, chatted with one another as they set up, but asked her only one question: "Where is Annie O'Rourke?"

As the television crew entered the cook shack, found the spiritual leader at the table, drinking coffee and consuming apple pie, the talent show began to take shape. Sweet Pea offered cordial greetings to the dark-haired woman in the green suit, because she was the only one carrying a microphone. The retired Disneyland waitress knew her show biz people, mentioned she had once served Charlton Heston and that one of her sons was an aspiring screenwriter. She did her Shirley Temple soft shoe: toe to heel, toe to heel, and a quick spin. Ethel was working at the closest sink, offering her

version of "Don't Sit Under the Apple Tree." As her voice strength-
ened, she moved into a half-hummed, half-sung medley of forties
swing tunes. Sister Claire was not surprised at the improvised Ama-
teur Hour. These two had come up with similar routines a year
before when a documentary team from her order had come to the
Kitchen to film her. Embarrassed and irritated by the confusion, she
walked out the cook shack door, followed closely by Grady.

The young woman in the suit held out her hand to Annie. "Ms.
O'Rourke, I'm Gabriela Vargas from KXON, and this is Bob Hersh-
feld, my cameraman. When you finish your pie, do you think we
could go outside for the interview? Perhaps you could show us some
of the features of your shelter."

Annie was struggling to get up. "My dear, I'm already finished
with the pie. And it would be a pleasure to show you all the lovely
features. Of course, it's not a shelter. No, it's my dream to have one
someday, but we're only a humble soup kitchen now. It's the Lord's
work we're doing here. He said to feed the poor, and we're doing the
best we can with the little money that we have."

Leading them outside—unaccompanied, thanks to a nun blocking
the egress against curious volunteers—the great nurse first showed
the television people her clothes bin, marveling aloud at the foolishness of donated high heels and evening gowns with spaghetti straps.
She also mentioned her new presence on the Internet and said it had
already brought more practical donations. They took a peek into the
supplies bin and the food bin, but Annie rushed them away, mutter-
ing about untidiness. She offered anecdotes about men who'd been
successful in finding jobs, sometimes returning to donate money and
in one case giving flowers to the female volunteers. As Annie and the
television people moved toward the canopy, some men avoided the
camera, others made sure they were part of the pageant. After
Gabriela got her fill of cheese shots, she guided Annie to a bulldozer
at the far end of the compound, began asking specific questions

about the financing of the Kitchen and how she felt about citizens and merchants who complained that the homeless were a nuisance.

Annie went rigid at the word *nuisance*. She gestured toward the street of warehouses. "Do you see any homes or children here to be bothered? They made us leave the public park when we were only trying to help people who had no other way. And now that we're here, and bothering nobody, those same people are still complaining. Some churches too! But on the great tree that is Christ's true church, people like that aren't even the tiniest leaf."

Gabriela signaled Bob to pull in close for a head shot. "Ms. O'Rourke, what is your reaction to the rumor that the diversion of raw sewage into the C & R Canning plant was the work of irate homeless people?"

The nurse drew her head back, adjusted her eyeglasses. "I hadn't even heard about that, my dear. Was it one of those accidental spills?"

"No, it certainly wasn't accidental."

"Well, I can't have an opinion, since I only know about the accidental kind. But I have something to say about the new disease everyone is talking about. It's much more important than a soiled factory. If we don't do something immediately, the Shadow Plague will be the end of us all. This is much more grave than doctors believe it is. I worked in hospitals for forty-seven years, you see, and though I love so many of our doctors, there are some who would fall into a pit for looking at the moon."

"Ms. O'Rourke . . ."

The great nurse reached out to touch the reporter's hand but pulled back, realizing she was beyond her reach. "My goodness, child, just call me Annie. No one ever uses my family name."

"Annie, why do you call the new disease the 'Shadow Plague?' Is that an Irish expression?"

"No, it isn't. It's what an angel of the Lord told me during his visitation. I don't believe he was Irish, though I never thought to ask.

He said that if we didn't stop the Shadow Plague soon, it would be the end of us—all humankind."

The reporter glanced back at the cameraman. "Did the angel say anything else?"

"Yes. He said it had started in America but was spreading over the world. He said it was caused by the way our natural things that God has given us are being mistreated: people and plants and animals. The angel told me there are 1,452,374 people with the disease right now, but that most haven't been recognized as such." Annie had become so agitated, she'd run completely through her blood sugar and was beginning to shake. After staggering forward, she reached out to hold Gabriela's microphone hand. She called out to Whiskey Ed, asked him to bring William, her nickname for Navajo Bill. When the interviewer tried to pursue the matter of the Shadow Plague, the nurse apologized and confessed that she was all talked out.

The chatter around the serving table at one o'clock was a good indication this was no usual day. It was far more celebratory than Thanksgiving or Christmas. About halfway through the commensal ritual, Navajo Bill quietly escorted Annie from the table in the cook shack where she had been recovering. They were well away from the tabernacle, unnoticed as Bill held Annie by the elbow and the two of them shuffled toward his burgundy pickup.

The great nurse stopped, nodded at a spot of pavement before them. "Will you look there, William? I've never seen the like."

Bill smiled his sad, embarrassed smile, swept his eyes over the designated area, but saw nothing. "Look where, Annie?"

She turned to her faithful chauffeur, pulled her elbow away from his grip. "Right over there at the boat!"

Bill rested a hand on the few hairs that remained on the top of his head, assumed his standard slouch. "What boat? I can't see any boat. What would a boat be doing in a parking lot anyway?"

"Well, of course you can't see it, because it's an enchanted boat, an invisible boat. You probably can't see the river either, but it's

running right through here as sure as the day you were born."
Annie took three steps forward unassisted. "Come over here and
step into it."

After pushing out a long sigh and shaking his head, Bill took several steps forward, testing the resistance of the pavement with each
one. But his attempt to humor Annie only made her more irate.

"No, not there! Over here with me. And mind yourself getting
in."

The volunteer who worked not one but every day of the week
stood next to his boss, looked around him for cues that would allow
him to proceed. "Should I sit down, Annie?"

The watershed seer grabbed Bill by the arm and gave him a gentle shake. "No, you don't have to do that. Standing is just fine in this
boat. But remember in the days to come what a marvelous trip we
took. And now that it's finished, would you please bring around
your truck and take me home?"

Annie stood alone, extended both arms before her face, palms
outward. She was chanting or praying, but the only sign of her
devotions was moving lips. Then she clapped hands, rushed down
the dark tunnel, drove the Mysterious Stranger out through the
hawk's eye and back to a trailer roof struck with the light of dawn.
The raptor, still perched on his sunset arm, cocked its head, allowed
the Stranger's eyes to break out of the spell, scan the pavement
below, register the presence of a silver coyote loping past a pile of
asphalt. The red-tail sprang into the air, beat its wings with great
force until it had pulled itself up to soaring height. The coyote, smiling its trickster smile at the rooftop conjurer, passed behind the
clothes bin heading toward the fence and railroad tracks. The Mysterious Stranger waited for it to exit on the other side. What reappeared instead of the wily animal was a familiar silver-haired thug
named Roderigo, crawling clumsily on his hands and knees, then
crouching naked by the cyclone fence.

CHAPTER SIX

PICARESQUE

A voluptuous young Latina wearing hard hat, khaki work shirt, and tight jeans pauses halfway up the oil refinery ladder, dips one shoulder, and smiles out from the television screen.

"Just because we at Seaco work day and night to make the best gasoline for the lowest price doesn't mean we don't care about anything else."

The oil company's logo, a leaping dolphin, flashes almost subliminally across the screen before the camera pans over a skid row cardboard shelter, incised with dramatic late afternoon shadows. Cutting back to the refinery, a freckled Huckleberry Finn of a foreman, also in hard hat, looks up from his clipboard in apparent surprise.

"We *do* care about all of our customers, and about the less fortunate as well. Seaco wants everyone to share in the great American dream, even if they've been experiencing a little hard luck lately. Seaco and its employees have joined together to contribute nearly one million dollars to shelters throughout Los Angeles and Orange Counties."

The scene shifts to a line of happy, grateful homeless pushing trays through what appears to be a well-lit cafeteria. No one in the line is drunk, pugnacious, or frantic: evidently this is a scene of deliverance. Once again the dolphin logo flashes by, and we return to the refinery, where a woman looking very much like a news reader—high yellow, tailored suit, and mandatory hard hat—walks briskly through a forest of vertical pipes.

"This month we salute Annie O'Rourke of Lemon City for her tireless service to her fellow men and women for over seventy years. Seaco is proud to help fund her soup kitchen and shelter."

The camera locks on the dolphin logo. Blurred patterns behind the mammal's silhouette rack focus into a huge American flag flapping in the middle of the refinery. The camera zooms in until the flag fills the screen. Soundless fade to black. Heavy white sans serif letters against the darkness: AT SEACO WE CARE ABOUT ALL OF YOU.

Sweet Pea was the first to see the Seaco ad on television. She called Annie and put her on alert. By the next Friday the great nurse had seen it several times and was furious. The volunteers, expecting the same kind of exuberance she showed after hearing about the Web page and watching her interview on television, were surprised at her melancholy demeanor, her unwillingness to talk. Annie excused herself from apple pie and coffee, walked out of the trailer into the compound, approached Whiskey Ed's van on the driver side, stuck her head in the window.

"Have you seen the television advertisement by the oil people, Edward?"

The electronics wizard was draped over his front seat, sleeping off a serious hangover. He sat up, attempted to knead his face into presentable form with the heels of his hands. "Oh, Annie. No. No. I haven't. But I heard about it."

Ed was lucky the great nurse's eyes were focused elsewhere, peering through a tiny window in the air into a parallel universe, a place where she could see some scheme of salvation materializing. "Saying we're a shelter! And no one asked our permission before they used the name of Annie's Soup Kitchen." She rubbed thumb against index finger. "Not a penny of the money they said they were giving us has come into my hand. As I am honest to my God, Edward, I don't think these are good people. They don't sincerely mean us well, and yet they're making themselves into princes."

Ed tentatively touched fingertips to beard stubble, realized his breath must be telegraphing the gross overindulgence of the previous night. Afraid of getting a lecture from Annie, he turned his head from her as he spoke, feigning thoughtfulness. "I'm sorry to hear that. The money would have done a lot of good around here."

Annie reached through the van window and clamped down on Ed's shoulder with remarkable strength. "Wouldn't it, though? With the amount of money they were telling people about, we could build the greatest shelter on earth. Now I've been pondering this business up and down, and I've decided we need to pay the oil people a night visit."

Those words galvanized Ed into a state of panicked alertness. It had been hard to sell her on the canning company caper; now Annie had metamorphosed into Edward Abby and wanted to plan guerrilla action herself. The monitor of exotic wavelengths agreed to gather the Seven but expressed doubt that the group could work well together in a job as difficult and dangerous as this. He asked if he might invite everyone but Roderigo. Annie began to break into a smile, but raised her hand to her mouth and coughed into it instead. "Numbers have great power, Edward. All seven of us must come."

For the next few days, Whiskey Ed wandered around Annie's compound worrying at his tenuous wreath of hair, even more electrified than usual from sheer anxiety. He'd linger near the cook shack door, wait for an opportunity to tug at the nurse's sleeve, then enumerate in a low whisper potential obstacles to the undertaking. When she refused to revise the plan, he'd retreat to his van, throw himself prostrate on the sprung front seat, and agonize over catastrophic scenarios.

At 2:00 A.M. the following Wednesday, a fully loaded Watershed Express chugged west on the 22 freeway. Ed's prophecy of internal dissent was being realized. Skulford, crouching in his usual spot behind Annie's seat, stressed the difficulties of monkeywrenching a target as large as an oil refinery and warned them there were limits and a high degree of unpredictability connected with his electromagnetic manipulations. Turning her head as far as arthritis would allow, Annie's eyes transfixed the pale phantom of a face. "All we need, my dear, is a very small spill."

As Skulford began to express his concerns—the heavy security at the refinery, full crews working around the clock, the sheer size of the complex, covering hundreds of acres—Whiskey Ed interrupted and complained about problems of his own. "Well, let me tell you all a little secret: the first and maybe biggest technical problem is just getting this van to Carson. There ain't no guarantees. Last week I was driving down Baker Street in Lemon City and the right rear wheel came off with part of the axle. I had to pound a new bearing in with a hammer. Cost me my entire reserve of twenty dollars. I'm not thrilled about driving on the freeway, even if we are going slow."

His back against the roped-together rear doors, the General had been laying down a bass line of monotone chanting through all the argumentation. As the van merged into the northbound 405, he surprised everyone by shifting from a shaman drone to lyrics. "You Don't Bring Me Flowers," then "A Rainy Night in Georgia" and Lionel Ritchie's "All Night Long." As he sang the latter, the creative warrior began to mix in lines from the previous two songs, until he had produced a rich medley. In the meantime, Roderigo, irritated by the sudden serenade, started to shout bursts of Spanish.

The General, rather than being put off by Roderigo's linguistic interventions, simply added them to his collage. Uncomfortable with the collision of words bouncing around inside the van—it reminded him of Babel, the point at which all human history began to go wrong—Perry leapt in as a simultaneous mediator and translator.

"Aaahhhhhhh. What the General seems to be saying, Roderigo, is that people need to take care of each other. You know, just think about it . . ."

Skulford was in no mood to hear about brotherhood. "I want to know why we do all this sabotage but never mention the Shadow Plague, which is what it's all about, right? Just answer me that, anybody!"

Perry grabbed Library Lady by the elbow, hoping she'd join him as a voice of reason. But even in the dim freeway light, her smiling face made it clear she was enjoying the free concert. After one more shot at mediation, Perry shrugged, picked up a paper bag full of old circuit boards, dumped its contents on the floor of the van, and pulled the bag over his head. There was a moment of silence, then he began to yodel at the top of his voice.

Skulford, suspending his tirade against the mismanagement of the adventures of the Magnificent Seven, asked his co-conspirator about the paper bag.

"Aaaaahhhhhhh. Terrific resonance, my man, almost as good as the shower. Just listen." The cowboy roared enthusiastically. "Sounds just like a lion, don't it?"

As the General swung into a spirited version of "She Works Hard for the Money," an octave higher than his usual range in order to sound more like Donna Summer, Annie closed her eyes and clapped hands together in prayer. Rocking back and forth in the front seat, she urgently requested that the Lord restore her fellow travelers to their full senses and that He turn the volume down to a normal conversational level. This, in spite of the fact that she was shouting the prayer in her hill to hill voice.

Whiskey Ed pounded the steering wheel, leaned on the van's anemic horn. "Shut up, shut up, shut up all of you! Damn it, we're already up to Long Beach, and there's not a chance in hell we can drive right through to Carson and do anything useful at this point. I'm getting off the freeway. Maybe we can find an all-night place and get some coffee. Personally, I'd like to cancel the whole thing right now and go home."

Annie took a long breath, looked over her shoulder at the folks in the back of the van, all of whom were utterly silent for the first time during the trip. "Coffee would be very good, Edward."

The General, in full battle regalia, led the Seven through the door of the restaurant. As the night manager, positioned behind the cash register, scanned the giant from knee-high rubber boots to Bedouin headgear, his face collapsed into terror. One hand dropped to the alarm button under the counter, but his panic was eased by the sight of a smiling Annie O'Rourke guiding her little community through the door. Since the corporate headquarters of this restaurant chain had just settled a multimillion-dollar class action discrimination suit, he had been instructed to make the best of what central management termed "difficult situations." Summoning a polite greeting, he signaled a waitress and pointed to a crescent-shaped booth in the back corner. The all-night's sparse population included two men sitting at the counter, separated by three swivel stools; a group of four young women in a booth against the front window, energetically ignoring the five surfers camped in the booth next door; and a table of four skinheads who had been laughing and playfully swiping at one another until the Magnificent Seven made their entrance.

After some bustling over who would have inside and outside positions, the inspired monkeywrenchers deployed themselves around the crescent and the waitress arrived with a full carafe of coffee.

"I can see you're holding a very nice pot of coffee, Miss, and I agree I'll be missing out by taking tea instead, but I still prefer peppermint. A pot of water, very hot, please." After making his order, Skulford took out his special deck, slipped off the rubber band, dealt them as if he were about to do a tarot reading.

The General had been utterly silent since leaving the van. He slurped his coffee as soon as the waitress poured it, finishing the cup before she had gone a full round. "I need more coffee. It goes a long way toward coloring my dreams. I'm celebrating my graduation into being somebody for a change. See these hands?"

Shirley, a gaunt night shift waitress who had seen pretty much everything, took a step back. This time she wasn't sure how to react. "Let's just give you another cup and find out how long that one lasts."

"Seaco." Chatting with himself again, the warrior looked into his brimming cup as if he were reading tea leaves. "Seaco, Seaco. Sho-do-ben-do-be-do. Been to Carson before, all right. But not in the still of the night."

Perry eyed the warrior sidelong, showing cheerful concern. "Aaahhhhhh, General—this here is Long Beach, not Carson. Now I know you understand what's going down. We're kind of like Spock and Kirk, trying to save the world from destruction."

"Yeah, real good, Perry. Why don't we call the cook in on this strategy session too?" Whiskey Ed waved his hand with a flourish, thanked Shirley, and said he'd call her if they needed more coffee. As she walked back to the kitchen, the chief engineer dropped elbows to table, head into hands, and whispered his anger. "It's going to be hard enough even if you nuts don't broadcast this thing all over the county."

"Wonderful coffee, isn't it?" Amazed at the discovery, Library Lady set down the cup and hugged herself.

Annie was beginning to vibrate again. She was working herself up to a lecture, but the sight of the boy with shaven head, swastika tattoo, and nose ring distracted her. She thought sympathetically about his mother and the state the woman must be in over such a transformation and glanced around the restaurant to assess the rest of the customers.

"Aaaahhhhh, Mr. Ed, I know you're in charge of engineering and high tech, but I think we all need to agree on the whole plan of action before we go any further." Perry was accenting his verbal rhythms with two pointing forefingers, a gesture he associated with political consensus makers.

Ed paused momentarily to decide whether to respond to the insulting use of his name. "As far as I'm concerned, Buddy, you're out of your league here. In fact, we're all out to lunch. I'd just as soon drive to the beach. Might as well . . ." Ed lost the thread of discourse as he watched Skulford finish a cruciform arrangement of his cards. The last two dealt were Jimmy Hoffa and Geraldine Chaplin. "Are you checking to see if we can pull this off? Whatever you find out, please let me know."

Skulford looked up from the cards and smiled.

Roderigo, who had entirely ignored the repartee around the table, was tugging at the collar points of his polyester shirt, fluffing his silver chest hair. Noticing that they were whispering, looking his way, he winked and waved slyly at the young women on the other side of the restaurant. "Man, did you see that juicy one? Look, she's getting up and gonna come right over here. Let me out." He nudged the General, to no effect. "Come on, man, let me out."

In spite of Roderigo's struggle to get past him, the lyrical warrior held fast to his position on the edge of the booth's crescent cushion. "That actress is coming to see *me*, Coyote Man. You just don't have no knack." The General rose and bowed formally to the young woman, whose eyes were opened so wide her mascara-caked lashes were in danger of sticking to her eyebrows.

"I know you're dressed up so nobody can recognize you, but you'll always be my favorite basketball star. Would you give me an autograph? My name is Lori." A cascade of blonde hair fell over her face as she searched through her purse for something appropriate to carry the inscription. However, all she could find was a ballpoint pen. "Oh, just do it there on my hand."

Roderigo was stupefied. Annie leaned over to Library Lady, asked if she thought the General was bothering the girl. Ed and Perry covertly studied her figure, a job made considerably easier by the thinness of her tank top. Skulford continued to consult his cards. He touched Will Rogers, the Gentleman of Situations.

As the General raised one hand to reject the ballpoint, he dug into his combat fatigues and extracted a felt pen. Signing her arm from hand to elbow, he produced a scrawl so illegible the young lady was entirely satisfied. Recapping his pen, he burst into song. "Going to the chapel and we're going to get married! Going to the chapel of love. Yeah—yeah, yeah, yeah, yeah."

Two of the surfers approached the semiround table the Magnificent Seven were occupying, joined the blonde. One of them, slightly less drunk than the other, complimented the General's headgear. "Man, that Arab hat you've got there is totally sick. I mean, rad. Like you could go on safari with it, some kind of caravan, dude."

"Where'd you snag it, man?" The one with the setting eyes giggled and pulled his hair to one side. "Wow, I'm totaled. Whacked. Started drinking our way from San Berdoo last night. Whoa! I mean, banzai! We're just here for munchies. Right, Corky? Figuring to make it to Seal Beach in time for the first dawn sets. Pit City, man."

The General had stopped singing and was benignly accepting admiration from all sides. Roderigo, who cursed the blonde's taste in angry Spanish, was the only flat note in the chorus. As this romantic moment was unfolding, no one noticed the approach of the skinheads. One of the four, sporting an earring that featured a raised middle finger, stepped up to the warrior, pulled out a switchblade, and snapped it open. In a protective gesture, the General pushed his female admirer behind him, and the low conversational hum in the restaurant stopped.

The armed defender of white superiority was sneering. "Haven't you heard? Niggers aren't allowed in this restaurant. Not your freak scumbag friends neither. Guess I got to teach you that niggers messing with white women are born to die." The skinhead lunged, but the General stepped back, parried the thrusting hand. "Oh, you're a kung fu nigger. Think you can handle all of us, boy?"

As three more knives appeared, Library Lady asked Annie to excuse her, struggled to her knees on the seat of the booth, pulled up her jacket, and removed a huge nickel-plated automatic pistol from beneath her jogging pants. Without a word she began ripping off shots, each one bucking the barrel of the gun to near vertical.

The skinheads, surfers, admiring women, and restaurant staff dove for cover, sending up shrieks and terrified animal sounds. Library Lady paused for a moment, suggested to her compatriots that they head for the van, then emptied the pistol as she backed toward the door. Ejecting a spent clip, she slapped another into the handle and began firing again.

Annie O'Rourke and her helpers were in the Watershed Express and on their way before people in the restaurant, having noticed that the restaurant's windows and furniture had remained intact, surmised that the woman in black had been firing blanks. All three groups left to pursue the Magnificent Seven, the surfers and women out of admiration, the skinheads in the hope of avenging their humiliation.

Inside the van, Annie looked over the seat as Library Lady wiped down her sizzling firearm with a white hanky. "That's a very big gun, my dear."

"Isn't it a beauty, Annie? It's a Colt special edition .45. I just love guns." Eyes moist with tears of joy, she held it at arm's length and admired its glister. "Just the bullets: that's the only thing I don't like. Blanks get the job done too. It's bullets that kill, not guns. You know I'm a pacifist."

Roderigo whined about having missed out on a chance to court the other young women, cursed the General in Spanish for having blocked him from his quarry. Skulford, leaning against the back of the front seat, still breathing hard, added his own complaint. "Ordinary fucking people, I hate 'em."

Annie turned again, this time with a stern look. "And who in this company, young man, would you say is ordinary?"

Skulford pointed to the back corner of the van, where the General was cuddling with the blonde from the restaurant.

In fear the restaurant crowd might follow him, Whiskey Ed steered his custom vehicle through the back streets of Long Beach, working north toward Carson. Suspecting that retaliation from the skinheads would not be in the form of blank cartridges, he avoided the freeway, believing it would leave them vulnerable to a broadside volley. His evasions, however, were less than effective. A Chrysler convertible and a '58 Chevy wagon piled with five surfboards shadowed his every twist and turn. The skinheads, in their '75 Ford Granada, would certainly have made the pursuing cars a threesome, but their engine had flooded when they'd attempted to fire it up back at the all-night restaurant.

Unaware that he was being followed, Ed pulled to the curb along the south fence of the refinery compound, raised the hood to cool the engine, and looked around to size up the possibilities. Skulford disembarked from the colorful van, sat on the curb, began to warm up with some mental tai chi. He proceeded from that point to an assessment of the earth chakras on location, knowing he was sure to be called upon again. As always, they'd expect something spectacular. Library Lady, her .45 safely tucked away in its holster, was warming up the dance of her *chi* in the middle of the street. Roderigo ran back and forth along the broken white line, shouting, "Can't catch the wind!" As he alternately crouched and leaped, flailing his arms and growling, the Coyote Man tuned in to the resident animal spirits. Annie had her face against the fence, peering at the refinery lights, the tall release stacks that pushed out great noxious clouds, some of them in flame, and the general leakage of gagging vapors from myriad pipes throughout the system. She meditated on the seductive beauty of the refinery, the way it looked like a city that had suddenly disposed of all its citizens—an evil mother putting strychnine in the family soup pot. Ed stood behind her, groaning out his lack of faith, offering immediate resignation from the project. The great nurse paid him no mind. Perry was on one knee next to Skulford, trying to get tactical suggestions from the card reader, but he too was being ignored.

As Skulford drew Wild Bill Hickok, it suddenly occurred to him that the city of Carson was probably named after Kit, the glamorized Indian killer. He stood up and began a diatribe. How could fifties television depict the scoundrel as a warmhearted cowboy in fringed buckskin shirt? How could we forget all his atrocities, such as cutting off the breasts of Navajo women and using them to play baseball? Whiskey Ed concurred with his just anger, pointed out that the projected sabotage was certainly justified and that Seaco was an entirely appropriate target. The electronics wizard seemed on the verge of getting Skulford to change his mind, but the card maker remained unconvinced and was still inclined to drop out of the monkeywrenching expedition.

Library Lady stopped the dance of her *chi* and listened to the exchange between Skulford and Ed. History excited her, so she was eager to provide any information she thought might be relevant. "Did you know Lemon City has more lemon trees per capita than any other city in the world?"

Roderigo, who had worked himself into a frenzy running and leaping like a predator, began to laugh with such viciousness even Library Lady was offended.

"Don't you believe me? It's right there in the Guinness Book of Records. I've got one at home. It's a few years out of date, but I don't think anybody has passed us up since."

The overaged punk attempted to still his laughter with a crisp slap to each of his own cheeks. Thrusting out chest hair, wiggling hips, he crooned in the smoky voice of Harry Belafonte:

> Lemon tree very pretty,
> And the lemon flower is sweet,
> But the fruit of the poor lemon
> Is impossible to eat.

Roderigo kissed the bouquet of his fingertips and flung it into the air. "Oh yeah, Sweetheart, you can believe I know how to suck a sweet one too."

Whiskey Ed turned and saw the alpha surfer, with his buddies and the other three women right behind him. The lanky kid shuffled in his huarachi sandals and laughed. "We thought it was just bitchin' the way the lady in the black warmups handled that restaurant scene. Man, she was going off the rail."

The chief engineer stared at the intruding hot dogger, dropped his head, and groaned.

"Hey, man. Don't lose it on me. We just figured we'd hang with you dudes for a bit. Got no place to go till dawn, and some raspberry Schnapps to share. You remember me? Hey dude, I'm F.B." The friendly surfer raised his hand for a high five, but Ed offered no response.

A colleague from San Bernardino stepped forward and decoded. "F.B. That's for Frank Beaumont Huggins. You ever hear of the Desert Goofy Foot? That's him."

The woman wearing the textured cotton zebra suit joined in. "Where's Lori? Is she OK?"

After crawling out the side door of Ed's van, the General approached the impromptu gathering with the blonde from the restaurant on his arm. "Says her name is Lori, but that must start with a *C*. A heart or kidney on the *i*, you know, instead of a dot. Or a smiling volleyball. The kind of a woman can turn a man into a pig, if he don't look out. But Allah protects the righteous. Lori's my woman now." The General put an arm around the blonde's bare shoulders, and she extended hers to encircle his waist.

"Jesus Christ Almighty!" Ed was pulling at his halo of white hair again. "How many people are we going to invite to this goddamned party? Why don't we just call up the TV stations and broadcast the whole thing live?"

Annie turned around at her station by the fence. "Edward, there's no call for cursing. We need all the power of the Lord to help us, and that's no proper way to ask for it."

"I'm sorry, Annie, but our window of opportunity is closing here. It's almost four o'clock in the morning."

"Edward, I think that man is going to tow your car away."

Ed turned and saw the tow truck parked next to his van, a small brown man in khakis and a straw hat doing a walk around the dilapidated vehicle. The electronics wizard galloped toward him, flailing air with the most uncoordinated gesticulations. "Whoa! Don't tow me away. We can move it. Don't write me up!"

The small man reached for his wallet, pulled out a business card as Whiskey Ed slammed down his hood. He took a few deep breaths, calmed himself enough to read the inscription:

JESUS YBARRA
freelance towing
24 Hour Service
Anywhere in California & Neighboring States.

Ed looked up from the card, pleading. "No, you've got it wrong. I just had my hood up to cool down the engine. This van is perfectly OK."

Jesus fingered his pencil moustache, pushed up on the rolled brim of his straw hat, offered a skeptical smile. Ed thought about amending his absurd statement, but Skulford was at his shoulder, pulling the business card from his hand.

"It appears Mr. Ybarra is a repo man." Skulford tried to hand the card back to the mobile entrepreneur, but he drew his hands back in refusal.

"Look, señor. The work of my boss, the big Jesus, is always repo."

Skulford pulled Whiskey Ed to one side and Annie joined the huddle. "I tried a little push-pull to get some movement inside the refinery compound, but nothing budged. The place is too big for us to work from this angle. Our only chance is to get directly over the complex and create an inversion cloud. Then the place will suffocate in its own filth." A curl of amusement at the thought of such a fate flashed across Skulford's lips, but it quickly turned to a flash of fear as he jerked up his head. It was only the sound of the tow truck driving away. He grabbed his hair and slipped a dirty rubber band around the ponytail. It was ninja time again.

Annie touched two fingers to her forehead. She was thinking hard. "Do you imagine the birds might help us get above this place? I mean the seagulls."

"Not enough for this project." Skulford was getting prickly and impatient again. "How close is the nearest airport?"

Ed leaped back into the conversation. "There are two. LAX is just north of here and Long Beach airport is back where we just came from. If you're thinking of chartering a plane, you've got to remember it's the middle of the night. Nobody is there. And anyway, what are we going to use for money?"

The great nurse was looking straight up—right where the Milky Way would be, if she could see it. "And where is the moorage for the dirigible?"

Perry had walked over, eager to take part in the strategy session. "Aaaahhhhhh, that'd be across the freeway. The blimp's right here in Carson. Good call, Annie."

Ed threw his ample weight from one foot to the other, one of his trademark gestures of frustration. "So what good does that do? Do you think anybody's there to take us up in it?"

Unimpressed by his lack of enthusiasm, Annie was deep in thought, leaning her forehead against a knuckle. Finally, she pronounced judgment. "Well, I know a man there and he might let us borrow it for a bit."

There was a murmur of excitement among the surfers and the women from the restaurant, who had also joined the discussion. F.B. stepped forward. "Man, that is so totally rad. Whoa." He dropped his head and concentrated, visualizing a glorious ride.

Ed leaned down to Annie's ear and whispered. "How are we going to do anything with all these strangers around?"

"Edward, don't trouble yourself over what these people might know. That can all be put to right later."

As the various contingents returned to their vehicles, Lori called out to the monkeywrenchers. "We're taking Handsome with us, OK? We'll be right behind you." The General paused, and his face, illuminated by the sick light of the refinery, showed a moment of doubt. After Lori reached up under his tunic and rubbed the skin on his back, he turned and climbed into the convertible.

～

Crazy love, lazy love. When a woman stands next to a large granite egg, is it a metaphor? What happens if it's a man instead, and he leans on the primal source? You can never cut straight to the chase— or spell a long word with two letters, although people in Southern California often try, conjuring linguistic distillations for their vanity plates. The car dealers in Carson, California, do the same with the encodements they spread in lights over huge computerized signs: philosophical aphorisms, time, temperature, and the salesperson of the month.

But when a schizophrenic embarks on a word voyage, there's no looking back. The result is a leap into the mosh pit of the collective unconscious, a return to the dark reservoir that feeds the blazing oil fields of crazy love.

～

As the skinheads closed in on the Seaco refinery, the monkey-wrenchers were already on their way to the blimp moorage. The boys did, however, notice the Chrysler convertible and Chevy surf-mobile whiz by, going down the boulevard in the opposite direction. Steel Deal hit the brakes, put the Granada into a 180-degree spin, TV chase style, but killed the engine in the process. After three or four grinds, it kicked over and he set off in pursuit. Much earlier, as the lead skinhead tried to get his stalled engine going back at the restaurant, one of his associates reached under the right front fender and retrieved a pistol. The young defenders of racial purity were ready to avenge their loss of face at the hands of genetic inferiors.

Lori was a great driver, but after exiting the 405 freeway her sense of direction wasn't good enough to keep her from digressing. She wound around and around the intricate roads of the industrial park. Since the surfers were following her, the whole entourage fell five or ten minutes behind the Magnificent Seven minus one. When the two chase vehicles finally pulled into the parking lot next to the blimp field, the airship's engines were roaring, its nose ring was free from the clamp on the top of the mooring mast, and it was lifting off. The General vaulted out of the convertible, ran across the field, grabbed the end of the blimp's nose rope, and hung on as it ascended. Lori was running close behind him, screaming for him to let go, while the San Bernardino contingent and the remaining girlfriends were grooving on the adventure, wondering what it would be like to catch a wave in the middle of the air with a rig like that.

Corky craned his neck and shaded his eyes from the field lights, trying to get a fix on the airship. "Dude, you could just drop in and park that sucker in the blue. Like a permanent jaws wall. The ride of your life, man."

F.B. was in a similar reverie. "Yeah, just bitchin.' Totally sick. How long do you think that big Black dude can hold on to the rope before he falls?"

Lori was already in a state of extreme distress, but as F.B. articulated her fears for the welfare of the General, she lapsed into complete hysteria. Her girlfriends and a couple of the surfers were trying to console her when the Granada and its crew of angry skinheads slammed over the speed bump into the parking lot. Steel Deal was out of the car and running across the field, his pistol aimed at the dangling General. He fired a quick shot in hope of dropping his nemesis fifty feet to the ground. Since his first attempt had no apparent effect, his buddies suggested switching targets. "Shoot the blimp! Shoot the blimp!" The sound of the first shot helped Lori recover from her grief and anguish. Just as Steel Deal squeezed off a second shot, she took him down with a flying tackle. The surfers and Lori's friends scattered as the other skinheads came to the assistance of their downed leader. However, three squad cars on silent approach, screeching to a stop in the parking lot, convinced Steel Deal to discreetly tuck his weapon under his leather coat, stand up, and recapture his cool.

Two of the three cops were staring in awe at the ascending blimp, but the tall one was busy with a worried survey of the facility. "I don't think this is right. All the lights are off in the office there. I'll go see if the night guy is in the tool shed."

Lori grabbed the big cop by the arm. "No, no. Look at the rope hanging from the front end! That's a famous basketball star! You've got to make them come down, or he's going to fall and die!"

The woman officer squinted her eyes at the dark form looming above her. "Holy shit, she's right! Look, just below the nose. Somebody's hanging on."

Steel Deal stepped forward. "I'm a witness. It was a bunch of degenerates that stole the thing. I'm a witness. And the nigger hanging from the blimp, I could identify him anywhere."

Lori yanked on the big cop's arm again. "Don't listen to him. He came out with a gun and took two shots at the blimp. He was trying to kill the guy hanging from the rope. You know, the basketball star."

All three cops drew their side arms, suggested Steel Deal drop to his knees, position his hands behind his head. When they snatched the gun from under the jacket, the woman cop pulled his arms behind his back, cuffed the wrists, and began to read him his rights. But the defender of racial supremacy was in no mood to listen to any part of the Constitution. "You can't do this to me, assholes! The perps are up there in that blimp. You must be fucking Jews or something. They were shooting at *us* back at the restaurant. What about our rights? I'm trying to help out and you put cuffs on me. Fucking nigger and his crippled freak friends. Doesn't it count for nothing to be a real white man nowadays? Nigger lovers like you make me sick. You're the reason we need a White People's Independence Day."

As the cops called for backup and the remaining skinheads scattered into the industrial darkness, the surfers and Lori's friends rejoined the circle, offered various observations and analyses of the crisis. Lori tried to keep focus on the physical danger to the General, who by this time was out of sight. "You've got to do something. Get a helicopter and throw him a ladder—or maybe another rope. I'm telling you, he's a famous basketball star."

Trish, the curly redhead in a leopard skin print, expressed skepticism. "Lori, like he never even told you his name. What makes you think he's Amir Muhammed?"

Lori held out her autographed arm with pride. "Of course he is—just look. And besides, if we don't know his name, then how do we know he *isn't* who we think he is? Be logical, girl!" Feeling vindicated, Lori turned to the big cop. "Do you think the people up there are in trouble, sir?"

He holstered his sidearm, rested hands on hips, and pronounced his opinion grimly. "Felony blimp-jacking? Yeah, I'd say they're in some pretty deep kimchee."

The roar of the blimp's engines, which had been fading for several minutes, suddenly increased in volume. The cops, girls, surfers, and lone skinhead looked up to see the airship, its nose high and tail dragging at an altitude of about twenty feet, coming right at them. They fell to the ground, protecting heads and ears as the monster churned through, heading west, barely clearing the cyclone fence on the far side of the field.

~

Annie's Friday volunteers once discussed their fond memories of California governor Earl Warren—excepting only that strange aberration, the commission he chaired as Supreme Court justice in the early sixties. Such an honest man presenting all those silly stories as truth, why would he do a thing like that? Even Orange County conservatives wondered at the frantic scrambling to lay to rest a crazy death. Key characters in the tragedy's ensemble cast were edited out silently, the gaps stuffed with comic interludes, nonsense deemed plausible only by official minds. Any kind of story can be motivated by crazy love. A man caught in his lover's lingerie will tell the most beautiful lies. But what kind of emotion would motivate that commission's improbable fictions? Is there a limit to the flexibility of truth?

~

POLICE REPORT

Officer Jack Lardner
Helicopter Unit #4
Los Angeles Police Department

5:02 A.M. Responded to hijacking reported by Carson Police Department. Intercepted lighter than air craft, flying at an altitude of approximately 2,000 feet, west of 405 freeway in the vicinity of Wilmington Blvd. Craft was listing heavily to stern and maneuvering in an erratic manner. A black adult male was attached to one of the nose ropes. As it approached the airspace over the Seaco refinery, the craft trimmed and began to fly in a tight circle. A large cloud of dark gas formed and blocked refinery lights and flames from burn off towers. The hijackers presumably released some kind of chemical agent. After said assault on the property of Seaco, the blimp proceeded west southwest toward the ocean. Helicopter units four and six attempted to force the blimp to an inland course by training spotlights on the gondola and making close passes across the nose of the craft. These cautionary maneuvers had no effect. The computer light displays on the sides of the craft were illuminated. The hijackers sent two messages:

1) "We're armed and dangerous, and we know where you live!"

2) An obscene hand gesture.

Lighter than air craft then headed over Palos Verdes and out to sea. Our units discontinued surveillance as the hijacked craft moved into Coast Guard jurisdiction. Their aircraft intercepted shortly after it passed over the water. Our helicopter units returned to base.

COAST GUARD REPORT APPENDED.

Lieutenant JG Ronald Tarkington
U.S. Coast Guard Air Support Squadron
Long Beach, California

Intercepted lighter than air craft 5:27 A.M., bearing 118°27″50′ by 33°30″25′. Unable to establish radio contact with hijackers. Craft did not respond to visual warnings. Lighter than air craft continued on a direct heading to Catalina Island, losing altitude at a steady rate, barely clearing the surf as it headed into a fog bank in the area of Avalon. Visual contact lost at that time.

REPORT OF CATALINA POLICE APPENDED.

Officer Webster Michaels
Catalina Police Department

Arrived at blimp crash sight, in a field southeast of the golf course, at 6:37 A.M. Apprehended one Uriel Jones, who identified himself as caretaker at the blimp moorage in Carson and a victim in the hijacking. When questioned about the hijackers and the black male riding the rope, he insisted there were seven of them, and all had disappeared because they had been abducted by aliens over the Catalina Channel. Our investigation of footprints leading away from the craft verified seven perpetrators. Subsequent search of Avalon and later the entire island of Santa Catalina produced no further leads. At approximately noon of the day of the hijacking, FBI agents arrived from Los Angeles and took charge of the investigation.

CHAPTER SEVEN

ANNIE
COMES OUT

As Sister Claire took another snip at Perry's left sideburn, he raised a hand as if he were in a dentist's chair signaling pain. She stepped back, hand on hip. "I can't give you a trim without taking off a little hair."

"Aaahhhh, sorry, Sister, but you know those two babies are my trademark. Don't care so much about the other stuff." Perry smiled, shrugged an apology, gesticulated with the eyeglasses in his other hand. Actually, he was looking over his shoulder not at Sister Claire but at the bathroom door. Without his glasses there was no way to differentiate the two forms even at close range.

Scissors cocked once again near his ear, she was on the attack. "OK, Elvis, but we've done this before, and you've always survived."

Perry raised his dilapidated cowboy boots into the air. "Honey, you can do anything but lay off of my blue suede shoes." He snickered, then gasped. "Oh, sorry, Sister."

Eyebrow raised but smile still on her face, Sister Claire wagged a finger. "That song was Carl Perkins, not Elvis. And, believe me, you wouldn't be the first guy to say something out of line to me. Just the other day, when I was working the crisis hot line, this man said I had a beautiful young voice and asked me out for dinner."

"Aaahhhh, sorry Sister, but Elvis did 'Blue Suede Shoes' too." Perry grabbed his nose bridge, in search of his glasses, then realized they were in his other hand. "Did you take the guy up on the date?"

Sister Claire turned aside and laughed. "Oh, sure. But I want you to know I don't have anything against sideburns. Now beards, that's something else completely. You never know what's set up shop in all that greasy hair. And, believe me, when I'm trimming around, I hate that kind of surprise."

"Aaahhh, last I heard, Sister, Jesus had a beard. Don't think you're going to file no complaints on Him."

The hairdressing nun looked stern, ready to scold the man in the chair for blasphemy, but instead burst into laughter. "Why did you do that? Mind you, none of these guys around here even vaguely remind me of Jesus, but now I'm going to have to stop complaining about their beards. You've gone and spoiled my fun."

At the bottom of the stairs stood a shock of gray hair attached to a greasy sports jacket. A blackened hand emerged from one of the sleeves and lifted the string-tethered pen, prepared to add a name to Sister Claire's haircut list.

"Don't bother signing in. Not that you couldn't use a shampoo and a good shearing, but I can't do any more of you boys today. They asked me to pack up early because the press is coming."

The eyes under the gray hair looked up at the haircutting station on the ramp, confused. "Why would press people want to come here?" He turned and looked around him. "Somebody important showing up?"

Perry tilted his head back, spoke to the nun out of the corner of his mouth. "Aaahhh, don't think this boy has figured out he's not in Kansas anymore."

Sister Claire didn't respond to either man but continued to peck at Perry's sideburn until the disappointed client returned to the tabernacle. She drew in a deep breath, then expelled an emphatic "Hmph!"

"Aaahhh, don't be mad, Sister, he probably just come in from someplace where nobody knows about Annie. Lots of places like that." After a long pause, Perry finally deciphered her frustration. "Don't like reporters, do you."

Sister Claire used a wrist to push the hair back from her sweaty forehead. "I have no problem with reporters. But don't they have anything better to do with themselves? At least giving haircuts and feeding hungry people serves some purpose in this world."

"They all want to talk to Annie."

Scissors to sideburn, the nun was back to business. "If you ask me, this was a much happier place before all the publicity."

"Aaahhh, Sister, but how do you say no to those guys? The reporters, I mean."

"I've heard Annie say no plenty of times, in very plain English." The liberation theologian dropped hands, looked up from Perry's mop toward the gate. "And here they come."

Two men carrying equipment cases had just walked in. There was no mistaking their profession. They were followed by various teams of cameramen, sound men, and reporters, all of whom assembled and began to set up below the area on the ramp where Annie delivered her premensal prayer. Each evaluated the layout to discover the most strategic location beneath the small podium that had been set up. As preparations proceeded, some of Annie's clients covered their faces and scattered. Bench warrants on a number of charges made the media people about as welcome to that group as an invitation to interview on *America's Most Wanted*. Others were attracted to the cameras like yellow jackets to an August picnic. Phil and Dracula were the first to approach two guys pulling gear out of duffle bags.

"Phil Tabangbang." Reaching out for a handshake as he delivered his most charming smile, Phil walked up to the man in the Lakers windbreaker. "I'd like to offer my full assistance to you guys. For free. Gratis. Just ask me. I know where everything is."

The man in the sweatshirt had yet to look up from his audio gear. "Thanks, but we're doing fine. We'll let you know if we need help."

Phil took another step forward. "Actually, I've always been a multimedia kind of dude. Tell me, just how does a guy get into this racket?"

The sound man and cameraman both looked up at Phil, then at each other. They snickered, returned to their work.

"I'm serious, fellas." Hands on hips, Phil flexed his biceps. "Just try me. Throw something at me. I can handle it."

Another of Annie's clients—tall and gawky, wearing a filthy ski jacket—stuck his head into the little circle. "Hey, I worked the circus. Twice. I can do set up. You know, like a roadie. Let me help."

Phil grimaced. "Man, circus work is shit. They bust your ass, then cheat you. Saying they'll pay you in the morning, and when you come back the assholes are gone."

Dracula shouldered in, smiled, showed off his irregular uppers. "The name's Jimmy. I'm the head security guy around here. So, if you're going to do something, you've got to clear it through me first."

The media men looked up, briefly evaluated the new arrival, then returned to the task of assembling their equipment.

Spotting the bulge in the audio man's breast pocket, Dracula decided on a down payment. "For starters, how about a smoke, Bob? That's your name, right?"

The sound man dropped his gaffer's tape, retrieved his cigarettes, shook one out, and offered it. Dracula reached down and took the whole pack. "Thanks. This is a good start. Listen, Bob, I'm a contract kind of guy. Nobody's going to lay a finger on your equipment. Bet on it. I'll kick their ass if they try. Got a light?"

"So do you think we can trust the line feed?" The cameraman was trying to concentrate on setup but was beginning to become anxious about the burgeoning number of the curious who were encircling his partner and him.

The sound man pulled out a collapsible fish pole, a hand-held boom for a microphone. "No, this looks a little rinky dink. Let me set up the pussy on a stick. There's a pretty stiff breeze going here."

As the sound man pulled out a zeppelin-shaped microphone mount and a gray fur sheath that looked like a soaked cat, Phil whistled and shouted out. "Pussy on a stick. They're talking about our girl! Hey, Madalene! You hear that? Damn, but who's gonna be the stick? Some poor hard up bastard, I guess."

Madalene, who had been primping both herself and her dog in anticipation of a close-up, was sitting at tabernacle table number four. She shouted back. "Fuck you, Phil. Maybe if you had a stick, you'd know what to do with it."

As the General strode up to the circle around the kneeling media men, Annie's boys suddenly pulled back, giving him significant elbow room. The cameraman noticed a quick shuffle of the onlookers out the corner of his eye and looked up. If he was anxious before, the General's appearance brought him close to panic.

His partner, unaware of the looming giant, was humming to himself as he assembled the pussy on a stick. "Alonso. Listen, I don't know about this. Think about the angle. I can't drop it in from above unless I can get to the side of her. Are we cleared to get up there on that deck? I mean, I can't push the fish pole up from below." Hearing no reply, the sound man lifted his eyes and flinched as the General leaned down into his face for a closer inspection, adjusting his Bedouin-style wrap to keep it from falling off his head. The sound man's eyes dropped to the sudsy water splashing out of the General's knee-high boots. That unsavory solution was getting closer and closer to the five-thousand-dollar portable mixer he was about to strap to his hip. Beside him, Alonso instinctively threw his body over the Betacam he had been calibrating.

"Don't worry, just doing recon. But I smell something else. Electronic white boys. Hmmmm. Agh. Hmmmm. Got to watch these boys from the upwind side. Do I know you?"

As the General thrust his face and shoulders toward the cameraman, he and his partner crab-scrambled backward with their equipment, flashed a panicked look at one another. Before they could take a defensive course of action, the General stepped on one of the camera bag's straps.

"You white boys ever been in the army? Do I know you? I never forget no kind of face. Doesn't matter how many beards you put on. Tip tap. Tippety tap. But don't you go and worry now. I been in the business a long time. You know, actresses. They can't let go of me." With a large smile, the General thrust out his monstrous hands. "See the marks they made?"

As this small drama dominated the attention of the media people and Annie's clientele on the lower level, Navajo Bill quietly escorted the visionary feeder up the ramp and into the Kitchen. She entered the cook shack door near the restrooms, her vibrant joy about to burst into the purity of language, expressed in her hill to hill voice. "Oh my dears, my dears, I have just bought the very best hearing aids known to man. Can you hear me? Can you hear me?"

Sharing her leader's joy, Sweet Pea clapped hands together and laughed. Everyone else smiled in the sharing of light, except Sister Gianetta. She took a step closer, squinted, then shouted back. "Yes, Annie, we can hear you. But the question is, can you hear us?"

Annie stared down at the little nun, paused thoughtfully after reading her lips, then beamed broadly. "No, my dear, not a word!"

Betty rushed forward. "My goodness, we've got to get those things out of your ears before the press conference. Let's go into the bathroom. There's no privacy out here."

With uncharacteristic docility, Annie allowed her Friday lieutenant to lead her away, still smiling with pride over her high-tech purchase. When the two reemerged, the ancient nurse raised shaking hands, drew the volunteers around her. "Now I want all of you to behave in a proper way when these reporters come to talk to me. We all want to be at our very best. This is television, you know."

Noting Sweet Pea's downcast eyes, she added. "And I want all of you to stand behind me while I speak to them. They must know that Annie's Soup Kitchen is far more than the work of a single person."

There was a collective gasp of delight. But as the volunteers were enjoying the prospect of their celebrity, Annie turned and shuffled slowly toward the homely formica table against the wall. "But until they call for me, I would like to sit down and rest a bit." She tried to ease into a metal folding chair but sat down hard as her legs gave out. Closing her eyes, drawing a deep breath, she pulled herself together. "Would someone be so kind as to get me a piece of apple pie and a cup of coffee?" As Marlene and Betty scrambled to fulfill her wish, Annie's eyes moved restlessly around the Kitchen. Head turned slightly to one side, her hair vibrated in harmonic sympathy with her palsy. A subtle smile passed over her lips. It was clear she was already somewhere else, listening to dialogue no one else could hear. Annie had spent her entire life on a permanent conference call.

The crews outside, both Annie's and the ones from the media, were getting restless. A Santa Ana wind blew vigorously from the east. Everything in its path—animal, vegetable, and mineral—lost life-sustaining moisture, vibrated with an edgy static electricity, and drew just a little closer to violent collision. Cops hated Santa Ana winds as much as they hated full moon nights. With each event the world went a little crazy and there was nothing anyone could do about it. If you tried to mediate, your only reward was to be dragged into the whirlwind.

Outside the cook shack people were wired with an unnamed tension, pushing through all their circuits toward a point of release. When Grady appeared in the doorway, steadying Annie on one arm, a cheer went up from the faithful. In response, the media people jammed a little closer in anticipation of the visionary's words. After delivering her to the podium and adjusting the microphones, Grady took his place among the volunteers who stood behind her. The great nurse cleared her throat and tapped one microphone.

"Can you hear me?"

The men shouted in the affirmative.

Annie swept a knuckle over her sweating brow. "There are so many things to talk about, I don't know where to begin."

Perry, in the midst of the crowd gathered in front of the tabernacle, raised a fist and shouted. "Tell it, Annie!"

"It makes me so sad to say it, but maybe the Shadow Plague is all for the better. Frogs are growing six and seven legs because of the terrible things we have put into the water where they live. Doctors in Los Angeles are telling pregnant women not to drink water from the tap, because it might harm their babies."

The reporters and sound men had stopped signaling one another and elbowing for better position. Like the camera men, they were now focused solely on the tormented figure behind the podium.

"If we're all headed for this terrible destruction, it's just as well . . . "

The large commercial van that had just flown through the gate spun small rocks across the pavement as it slammed on its brakes, just feet away from the congregation. The dramatic interruption made Annie lose her thread and go silent. Cameras swung left to record the intrusion. The logo on the truck and the accompanying large red letters identified the local upscale caterer who had designated Annie his preferred tax write-off. Men in double-breasted cooking smocks leaped out of the van, retrieved several large trays of food from the back. As they worked their way up the ramp toward Annie, the one in charge began an apology.

"I hope we aren't interrupting anything, Annie, but we wanted to be sure to get these Beef Wellingtons to you today. Two dozen of them, and they haven't been touched!" As he approached the visionary feeder, she stared and sputtered, her face alternating between a smile and a frown. Pulling back the aluminum foil, he tipped a tray

toward the cameras, revealing his pristine creation like the denoue-
ment of a cooking device infomercial.

The men by the tabernacle were whispering, wondering who the
man was, and where he'd come from. They'd never seen the van
before. One of the Kitchen volunteers had to drive to the caterer
and fetch those leftovers daily. This was the first time they had
been delivered. As the confused whispers coagulated into grum-
bles, the caterer delivered the trays to Annie's volunteers, leaned
toward the microphone, plugged his enterprise, waved at the
restive men. "Thanks for all you do, Annie! I'm just so happy
you've allowed me and my employees to participate in your wonderful good works!"

Back into the van, a tight turn and he was out the gate as quickly
as he had entered. Behind the podium, Betty beamed and applauded
the contribution. *Alta voce*, for the various microphones, she extolled
the generosity of the caterer. Annie looked around at her volunteers,
then turned and faced the media. Confused by the sudden intrusion, she fell back on her automatic response to almost any stimu-
lus: pitching the Kitchen's need for contributions.

"Well, the Lord provides all the food we serve here. He provides
it through the good people who give it to us. We take nothing from
the government."

"Hey, Annie, did he really give us Wellingtons? Or are they those
chicken things? Those are all right but not as good as the beef."
Whiskey Ed was particular about his food. And he had serious issues
with intentional misrepresentation of motive.

"Well, I am sure I don't know what the man gave us. But we are
so thankful . . . "

Dracula waved his hand in the air, like a second grader asking
to be excused to the restroom. "Yeah, that's the question. Are they
really beef?"

In the midst of the rising murmur, Sweet Pea's high giggling
voice rang out behind Annie. "Where's the beef?"

Such temptation could not be resisted. The crowd began the familiar chant, enjoying it more the louder it got.

A reporter in the front grew impatient with this spontaneous demonstration, knowing it would be trimmed from any news story his station might run. "Speaking of beef, Annie, what about the Shadow Plague? You were just about to explain the ins and outs of that."

Annie's head jerked as if someone had pinched her. "Was I?"

"Yes, ma'am. Remember the frogs and the pregnant women?"

She reached up and touched the microphone, as if to assure herself of its material presence. "Yes, the women and the babies. I remember now. Well, if we're all going to be destroyed with such terrible suffering, maybe our minds should be wiped clean before we get to that point. Everything in God's kingdom has a purpose. Maybe that is why the Shadow Plague has come to us."

A woman in the back of the media gallery shouted out as Annie finished her sentence. "Does that mean you've lost all hope for humanity?"

The ancient nurse pulled herself as straight and tall as she could. "Do you think I would be feeding people all these years if I had no hope?"

As the young woman was about to extend her inquiry into the nature of hope and mercy, a white stretch limousine pulled up to the edge of the crowd and stopped. A rear door swung open and the mayor of Lemon City emerged, cradling a framed brass plaque in his arm. In spite of his short stature and chubbiness, it took only seconds for His Honor to make it up the ramp and take his place at Annie's side.

"My goodness, I had no idea the press was here, but what a perfect opportunity to bestow upon you this commendation from me, the Mayor, and the Council of Lemon City."

Recognizing the mayor as Annie's archenemy—the one who had tried many times to shut down her operations because they endangered innocent children, impeded the engine of commerce, or any number of other preposterous fabrications—the men began to boo and catcall.

Nervously smoothing his black hair, the mayor shouldered his way behind the podium, leaned into the microphone. "Yes, yes, we're all friends here. I know we all want to honor Annie and her exemplary service to the community."

Grady stepped forward and put a hand on the mayor's shoulder. "Hey! Get away from that podium. Go find your own press conference!"

Annie's clientele cheered Grady's challenge and surged forward, pressing the media contingent hard into the wall at the base of the ramp. Protective of their equipment, the cameramen and sound men began to shove back. Then the first punches and kicks were landed. As the initial confrontation began a descent into chaos, Alonso followed his instincts and eased himself to the edge of the crowd. Evaluating various escape routes, he noticed Perry slipping around to the back of the cook shack. Alonso tugged at his sound man's jacket, silently signaling a retreat in that direction.

As they turned the corner, they found Perry on his knees, speaking eloquently in some ancient tongue before the scruffy fan palm. As Alonso reset his focus and white-balanced, Bob swung his pussy on a stick close to Perry's mouth. At that precise moment the palm burst into flame and the pitch of Perry's wild utterances passed the threshold of pain. The media men continued to record, even as the event in which they were participating burned at their eyes and ears.

CHAPTER EIGHT

SUPERKITCHEN

It wasn't just the eyes. The ravaged hills of her cheeks, tunneled by the Shadow Plague, appeared as unstable as the Southern California coastal heights that slide each rainy season, dumping luxury view houses into canyons. The forehead and nose of the fortyish beach bunny had a waxen cast, mimicking the grotesque lies of mortician's clay. Annie stared at the former volunteer and was horrified. When Sally crossed over into zombie land, the new scourge had unequivocally arrived at Annie's Soup Kitchen. Dozens of Chlorox and rubbing alcohol bottles, used by Sally to sterilize counters, cutting boards, utensils, ice trays, everything she could get her hands on inside the cook shack, had done her no good at all. She'd succumbed in exactly the same way as the others. Annie waved a hand in front of the victim's eyes, but the pupils, viscous black surrounded by striated caramel irises, did not respond. There was no more luster in them than in polyvinyl chloride milk jugs.

Skulford flashed cards before Sally's eyes—Charles Lindberg, Marlene Dietrich, and Raquel Welch—but got no response. Whiskey Ed improvised electrodes and attached them to various points on her head and neck, attempting to detect alpha, beta, or gamma wave anomalies. Library Lady stroked Sally's frizzed-out hair. The blonde tint had not been touched up since she'd fallen into the gulf of her illness: her dark roots were nearly two inches long. Since Library Lady had no insights to offer and could not think of an appropriate avenue of analysis, she turned to the forces she could always trust: *chi* and compassion. Perry walked around and around the plastic chair on which the subject had been placed, there in the middle of the mall food court. He was looking for any clue to the pathology of the Shadow Plague, something that would mark a point of entry. Maybe the disease started with a sting or a bite; encephalitis had an insect vector and similarly devastating effects. But Perry could find nothing out of the ordinary. Roderigo teased his frozen yogurt with his prehensile tongue and watched the surrounding foot traffic, people carrying trays loaded with a dozen different styles of food, searching for a free table. He showed absolutely no interest in the group medical consultation taking place next to him.

When the General returned from the restroom, he sat down next to the fallen Martha Stewart disciple, scooted his chair closer, and began to speak in her ear.

"Striped tooth lizards. You know, those grotto Hawaiian things with twelve legs. When you spot 'em, just blink your eyes twice. Every hill's got another side you can't see, one that'll take you down into darkness, carrying a branch with golden nowhere leaves in your hand. Sulfur and smoke. Or Bavarian gentians, smoking blueness to windward, darkening daytime. Hades in dark blue funk, smoking daytime and darktime all rolled up into a single joint. When you hear me, lift your little finger. Give me a sign, woman."

Annie looked from Sally's impassive face to the General's animated one. She contemplated the huge warrior's furrowed brow, beads of sweat running laterally over its terraces. Although he was undeniably talented in a number of areas, particularly chants controlling visibility, the great nurse worried he might be pushing the unresponsive woman even farther from her fellow humans into the darkness of her disabled mind. Or, more immediately, she worried the General's presence would cause such a stir in the mall that the Magnificent Seven's plot to retrieve and recycle the volunteer might come to light. Earlier that afternoon Annie had told Sally's husband they were going to take her out for some air and exercise, that it would do her a world of good. He had agreed without hesitation, glad for a break from his twenty-four-hour-a-day caretaking.

The plague victim and her escort began attracting casual attention among the patrons of the food court as soon as Whiskey Ed attached his electrodes. People at the surrounding tables, where burritos, slices of pizza, and two-item Chinese plates were being consumed, whispered to one another. But there was no sense of alarm; in the land of televised freeway pursuits, an incident as tame as this would have to be considered normal. After the General's conjuration, however, the crowd was somewhat more aroused.

Noting this unwanted attention with some urgency, Annie wished the warrior would hurry and finish his therapy. She pressed him with a loud whisper. "Did you see any light come from her eyes?"

The General looked up at the nurse, eyeballs and temple veins bulging with exasperation. When a man is getting down to serious conjuring, it's no time for Q & A. He refocused his attention on Sally, touched her shoulder twice, then proceeded.

"Lead me down, woman. Show me the way. Let me talk to Demeter, Persephone, Eurydice too. They all know me; they've gone out with me and dig the stuff I do. Underwater martial arts, the movie thing. Rise up from that sightless realm; bring me a torch of darkness, a Cadillac full of lost brides. The blue, forked burning flower is a long gone voice to take us down the stairs and back up again. Persephone's on the telephone to you right now, Baby, talking to your message machine. Pick it up. Pick up!"

This intense psychic assault had no visible effect on Sally. Annie told the General she'd relieve him for a bit, then stepped behind the plague victim's chair, began massaging her neck and back, careful to avoid the electrodes Whiskey Ed had attached. Annie had been practicing this variety of effleurage since her earliest days as a nurse, and her touch was miraculous. Not only did she dispel tension with the light application of pressure, but her fingertips could pick up signals coming from deep within the body. The great nurse looked away as she worked, allowing all sensory acuity to travel to her fingertips.

Library Lady, still somewhat intimidated by the General, approached the chair again as Annie ministered to Sally. She had information she'd been meaning to convey to the chief. "Did you see the television program on the Shadow Plague last night? Well, you know they don't call it that. I think they call it the Cronkite syndrome now. That's the official word for it." Annie appeared to be ignoring Library Lady but didn't ask her to be quiet either, so the black and gray *chi* dancer continued. "I really can't believe what they're doing in Japan. Setting up those quarantine areas for people who are sick. Villages of the damned, they call them. You know, they also mentioned Annie's Soup Kitchen at the end of the program."

Annie looked up with raised eyebrows. "Did they, my dear? I hope they didn't give out any wrong information."

Library Lady lowered her head in embarrassment. "Well, I'm afraid what they said wasn't very good. One of the experts they talked to claimed the things that have been happening at the Soup Kitchen are signs of mass hysteria. I never heard of the guy who said it, but they called him an expert. Oh, there was some good news too. A French reporter has been calling us the "superkitchen." But when the other reporter told that story, the American reporter I mean, he had a sarcastic smile on his face."

"Never mind, my dear. They'll all come round, and sooner than you think." Just as she uttered that confidence, Annie pulled back her hands from Sally's neck. The woman had gone rigid, rolling her pupils up under her eyelids. Shudders and spasms swept through her body. "My God, something's happening to her. I don't have the least idea what to do."

The General leaned against a nearby column, arms folded, observing the blossoming of the medicine he had planted. "Back off and let the darkness drip away. The woman's gonna speak her mind."

Sally worked her mouth, trying to moisten the tongue that had had been useless for weeks. She moaned and let loose a torrent of speech, unlike anything the nurse had ever heard before. On the chance something satanic might be unfolding, Annie quickly crossed herself. Perry said he was pretty sure she was just speaking ancient Chaldean, nothing particularly dangerous, and gave a running translation.

Annie turned to one after another of the Seven, each of them staring at the resurrected Martha Stewart disciple, and asked if anybody understood the meaning of what had been said.

The General, still leaning against the column, began to laugh and shake his head. "Mercy, she been deep in the darkness, and got herself all the way back, if only for a little while." He laughed and whistled.

Surveying the area to make sure the huge warrior was not causing a disturbance among the eaters, Annie was struck by the number of people who had gathered into a tight circle around them, just since Sally had begun her strange proclamation. When the great nurse looked at their eyes, she felt a chill travel up her spine and into the shoulders. They all had Sally's look, the zombie deadpan that characterized the Shadow Plague. Since Sally's Chaldean had apparently attracted the wandering lost of the mall, the nurse cleared her throat loudly and suggested the Seven prepare for immediate retreat. As she turned back toward the conjuring warrior, she witnessed the food court manager and two security guards push through the circle of threatening zombie passivity to confront the General.

"There have been complaints and I'm afraid you will have to move on. You're causing a disruption of our eating and shopping traffic."

As the General looked down at the portly man—his green jacket with mall insignia and flushed face creating a holiday effect—he snorted, as a lion might when encountering a rat. The General glanced at the security guard who flanked the manager to the right, an older man with bifocals who looked more confused than secure, and the one on the left—young, crewcut, with a brilliant acne-scarred neck. The young one was ready for action, massaging the billy club in his belt with one hand and his walkie-talkie with the other, as if one of them might suddenly transform into a gun.

Annie stepped forward. "We are all here together. If our friend has to leave, then we all must be asked to leave. We've just taken this poor sick woman on an outing to the mall. How has that done anyone harm?"

As the older security guard whispered that he'd seen the old lady on television, Skulford Elephant leaped between Annie and the manager, raised his bad hand. "So we're defending the marketplace today, are we? Maybe I'm the one you should arrest. I hate commerce, on general principles, and I hate pathetic drones like you who fancy they represent authority." Skulford lifted his wrists, taunted the young security guard. "Why don't you cuff me, tough guy? You could call it 'intent,' because I've got a lot of ideas about things I could do around here just for fun." As he delivered his threat, the card maker's hands were covered in blue flame. The young guard, who had one hand on his cuffs, gasped and stepped back. Stunned but trying to maintain control of the situation, the manager encouraged the guards to stand fast, dismissing what he had witnessed as an illusion, a Las Vegas magic trick.

As his hands returned to normal, or as normal as his hands could ever be, Skulford stretched onto his toes so he could get into the manager's face once again. "Sure it is. You like magic? What kind of fakery do you want? We were just trying to heal this woman. But if you like, we can saw her in half. What about it? Which will it be?"

Perry stepped forward and grabbed Skulford by the arm. "Aaaah-hhhh, my man, I don't think we want to get these fellas mad. Maybe it's time we all went home."

The manager, who had been transfixed by the little man's harangue and demonstration, shook his head in agreement. "We're only asking that you people move on, quietly."

Skulford pulled away from Perry's grasp and went nose to nose with the manager again. "Tell me, do you think I could stand here and bring down this mall—every stone and brick? Do you think I could? Maybe we should start with something smaller, like a little test."

The manager and security guards took a step back, scanned Mr. Elephant's body for any sign of a weapon, some rational explanation for his cocky attitude. The older guard slipped his walkie-talkie out of its holster and called for backup. But Skulford pursued them as they retreated, got right back in the manager's face. Meanwhile, the circle of zombies was tightening on the foursome, reaching out and touching the uniforms of the officials, as if to ascertain their reality.

An enormous explosion came from behind the food counters, splattering bits of mushroom and pepperoni over every column and bystander in the food court. One of the ovens in the pizza concession had blown up. There was a momentary pause, an aftershock of silence. Then hundreds of shrieking people stampeded, trampling fellow mall denizens underfoot, including the manager and his two security guards. As Sally and the Seven slipped out one of the emergency exits, Annie turned to Skulford.

"I hope, young man, you had nothing to do with that explosion."

Whiskey Ed was scratching his large patchy bald spot. "Yeah, I thought pizza ovens were all electric. How can an electric oven explode?"

Skulford was giggling, scampering along at the General's side. When he arrived at Ed's van, he offered his analysis. "Must have been an overripe calzone in that oven. Just lucky nobody got hurt."

～

In the convent chapel, late on a Thursday afternoon, Annie knelt alone. She wore her gray blazer of penance, held clutched hands against forehead, and it was a mixture of sweat and tears that dampened the back of the pew she leaned against.

"O Blessed Mother, I pray that you will guide me, show me a way to put an end to this terrible Shadow Plague. I am deeply sorry for the bad things I have done, and the people who were hurt at the refinery. Thanks to Your intercession, Blessed Mary, none of them died. It was anger that made me do those things, and I'm ashamed of it."

Sister Claire had been standing at the chapel door for some time, trying to decide whether she should join the tormented figure in the second pew and try to console her or just leave her alone. Annie, head still down, was mumbling Hail Marys when the nun slipped in beside her. The Soup Kitchen director raised her head, shocking the nun with a blotchy contorted face.

Sister Claire was afraid she'd intruded but also worried that the suffering the ninety-five-year-old activist was undergoing might imperil her physical well-being. She wanted to distract her. "Would you like me to pray with you, Annie?"

"Oh yes, Sister dear. I'm so glad you've come."

The nun leaned one shoulder against the pew in front of her and began to converse. "I don't think I've ever seen you here in our chapel before."

"No, I've never been. Sister Gianetta invited me, and I wanted to be alone, without Father Michael seeing me. Please don't tell him I said that."

"Is there anything I can do to help?"

Annie wiped her eyes with the back of one hand, straightened her lapels, tried to reassemble herself. "Would you help me up then, Sister dear? My joints can't take any more of this kneeling."

The nun stood, pulled Annie from her knees, and both settled back in the pew. "This isn't about your oldest son again, is it?"

"Oh no, no. He's a great-grandfather himself now. If he can't lead a good life at his age, then I have doubt he ever will. No, I'm worried about the whole lot of us, Sister Claire. The Shadow Plague may take us all. I'm afraid it's even worse than we've been thinking. I hope you won't call me a fool, but I've tried every way I could to understand what is happening, and I can't. We looked over poor dear Sally top to bottom, and I have no idea how she got sick or what we can do about it. You know she was so afraid of germs. I've thought about all possible causes, like rats and fleas in the time of the Black Death, or deer mice with hanta virus, or flies, or killer bees, and even snails. I remember so many people getting terribly sick when they built the dam in Egypt. It was from the snails, my dear. I've been thinking particularly about snails, because I have such a number of them in my garden. I've never seen so many before. But sometimes I don't think germs have anything to do with this new disease."

Claire rested a hand on Annie's shoulder. "I thought you'd already figured this out. You told the reporter racism and religious bigotry were caused by damaged genes, and they in turn led to immune system dysfunction."

Annie looked down thoughtfully, then lifted her eyes and smiled. "Oh, I was just making all of that up. I needed something to tell them."

Sister Claire coughed as she tried to suppress her laughter, rested a consoling hand on Annie's shoulder. "All the important medical facilities in the country are devoting time and resources to solving this problem. I'm afraid a couple of obsolete old nurses like you and me will just have to be content to wait until the experts figure something out."

"But there's no time to wait." Annie looked up at the rose-colored stained-glass window in the apse. She paused, then spoke slowly and deliberately. "Last night an angel visited me. It was the one with the green suit and wonderful sparkling wings, the one that gave me the instructions for the tabernacle. The Lord's messenger told me that the health and survival of this world has everything to do with the palm tree behind the trailer."

Sister Claire knew what Annie was talking about. She always stared out the window at that tree as she washed dishes, taking solace from its sturdy presence in a place where nothing else could survive. "What are you saying? If the palm dies, we'll all go with it? Why would the Lord put such a terrible burden on us?"

"The angel didn't explain why. He just gave warning. You see, the responsibility for curing this sickness has been put on me, not all those doctors at the big hospitals. The angel came to me, not them. I have no idea why I was chosen, but I must do my best, Sister dear. I've been praying here in the chapel for guidance. You're the only person I've told. If I tell the others, the people from the newspapers and television, what do you think would happen? Would they believe me? But if I say nothing, how can the world know how close we are to the end? And if I do tell them, what if some crazy person tried to harm the tree? Or other ones might give it too much attention and end by worrying the poor tree to death. It's so hard to decide."

The nun looked at her friend. She too had experienced miraculous things in her life, and was particularly fascinated by charismatic sects, but Annie's visions often took her to the limits of her own faith. "Whatever you decide, Annie, I'll do everything I can to help you."

The eldest nurse looked quickly over her shoulder, began a conspiratorial whisper. "Do you know the man at the Kitchen with the dirty wool cap and long beard?"

Sister Claire's face slipped into a smile. "Have I ever cut his hair?"

"Oh no, Sister dear, I don't think anyone has ever cut his hair. He's the one who always comes late, when there's not much food left to give."

"Yes, I know who you mean. He looks like an old hippie. I'd sure like to get my hands on him, but I know he wouldn't sit still for a trim. Why are you telling me about him? Do you think he's an angel too?"

Annie raised a finger to her lips, pondered hard on the possibility. "He might be, though he doesn't look a thing like the others I've spoken to. Let me tell you the message he gave me. He said, 'Don't forget the river. The hawk, the snake, the palm tree, and the river.' I know he meant that the river has something to do with the Shadow Plague, and if we could only understand what it is, we would find the cure. My God, the poor river has been so blocked and broken it can't travel the way it should. In some places it's nearly impossible to find, just like the minds of these miserable lost souls who have fallen to the Shadow Plague, like poor Sally. Sister Claire, would you come with me on a pilgrimage, following along the Santa Ana River? I'm sure if we go there we will find what we need to know."

The next morning Sister Claire arrived at Annie's house in her blue Jubilee 2000 sweatshirt, and the two of them set off for Fingerly Park in Yorba Linda, the burial place of Richard Milhouse Nixon that styles itself "the land of gracious living." After exiting the 91 freeway on Gypsum Canyon Road and pulling up to the park's entry gate, Annie and Sister Claire argued briefly over who should pay the five-dollar fee. The nun paid, steered her dilapidated vehicle down a dust-clogged crunchy road that paralleled the river, eyeing a scatter of people, tents, and campers along the way. Sister Claire fussed about the legality of several parking spots before she finally chose a dusty patch shaded by a carrotwood. The two pilgrims achieved a precarious balance by clutching one another as they moved over the soft dry silt along the roadside. Their first clear view of the Santa Ana River: not impressive in size, but it rushed between flanking cottonwoods and willows at considerable speed, whipping the weed that grew on submerged rocks in one direction, then another.

Sister Claire saw snags and sandbars, railroad ties and telephone poles driven into the riverbed by the force of winter floods. Then at her feet, among large rocks dumped to stabilize the banks, there were fat geckos darting in all directions. Only one cheeky lizard held his ground on a rocky prominence, doing push-ups in the sun. Upstream a large, lazy S-curve in the river was a miniature version of Huck Finn's Mississippi. Sister Claire remembered the mother superior insisting that all the nuns in the convent watch an Army Corps of Engineers tape on flood preparedness. In fact, it was more a hustle for public funds to be spent on dams and channels. However, the tape did declare the Santa Ana the most dangerous river west of the Mississippi. Sister Claire turned to relay that bit of information to Annie but found her partner craning her neck, looking straight up into the sky.

"Do you think it's a sign, Sister dear?" A large and perfect circular rainbow ringed the noonday sun. The misty sky within the circle gave the illusion of a huge three-dimensional globe, as if a planet were about to collide with the earth.

Sister Claire stared in amazement at the miraculous phenomenon. Turning to Annie, who crossed herself in multiples, Claire realized her fellow nurse had already interpreted the significance of the sunbow.

"Annie, do you want to walk along the riverbank?"

"Oh yes, you see we were meant to come here. We will find the path now." The visionary feeder's eyes were intense with excitement. She was ready to move to the next station of her enlightenment.

Finding a path was not easy. Since the course of the river was unpredictable and there was no continuous clearing along either bank, they cut through thick brush to find a way to proceed upstream. Walking over peeling dried mud, they found their way to the river but were blocked by a wall of battered cattails and bamboo. Looping back, another trail took them farther from the river, almost to the high concrete bridge that carried Gypsum Canyon Road over the floodplain.

Both women perspired heavily, but Annie's silence spoke only determination. Sister Claire wasn't counseling surrender, but she was not beyond complaining. "Annie, this river is not cooperating. Don't you think the water might be hiding from us on purpose?"

Annie turned her head and shoulders, scanning a complete 360 degrees. She hadn't heard a thing Sister Claire had said, but this nun was not easily ignored.

"For a river as dangerous as they say this is, it sure is hard to find. Downright stealthy, I'd say. Let's try this way in." Sister Claire grabbed Annie by the elbow and steered her through a low opening in the heavy brush, a tunnel more appropriate for four-legged animals. When they broke through to the other side, they were at the edge of the sandbar that had been their goal. As they walked through torn prickly pear paddles, a small snake slithered across their path. They stopped, held each other tightly, looking for others. Proclaiming in loud voices that snakes were not evil by nature, they mounted the sandbar and continued along the sinuous course of the river.

Annie stopped and looked down. "Sister, what are seashells doing here?"

Claire picked up and inspected the shell, which looked like a small steamer clam's. "I can't imagine the ocean ever came this far inland." Observing her partner's face, she added a warning. "I'm not at all sure we can read this little shell as a sign from the Lord. Other than the fact that all of creation is a sign, the fingerprints of the Father."

Annie did not heed the warning. Her attention was seized by skimming swallows, darting back and forth over the swift water. The nun watched them as well, until her eyes drifted up to the symmetrical lines of pink and white development houses deployed over the hills of Yorba Linda. She was about to remark on the pity of it when Annie jerked her elbow and pointed to a red-tail as it descended slowly to a tree snag farther downstream. The nun's eyes were dazzled by the sunlight and even more confused by the sudden transformation of the hawk into a snowy egret. Annie had already gotten down to business, kneeling in the sand, pulling clasped hands to her chest in prayer. This was the revelation the leader of the Magnificent Seven had been seeking.

~

First they flavor the water table and ocean. Little by little, when no one is looking, toxics here, an accidental spill there. Depending on the weather, slow seepage or the mad rush of pesticides, herbicides, and chemical fertilizers we're convinced we cannot live without. If the authorities don't create serious penalties for our transgressions, how can they be such a terrible betrayal? It's said the body is 75 percent water. But the question remains, just what kind of water are we made of?

~

The morning after the river pilgrimage, as the liberation theologian drove toward Annie's Soup Kitchen for her Friday haircuts, she pondered the remarkable vision Annie had carried away from the trip. Returning from Featherly Park, the Saint of Lemon City had articulated the whole thing so clearly, even the nun had begun to accept the experience as some sort of divine intervention. All the way back in the car, she'd talked about the world as the body of Christ and rivers as His blood. Pollution, overbuilding, the general degradation of the land, air, and water were more than an ecological disaster. They were a desecration of the Sacred Body and Blood. That much Sister Claire could accept. In fact, it made perfect sense. Then Annie declared that through divine grace she'd been allowed to see the vector of the Shadow Plague. It was humans, all of humanity, who were the disease, rather than the victims. Since people were sickening the holy body of the world, the human virus needed to be purged, washed out of that system by a terrible flood. Only then could the body of the world regain its health.

The nun was horrified by the last part of the revelation. She could not believe Annie, the epitome of compassion, would see her fellow humans in such a way. She asked the pilgrim why the Lord created humans if they were only a disease. Annie's reply was quick and sure. She said the Lord was giving humans one more chance to change their nature, to stop being a disease and help bring about a cure. She had a plan. If people came back to the river, touched it, waded in it, were rebaptized in it, maybe the Lord would relent and not send the flood. On the other hand, since her message had not come from an angel—more of a voice inside her head that made everything clear—there were no specific instructions. Annie said she hadn't been told to warn anyone, build an ark, or gather the various species together. So she didn't want to let her own personal softheartedness interfere with the divine plan. Maybe God was as angry as He'd been in Noah's time. And if that were the case, who could stand in His way?

Driving toward the Kitchen, Sister Claire's mind's eye brought back the sandbar in the brilliant light of midday, and the strange accidental sculpture that stood in the middle of it. An L-shaped piece of iron conduit pipe rose out of the sand to a height of fifteen feet. Around its waist hung a layer of fractured concrete, all that remained of some former superstructure. A pipe of the same dimension shunted off the horizontal top piece, and at the end of that shunt an enamel blue gadget was attached, its label declaring it a McChrometer manufactured in Hemet, California. The last reading, likely taken at the moment of the waterwork's destruction, was 21,259,900 gallons per minute. Sister Claire had no idea what that figure meant, but she shuddered when she thought about the coming flood.

As the nun drove through the gate at Annie's Soup Kitchen, she did not notice Whiskey Ed holding Annie in earnest conversation near the clothes bin, where he'd intercepted her on the way to the trailer. Ed looked furtive and disheveled, his eyes betraying all the agony of the usual postbender penance. "I'm telling you, Annie, I checked it out more than once. Lucky I just got this piece of equipment the other week. Microwave transmissions like this are not from television or radio. They're not from these media guys around the Kitchen either. These channels are only used by the military, the feds, and the CIA. They've set up somewhere around here, so I think it's safe to assume surveillance. Probably even the conversation we're having right now."

Annie looked at the pavement and tugged at her maroon blazer. "Why on earth would the government want to spy on us? We're only a soup kitchen."

Ed shook his head slowly and miserably. "Have you forgot all the stuff you've been saying to reporters? Or the pictures they got when Perry talked to the palm tree? If the plan was to keep the action around here a secret, it hasn't been working too good."

Annie raised both hands in bewilderment. "As I am true to my God, I forgot about the tree. So many things have been worrying me, I forgot about the tree. But we mustn't let the government in here, especially now. They'll poison everything they touch, even when they try to help. That's why I've never accepted their money. What will happen if they come in and kill our precious tree? Can you tell me what will happen to us and the whole world then?"

Ed shrugged his shoulders and pulled up his baggy pants by the suspenders. "I don't have any ideas, Annie. Taking on the government is even harder than the other, you know, things we did. But I wanted to warn you."

"Well, you can be sure we won't be doing any more of those illegal things. I'm ashamed to have done it, Edward, and that's the truth of it. Maybe I can talk to these reporters and it will scare the government people away."

Annie marched past Navajo Bill, who was leaning against his pickup watching the circus. There were two rings of cameras and reporters, one around Sweet Pea, who was singing, dancing, and laughing, and the other around Betty, who was lecturing assembled media that the quality of mercy is not strained. There was so much flashing, whirring, and commotion, an overwhelmed Annie blinked and turned her head away. Having carried the terrible burden of prophetic knowledge for almost twenty-four hours, this foolishness made her forget all strategy. She lapsed into a classic Annie O'Rourke fit of rage.

"Is all the work in the Kitchen finished so the volunteers are out here having a tea party with you people? And has everyone forgotten what we're here for? We're here to feed the poor and homeless and out of work. There are so many of you other people in here, there's no room for the ones I need to look after." She glanced at the fence on the other side of the trailer, where a sullen Skulford stood with Perry and John DeLorean. Just beyond, the General stood alone, holding his looseleaf Koran and chanting his most vigorous prayer of purification. Annie began to wave her hands wildly. "You're bothering the men! Just be off with you! Right this minute." She rushed at a cameraman, but he jumped out of the way. "Go outside the gate and mind your manners! If any of you wants to eat, you're welcome to stay, but you must leave your cameras and machines outside. And if you don't want to eat, I want all of you out right now!"

Ed stepped forward to remind Annie of the news item she was going to convey, but as he did, her knees gave out and she collapsed. The electronics wizard caught at her arm but could not stop her from hitting the pavement. There was tentative laughter, then a collective gasp, as everyone realized what had happened.

The crowd fell back and formed a wider ring, cameras continuing to whir and flash. Betty knelt by Annie's side, held her hand, and sniffled. Sweet Pea ran to the trailer to get Grady. The General pushed through the circus ring and stalked to the ancient nurse's rescue. He picked Betty up by the elbows and placed her a few feet away, then arched his body over Annie to protect her from a relentless sky.

After packing Annie into the back of an ambulance, the paramedics accelerated down the street, siren drawing passing notice from the officers milling around squad cars in the parking lot of the Lemon City Police Department. Back at Annie's gate, Roger Fitzpatrick tousled his hair, brought the mike to his lips, and signaled the cameraman with his other hand. "Well, this is certainly a surprise development here at Annie's Soup Kitchen. Of course, considering Annie O'Rourke's ninety-five years, it comes as no surprise . . . Hey, get a shot of that ambulance before it turns the corner! OK, let's start over. 3, 2, 1. Annie O'Rourke—hero to some, charlatan to others—is on her way to the hospital after suffering a collapse at her renowned Soup Kitchen. Stay tuned to KFRG for further details of this tragedy, as they become available. OK, cut. Let's get to the truck and send this to the station *tout de suite.*"

CHAPTER NINE

VERONICA

Friday morning the tabernacle contained its usual congregation of lions and lambs. DeLorean sat at number seven with Skulford. Smoothing his silver hair, he marveled at the diminutive card maker's newest works, laid out over the surface of the picnic table.

"Skulford, those definitely are the real McCoy. You've got natural talent for what you do."

Mr. Elephant's ambiguous hand was still at work detailing a face. He refused to look up and acknowledge the compliment. "Of course, it's natural. But I can tell you a lot of the people on the cards aren't, nothing natural about them. That's why we call it history."

This exchange between DeLorean and Skulford attracted the attention of Phil Tabangbang, who sat at the other end of the table with Madalene. Tilting his head so his long black hair deployed into air, a gesture that almost never failed to attract attention, he jumped into the conversation. "Say, you ever think about going into production with those things? I bet you could make a pile of money."

The little man looked up, defied Phil's good-natured smile. "You mean, make reproductions of my originals? Get real."

As always, it was particularly irritating to Madalene when Phil's interest was deflected from her feminine charms. Under the table she thrust her foot toward his private parts, but he intercepted it between his knees. Business was the only thing on his mind at this particular moment. Phil wanted to reason with Skulford. "What's wrong with reproductions? Even famous guys like Salvador Dali made prints. Are you trying to tell me you're more of an artist than him?"

Slipping a leg over the bench, Perry the post-Babel linguist took up a position facing Skulford and joined the debate. "Just let the idea percolate a little, guy. Drive it around the block. What if you could get your stuff out all over the country? Forget the money. Everybody on those cards would be alive forever. And look at the influence you'd have."

Continuing to concentrate on his fine pen work, the card maker had not yet lifted his eyes. "There'd be only one significant effect: going from making art to distributing trash."

Looking around the table for allies, Phil hit on the tall, dapper baseball fan. "Hey man, give us your take on this. Like how much money do you think he could make mass producing these cards?"

DeLorean smiled shyly. "Well, it's all pretty much out of my league. Ask me about trucking. I could give you a reliable opinion on that topic."

Phil touched his temple. "Just think about it, gents. I bet old Skulford could turn this hobby into a nice piece of cash. A sweet little operation. And we could help."

Sweeping his hair out of his eyes, Skulford finally looked up. "Whose operation? I have no intention of moving to mass production. But if I did, why would I need any of you? I already have access to means of production."

DeLorean studied Skulford, then glanced at Perry, Phil, and Madalene. The little man's response had taken everyone by surprise. But Phil was not ready to let things go.

"Sure, Skulford, whatever. We know you got connections. Hey, I'm not trying to piss you off or anything. I'm just saying, you got something really hot here if you want to run with it."

Perry massaged his furrowed brow, adjusted his glasses, and pulled at his walrus moustache, contemplating possibilities far beyond the extrapolations of his eager colleagues. "Man, just picture it. You could put biographical and historical stuff on the back. You know, George Armstrong Custer: massacred a bunch of unarmed Indians and then got his ass kicked by Crazy Horse. J. P. Morgan: terrorized the country with his cronies for decades, then over-reached trying to corner the gold market and never recovered."

Throwing her head back in a mirthless laugh, Madalene dropped in a cheap shot. "What do you think about overreachers, DeLorean?"

Perry continued his contemplation of the possibilities. "Madonna: parlayed no looks and no talent into a multibillion-dollar media scam. And what about a guy like Earl Warren? How would you do your card on him?"

Flexing his bad hand at the wrist, Skulford dismissed the question. "Already got him in my deck."

Phil took a punch at the air. "So what did you say about him on the back?"

An enthused Perry jumped in. "Two strikes for his Nisei concentration camps and the Kennedy Warren Commission, home run for the school desegregation decision."

At work detailing an emerging face, the card maker was beginning to resent the attention. "Listen, I never say anything on the back. That's your idea, not mine. I'm more interested in collective memory. Data erodes memory."

Since Madalene had begun monitoring this eager speculation, she had been allowed few words. Her frustration and sarcasm had now reached critical mass. "Hey, DeLorean, what about you? Do you get a good guy bad guy card too?"

Pulling on both sides of his walrus moustache, Perry was still running with the concept. "Interesting. Yeah. Aaahhh, what about Nixon?"

Madalene lifted her yipping dog into her lap, prepared to continue her critique. "How about some more women?"

Mr. Elephant was ready to bail out of this commercial invasion of his privacy. "Hey! Leave my fucking cards out of your plans. You guys don't know what I've got in this deck. I could have the whole fucking population of the United States, for all you know. You have no idea how fast I work."

Staring straight up, still brainstorming, there was no way to discourage Perry. "What a concept, my man. You get everybody on cards, then you throw them together into different populations. See how they get along."

~

Sweet Pea clutched her hips with both hands, attempting with little success to contain her eagerness. "But how's she doing? She's going to be all right? I mean, like ever coming back to the Kitchen?" The half-eaten, day-old maple bar lay abandoned in the retired waitress's hunger for news. "A lot of times when bad things happen to old people, they never get any better. They just fade away and die."

"Did you ever know Annie to do anything quietly? Lord, I'll tell you she put a few bruises on the people in that emergency room. Her doctor got off scot-free, but only because he moved faster than the rest of us." The liberation nun flailed her arms, reenacting Annie's epic struggle. "She was hitting and grabbing and scratching. If you'd asked me at that moment, I'd have told you she had more arms than an octopus. But the poor thing had no idea where she was. In a complete panic, hollering that the whole lot of us were trying to kill her. She landed a right hook just under my eye."

Grady and Wanda leaned closer to the narrator, inspecting the nasty discoloration they'd previously been too polite to acknowledge.

"Just went crazy on you, huh?" Sweet Pea paused and savored the image of a ninety-five-year-old terrorizing younger people. "She's still plenty tough, even after all these years."

The lanky nun reached her arms around behind her to knot the ties on the plastic haircutting apron. "Sure she is. If she weren't so stubborn, she'd be long gone by now. Turns out she didn't have a heart attack at all. She had a fainting spell, and dislocated a shoulder when she fell on her arm. It's all my fault, since I let her talk me into that foolish trip to the river."

At the other end of the trailer, Betty knelt before a refrigerator. Her distance from the conversation was indication she'd made visits to see Annie at the hospital several times over the past week and didn't need an update.

Sweet Pea took Sister Claire's cue and began to confess her own remorse. "What about me? Last week Annie was awful mad at me and Betty, and I feel bad about it. Maybe she didn't want us talking to reporters anymore. But why is it all right for her to talk to them all the time, and not us?"

Grady studied Sister Claire's haunted face. Neither she nor anyone else in the room was paying attention to Sweet Pea's rhetorical question.

The nun raised her haircutting shears by the points as if they were an object of veneration. "How do you think I feel? When I agreed to go on that river trip, I knew it would wear her out."

Since Sister Claire's father died the night of her birth and she was blamed by her family for the catastrophe, Grady could imagine how crushing it would be if she held herself responsible for the death of another beloved. Especially the Saint of Lemon City.

The hairdresser nun began to wave her arms again. "When they got her into the emergency room, she just had a complete and total fit. It took three big orderlies to hold her down when the doctor reset her dislocated shoulder. She kept telling me she'd been kidnapped by the government. To tell you the truth, I don't believe she had any idea who I was for a day or so. And she was mad as a wet hen. She thought everyone in the whole hospital, including me, was part of a conspiracy to do her in."

Sweet Pea had the odd smile on her face that always indicated she'd gotten lost in a transition. "Sister Claire, do nuns work for the government? I mean going undercover, or something like that."

Arms dropped to her sides, the nun searched the retired waitress's eyes before replying. Was it possible to be completely sure this aging Shirley Temple wasn't taunting everyone? "Lord knows they accuse us of enough things already, but as of this moment I don't know anybody at the convent working for the FBI or CIA. I don't need to tell any of you that Annie gets a lot of ideas, and some of them are pretty darn crazy."

Marlene called Grady over to the stove, asked if he thought the vegetable soup and the black bean soup they'd received in plastic sacks from the caterer could be combined. He said it was up to her, but he didn't think it was a good idea. As he turned his back, she prepared to dump both into the same pot.

"Getting back to what I was saying, Bill. People have got to live somewhere, don't they?" Sweet Pea was trying to rekindle an argument she'd been having with Grady half an hour before, when he'd been haranguing about overdevelopment in Orange County. She still dreamed of living in a Newport Beach mansion.

Standing up and brushing hands against one another, Betty was ready to mix. As usual, she made her acerbic comments through a large smile. "All this talk about real estate developers poisoning the environment is so silly. I grew up on a farm, and Lord knows all the poisons we had to put up with. We got through it, and all of us turned out just fine."

The cook ignored Betty's contribution, thinking that for someone who'd had cancer three times, it was an astonishing example of self-delusion. "By the way, Sweet Pea, my name is Grady."

"Oh sorry, what did I say?"

"You called me Bill. He's the guy who transports Annie and picks up the vegetables. Have you ever tried *Ginkgo biloba*? If you took that, you might start calling all of us by our actual names."

Sitting at the table, Wanda chuckled, stopped for a sip of coffee, then laughed again. "Try it, Sweet Pea, it works. I used to swear by it, tell everybody about it, until one day somebody asked me what it was called and I couldn't remember."

The teacher-cook smiled, thought for a moment about his own struggle with dementia. "Guess we all better double the dose, Wanda."

Throwing her hands over her head and rolling her eyes, Sweet Pea was ready for a change of subject. "Oh boogers, I don't care a fig about my memory. If that pinko beluga stuff would take away my wrinkles, I'd sure give it a try. Grady, tell me what you think about these Vigoro pills."

He paused contemplatively. "You mean Viagra? But then again, I can see your point. When you put Vigoro on something, it grows. Of course, Vigoro's a lot cheaper than Viagra."

Her eyes bulging, Wanda tried to suppress a laugh. Ethel, the moral rudder of the crew, shook her head and continued to dice tomatoes. Betty marched to the other end of the trailer, uttering, "Sweet Pea, Sweet Pea, Sweet Pea, what are we ever going to do with you?" Shy Marlene was the only one who could not avoid overt laughter. She started out with a small, low-range giggle but ended with a high-pitched cackle no one in the Kitchen had ever heard from her before. Sister Claire shook her head, announced that things were getting far too silly for her, stepped outside to the portion of the ramp reserved for haircutting and checked the sign-up sheet.

As she arranged her improvised station—beach umbrella, side table, and mirror—the nun felt a presence behind her. "Sign your name on the clipboard there on the railing. A couple of people are ahead of you, but I can get to you in three quarters of an hour or so."

Instead of hearing a voice in reply, she saw a man's arm reach around her waist, holding an open wallet with a star pinned to the leather. "Ma'am, I'm a parole officer. Please don't turn around. If you'll just continue to face the wall, nobody'll be able to lip read us." The man's voice was low, little more than a whisper. He moved forward until he was standing side by side with the startled nun. She glanced toward the source of the voice without moving her head. Sister Claire couldn't see his face clearly, but noticed an embroidered alligator on the beige knit shirt.

"I think you want to talk to Betty. She's in charge."

The officer continued his briefing. "No, I know who you are. Don't be alarmed. At least not of me. Just listen and don't say anything. When you go back into the kitchen, remember it's bugged. This whole place is under a cloud of surveillance. I want you to know that I don't have anything directly to do with it, but some federal agencies are very upset with Annie O'Rourke. There's been talk about a plan to do her harm."

The liberation theologian allowed a fragment of a laugh to escape her teeth but caught and held back the rest. "What do you mean by 'harm'?"

"I mean there are people who would kill her if they could get the job done cleanly. Understand I can't do a thing about this, other than tell you. If they catch me, I'm in as much trouble as she is. Listen, I have great respect for Annie, or I wouldn't be here. She's one of the good ones."

The nun breathed shallowly for a time. When her voice resurfaced, it sounded like a whisper. "Well, now you've told me all this, what am I supposed to do?"

"I have no idea. That's up to you. But don't call the police or FBI."

After the officer walked down the ramp and over to the tabernacle, engaging one of the regulars in conversation, Sister Claire continued her usual preparations for cutting hair. She tried to study the man without making her attention obvious, wondered how seriously to take his warning. How much can you trust such an encounter? Then she thought about his motivation. None of the various alternatives were good. If he was telling the truth, everyone was in danger. If it were all a bluff and he had been sent by someone to intimidate them, that was pretty sinister too.

"Should I sit down, Sister?" It was Whiskey Ed, with his electrified shock of thin white hair. He was ready for his biannual shearing.

The nun waved him into the haircutting chair, then continued through the trailer door into the Kitchen, having decided to pull Grady aside and ask his opinion. Standing in the far door, looking toward the gate, he was just announcing an arrival. "You guys are not going to believe who's driving up inside Bill's truck."

Along with the rest of the volunteers, Sister Claire pushed to the door. "What on earth is she doing out of the hospital?"

The men outside gave three cheers as Joe helped the great nurse out of his pickup, her left arm in a sling. Even the encampment of media people outside the gate joined in the jubilation. Annie gave them all a weak but continuous salute by pivoting the wrist of her good limb, like Queen Elizabeth on a motorcade through London.

When she entered the trailer, the volunteers crowded around the saintly director of Kitchen activity, kissing her on the cheek, touching her shoulder to feel the healing magic. Annie caught the nun's stern look from the other end of the trailer and decided storytelling was a good way to smooth things over. After sitting down at the formica table and propping her immobilized arm on its edge, she laughed, rolled her eyes, and began. "You know, my dears, when I was in the hospital, someone paid me a visit and burglarized my house."

Sweet Pea was horrified. "Did they steal all your nice dresses and the VCR?"

After a questioning pause and a troubled look, Annie continued. "Whatever that is, I'm sure I don't have one. Well, it was all a mess when I came in, you see. I went to the telephone and called the police, before I'd truly taken notice of what was missing. When the officer on the telephone asked what had been taken, I said a sack of diamonds. She asked was there anything else missing, and I said my bag of rubies and bag of emeralds as well. The woman didn't even laugh. Not a bit. So I said, well there's nothing to worry about, because I have a sack of diamonds in every room and they only took the one."

After Grady served his leader the usual bowl of mashed potatoes, volunteers returned to their cooking and prepping chores. Annie asked Grady to help her up and proceeded outside to talk to Sister Claire, who had retreated earlier, not a bit charmed by her storytelling. Noticing that the ancient nurse had the look of a remorseful child, the nun stopped in the middle of a haircut, walked over to hear her explanation. "Well, this better be good. Not that you can't talk your way out of most anything."

"Oh, Sister, Sister. I had to get out of the hospital so I could come today. The angel was very precise about it. I had to come Friday and look into the clothes bin. That's what he said. There must be people who are in dreadful need of something to wear."

Releasing a huge sigh, Sister Claire walked back to the partially shorn Whiskey Ed. "Well, the length of time you stay on this earth is between you and the Lord. Don't believe I or anybody at the hospital will have much say in the matter."

The ancient nurse continued around the corner and down the ramp, walking slowly toward a huge beige bin. It was ribbed in steel like a garbage dumpster but offered access via two doors on the front rather than a hinged lid on top. She slipped key into padlock, swung open the double doors, and let the late morning light shine into the temple of her promised revelation. Annie entered her treasury house of raiment and grace, the recycler's answer to the beautiful lilies of the field. She was prepared to see disarray after her stay at the hospital, but the clutter of unopened bags and bundles, piles of stuff that had been worked over, doubly castoff, torn and broken—it would have been overwhelming even if she didn't have a tidiness fetish. If there had been any place to sit down in the clothes bin, Annie would gladly have done so. That lacking, she grabbed the wooden shelf dedicated to shoes and tried to hang on through the palpitations precipitated by anger and disappointment.

"How long will it take to put all of this to right? I only ask of people that they make no more of a mess than they found. As I am honest to my God, some people who say they want to help have no respect at all for what we're trying to do here. My dear mother would turn me out if she saw me in the middle of this pigsty. Or she'd roll up her sleeves and set to washing down the bin, top to bottom, before she'd even grant me hello. This is no tidying job: it's a task for Hercules.

"And those men outside with the cameras everywhere. Do they think I have nothing on my mind but foolishness? Do they think there's nothing in the world to trouble me but the bad things they say about Annie's Soup Kitchen? When the world comes to an end, every one of them will be washed away. Those cameras will be no use helping them float when the flood comes. It'll carry away every last television too."

As Annie fussed, she bent over, picked up shirts, pants, and bundled white socks with her good arm. She was in her fortress against poverty, impregnable from without but vulnerable to betrayal by false friends from within. The bin may have looked like a garbage dumpster from the outside, but she had turned it into a horn of plenty. There were some, she worried, who were set on destroying everything she had worked to build, turning it all into garbage. They were of the same ilk as those who wanted the whole world to become a pile of foul-smelling rubbish. But no setback could daunt her. Annie's heroism was based primarily on one principle: she refused to be discouraged, regardless of what the external world handed her. Her inner light could not be extinguished, and she was so stubborn she'd give a furious fight to any who were bent on such snuffing. However, even the ostensibly charitable in Lemon City put her to the test. Looking at her treasures—wardrobes of the dead and rags most people would be ashamed to give the Salvation Army—only Annie could see a way to turn this dross into gold.

"Did someone spill coffee in here? You must never bring food or drink into the clothes bin. It's not allowed." Annie's exhortation, aimed at her own ears or the air, came after she'd spotted the piece of wadded cloth pushed into a back corner, as if someone were trying to block a hole in the floor. Whatever the garment's original color, it was now sepia, the washed out brown of old photogravures. The great nurse struggled to lean over and dislodge it. She was afraid to bend her knees, because they hadn't been trustworthy for many years, and she was in no mood to fall and return to the hospital. There was serious work to be done. She held the edge of a shelf, crooked her knees, let go, and made a grab for the piece of cloth. Having snatched it out of the corner, she tipped her good shoulder into the shoe shelf to keep from falling to the floor. The exertion sent a hard pain through the damaged shoulder and took her breath away. Wiping a knuckle across her wet forehead, Annie caught sight of the Fruit of the Loom label. The object in question appeared to have been a T-shirt. As nasty as it looked, Annie decided to open up the wad and see if it couldn't be reclaimed one last time.

A pattern of mildew stain had penetrated the cotton fabric in the manner of a tie-dye, setting dark in some areas, light and splotchy in others. She stared at the unfolded shirt, about to exclaim against ruinous wastefulness, but forgot her anger as an image began to take shape. Emerging from deep shadow was the suggestion of a gaunt, elongated face, framed by shoulder-length hair and a thick beard. At the top of the forehead were slashes and blots, imprint wounds from a crown of thorns. The dominant nose was flattened and bent to one side, as if it had been broken. The power and peace radiating from this image of violent death made it seem more alive to Annie than the people just outside the bin.

"Blessed Mother of God!" Annie crossed herself and checked the shirt once more, to be sure she hadn't been looking cockeyed out of her bifocals. She hadn't. "It is an image of Our Lord! That's why the angel at the hospital wanted me to be here today. It's a sign!"

The nurse felt awkward in these circumstances, because there was no proper gesture of veneration she could make in her impaired physical state. Kneeling was out of the question, yet what event since the revelation of the Christ child to the Magi would be more worthy of prostration? She held her fist to her mouth and struggled with the joyous laughter that was rising within her. The visionary feeder began to understand the full implications of this miracle.

"Are you Annie?" A customer in blackened jeans, ruined cowboy boots, and shirtless vest stood outside the bin doors. "They told me if I could find you, you'd give me some soap and a razor."

"Oh, young man, it's such a happy, happy day! But I have no razors or soap, not in the clothes bin. You must go to the trailer and ask for Betty. She'll find what you need."

After he departed in search of toiletries, Annie stood looking out the doorway at the sky, the hard and brilliant light of Southern California at midday. She was as content as in the good days before her husband's death so many years before. Joyful that she was still standing and breathing on her own, amazed to be alive at the age of ninety-five. Annie fell into a trance and was so deeply in the moment, she forgot what had brought her to this state of consummate joy. Confused but smiling broadly, she looked around the clothes bin to find her way back into a reality where the rest of the world awaited. When her eyes fell on the T-shirt once more, stretched flat over a shelf devoted to women's dresses, she grasped the thread of causality.

"He wants me to tell the people about the flood! The Lord wants me to save them!"

Arranging the T-shirt on a hanger, Annie headed for the cook shack. She'd decided the first people who would see the veronica and hear of revelation would be the volunteers. Of course, Sister

Claire had heard about the promised flood on the day of the pilgrimage to the river but had long since put the prediction out of her mind with worry over Annie. The great nurse had not gotten beyond the door to the clothes bin when the tabernacle came alive with excitement.

Dracula, having overheard Annie's exclamations, ran up to the picnic tables, displaying his ventilated uppers as he burbled enthusiasm. "Hey, you guys. Come and see what Annie found. It's Jesus on a T-shirt, swear to God."

When Skulford, DeLorean, and their group approached the clothes bin, they squinted at the filthy T-shirt she held in her hand. One of the men, who was looking at the object of veneration from all angles, was exasperating her. "Can't you see it, my dear? Look again. It's clear as day."

Feeling that a little religious history was called for, Dracula walked over and tugged the doubter's sleeve. "Remember the time they found Jesus on a tortilla? This is just like that. Or that other time, when there was a mossy stain on a gas station wall."

The day laborer who frequently gave cash donations to Annie, and sometimes brought flowers for the female volunteers, shouted out from the back of the crowd. "I see it! I see the face and the scars and the blood." As he dropped to his knees and crossed himself, the men parted and provided a visual corridor between the kneeling worshiper and the holy object.

Busily sketching the T-shirt on his card stock, Skulford stood to one side. Library Lady held hands to cheeks, exclaimed on the object of veneration and its remarkable range of color. The gentleman standing next to her snorted. "Yeah, and all of them brown."

The talk and energy of the crowd surged back and forth, then another man knelt, and another. Soon the skeptics had to flee back to the tabernacle to avoid the accusation of blasphemy. Annie was pleased her people had been appropriately moved. She was about to deliver the news about the impending flood when Whiskey Ed walked to her side and whispered.

"I've been picking up tremendous low-frequency anomalies on my oscilloscope, coming right from this bin. I believe the T-shirt is the real thing."

The visionary nurse looked at the electronics wizard in astonishment. "Of course it's real, Edward. The Lord has given us the gift of a miracle. It means we can all be saved now."

Annie stood silently for a few moments, fingers on lips, trying to decide how she would tell everyone about the danger that lay ahead. Looking beyond the circle of worshipers toward the street, she could see the press contingent was pressed up against the fence, trying to glean as much information as they could. As unfond of them as she was, she decided it would be better to tell the story once and let the newspapers and television spread the news. They certainly were better at this kind of work than she was.

"Edward, would you please go ask Sister Claire for the key to the padlock? Unlock the gate. I want the news people to hear what I have to say as well."

Whiskey Ed and the nun who groomed him strolled down to the entrance to let the media in, Ed warning them they'd better prepare themselves for a miracle. As Sister Claire began to open the gate, a cameraman pushed his way through, knocking her to pavement. After hitting flat on her back, she lay stunned and breathless. As the stampede continued, a woman reporter stumbled and came down on Sister Claire's chest with the other foot. The nun could hear the crunch of her ribs, but evidently nobody else could, because not one of the onrushing press tried to help her. By the time Grady, who had witnessed the incident from the cook shack ramp, ran to her assistance, she lay alone and isolated, staring straight up at the sky.

"Are you all right? Can you move?"

The liberation theologian nodded her head slightly but did not move her body. She could barely whisper. "I heard something in my chest. I think it's my ribs. They hurt like the devil, especially when I try to take a breath."

Grady was waving at Ethel on the ramp, but her attention was directed toward the surging crowd. "I'm going to call an ambulance. You could have internal injuries."

The stubborn nun remained motionless on the pavement, blinking tears out of her eyes. She panted for small breaths. "No! Don't do that. I'm all right. I'm just going to go back to the convent and rest. Help me up now."

Reluctant to move her at all, he helped Sister Claire to her feet by lifting her under the armpits. "Are you sure? This is really crazy. You could be seriously hurt. Why don't you let me drive you to the emergency room for x-rays?"

Her stubbornness undiminished, the nun stood with head down and shoulders tipped forward. "I'll be all right. It only hurts when I breathe."

"Great, then all you have to do is stop breathing for a month or so until it gets a chance to heal. Listen, Sister, will you promise me you'll go get x-rays if the pain doesn't get any better?"

Walking stiffly toward her dilapidated gray Ford, she had already waved him off. Sister Claire got in, cranked it up, and edged out the gate against a stream of foot traffic, the pious and the curious, all heading toward the miracle. She turned the corner onto Marston, headed back to the convent. With this powerful guardian of sanctity out of the way, demons began to gather on Palm Street.

~

The current media popularity of the word *communication* implies the existence of new information; some people out there have it and the rest of us are in desperate need of it. However, if the contrary is true, and as Socrates has suggested we are all born knowing everything, then the only question is whether to act on the knowledge we already possess. Thus, a metaphorical cyclone churns in the storage yard of the Lemon City DPW, the home of Annie's Soup Kitchen. It swirls around a pavement scraper, leaps over a bulldozer and backhoe, picking up speed. The whirlwind remains inside the enclosure, bouncing from one permeable wall to the other. The plastic screen on the side of the tabernacle is still, scraps of paper scattered over the pavement have not lifted, yet the storm is nearing its peak.

$\sim$

A convoy of incongruous vehicles speeds down Palm, taking up both sides of the street: a Roto-Rooter van, a beer truck, two Ford Explorers, one beige and one white, and an ominously dark UPS truck. They go into side spins, deploy in formation to create a blockade. Out of the vehicles pour eighty-two federal agents wearing bulletproof vests, appropriate initials inscribed on the back, gas masks slung loosely around their necks. As they charge through Annie's gate, Skulford Elephant makes an accounting of every shotgun, automatic rifle, sidearm, and tear gas grenade launcher. The agent-in-charge steps to the side of the phalanx and raises a bullhorn to his lips.

"We are federal agents. All assembled here, including press, must vacate these premises immediately. Veronica needs to step forward and surrender peacefully. We have orders to take her into protective custody."

Annie watched and listened from her position beside the clothes bin. Mouth open in genuine astonishment, it took a few moments for the ancient nurse to process the outrage, realize these rude people were some terrible kind of police. When she did, there was no holding her tongue. "A woman named Veronica? You foolish man, it's the image of Our Savior you're talking about! It's the Holy Cloth! Your behavior is so shameful, you should get down on your knees to the Lord and hope He'll listen when you beg for mercy." As she held the hanger and T-shirt aloft, Perry, Dracula, and Phil pushed in close to their leader, ready to repulse assaults from any direction.

Twenty yards away Navajo Bill stood by his pickup, shouted for the men clustered by the tabernacle to help the trio of bodyguards escort the visionary feeder to safety. After they had hoisted Annie into the back of his pickup truck, he made an attempt to drive out the gate. As the truck slowly approached the phalanx, the agent-in-charge ordered the donning of gas masks. Annie's chauffeur and protector threw his vehicle in reverse, tires spinning up gray smoke as he backed toward the trailer, throwing her to her knees. The Friday volunteers lined the ramp in front of the cook shack, watching the evolution of a debacle. Betty shouted out her admiration for police of all sorts, said she was sure there was some mistake and that any problem could easily be resolved. At the same time the men dashed toward the gate, throwing up a human wall between the intruders and the Saint of Lemon City. Each time Bill jammed his truck into forward or reverse, in a panicked search for an escape route, Annie leaned her slinged arm against the side of the load bed and thrust the miraculous T-shirt into the air with the healthy one. Each time she made this gesture, there was a cheer from the crowd, press included. Bill was driving the truck in a tight circle, and Annie, having struggled to her feet, was once again lifting the shirt like a banner for the Crusades. Her defiance stirred even the patriotic Ethel, who observed the unfolding of this morality play from the apparent safety of the trailer's ramp. Up to now she had been convinced that authority was beyond question, but this insane pageant was beginning to trouble her. A spontaneous celebration of Annie's declaration of independence went on until the first smoking tear gas canister struck the side of Bill's pickup and fell to the pavement.

Perry took off his shirt, wet it at the laundry tubs, wrapped it around his nose and mouth to improvise a gas mask. But after chucking two of the tear gas canisters back at the agents who fired them, he too was overcome. DeLorean and Phil tried to rally the irregulars, but the majority of them ran behind the cook shack in an attempt to escape through the break in the cyclone fence. No winged creatures came to the aid of the Kitchen saint or her charges. The General, who might have been an ideal candidate for a rescue mission on this occasion, had disappeared. After brief quixotic resistance, the battle was over, and all demands were resolved to the satisfaction of the authorities.

CHAPTER TEN

WORLD
SURVIVAL

O-chlorobenzylidenemalononitrile, better known as tear gas or CS, is in fact not a gas but an aerosol. It is popular among law enforcement agencies for use in what they like to call crowd control situations. Although police and army recruits can be trained to endure a few whiffs, no one can take a large dose without involuntary physiological breakdown. Predictable results include (1) excruciating pain in the lungs, (2) such difficulty drawing breath you think the air has turned liquid, and (3) extreme irritation of the skin, exacerbated by any application of water. This partial list serves to explain why Annie and her partisans were defeated in their brief confrontation with the feds. The pig-masked keepers of order confiscated the veronica, hanger and all. Only then were the great nurse and Navajo Bill allowed to flee in his pickup from the suffocating cloud that hung over the DPW yard. After the driving out, the authorities blockaded the intersection of Marston and Palm, allowing only Lemon City squad cars and federal vehicles to pass. Since the large press contingent at the Kitchen had experienced precisely the same unpleasant effects as Annie and her entourage, newspaper articles and television coverage began to run heavily in favor of the Kitchen director and her mission and against the heavy-handed methods of the government agencies involved.

Two days after the rout, Annie lifted her eyes once more to heaven, refuge of martyrs, hawks, and angels. She scanned the living stretch of blue that pushed hard to the greatest ocean on earth and to the void beyond. She was trembling but in spite of that could sense the drifting continental plate beneath her feet. It did not frighten her. The great nurse accepted the perils of the terrestrial ride named after a Black queen, the improbable utopia named California. And those risks had existed long before this nastiness began. But now the politics of total possession, both material and spiritual: how could anyone fly above that? Setting her jaw, the refugee from British war crimes always tried for the highest overview, the compassionate perch that would allow her to love her enemies. But when she arrived there today, Annie knew she'd have to count on divine mercy to stave off anger and hatred.

Breathing deeply, she pulled her eyes away from the heavens, ready once more to speak to the world. Head tipped down to the level of the crowd gathered before a dilapidated store front, she peered through a cluster of microphones. Her press conference had been arranged as a gesture of solidarity by the Santa Ana Hunger Mission. The feeders of the world were ready to unite and resist oppression.

Annie stared at the tabletop podium, shifted the single piece of paper she held, touched a swollen knuckle to her forehead, and began. "I would like to read to you something I've written down." After clearing her throat, she paused. The palsied vibration increased and her halo of wispy yellow and gray hair blurred with motion. "So many things have happened to us, it would take a day and a night to tell the whole story. But the most important thing I have to say to everyone is this: there is a terrible flood coming. The Santa Ana River will rise and sweep everything before it. I'm afraid we are all being punished for the bad things we've done to the world God has made for us. I pray it's not too late for us to change, to show the Lord we can do better. I believe when He sent the blessed veronica He was telling us there's still time for humankind to be spared."

Just as Annie began to cross herself, the video clip ended and the television commentator turned to the man seated beside her. "Denise Rodriguez here with Douglas Parnell, assistant director of the Orange County Flood Control District. Thank you for being with us today, Douglas."

The gentleman smoothed his sparse gray hair, tried unsuccessfully to adjust his shoulders inside an undersized tan check polyester jacket. "It's my great pleasure to be here, Denise."

Leaning forward to sign intensity, the commentator gestured with a grasping hand. "Now we've all heard about Annie O'Rourke. She's dominated the news in recent weeks, first predicting the world would be wiped out by plague and now saying it will be by flood. What the public wants to know is your opinion, as an expert on the Santa Ana River, of the likelihood her recent prediction could come true. Is a flood disaster of this dimension a real possibility?"

The camera zoomed in for a close-up, catching Parnell as he sucked in his cheeks, took a deep breath, then returned to his unvarying car salesman smile. "Is it possible? Yes. Is it probable? I don't think so. But before I explain what I mean by that, let me fill you in on a little history. We've had some humdinger floods of the Santa Ana River. People tend to take it very lightly, since most of the year the water level is pretty low. But they shouldn't do that. Some of the viewers out there are likely to remember the flood of 1969. Damages in the millions of dollars, a lot of roads and bridges washed out. Terrible loss of crops. The flood in 1938 was much worse. At that time all of northern Orange County was underwater and there was a significant loss of life, considering we didn't have much of a population at the time. But the granddaddy, a real thousand year flood, came back in 1862."

Denise straightened the navy blue lapel that held her clip mike, pensively stroked her chin with thumb and forefinger. "That's going a long way back, all the way to the Civil War."

Director Parnell paused and glanced toward the studio ceiling, nodding his head. "Yeah. You're right. The Civil War. Haven't thought about that one for a good long time. By the way, on this particular occasion it rained fifteen days and fifteen nights without stopping."

Caught off guard, Denise held her shoulders as if she had stumbled forward and was waiting to feel the impact of the pavement. "What do you mean 'without stopping'?"

"Just what I said. It kept on coming down." Parnell shook his head, grinned in admiration of the power of nature.

The commentator half smiled. "How is that possible?"

"Can't tell you." Parnell pursed his lips in a facial shoulder shrug. "I'm an engineer, not a meteorologist. But that's what happened."

Denise had her hands out, boxing the air, trying to regain control of the interview. "I'm doing my best to picture this. Help me out now. Was the storm parked right above Southern California?"

"Oh no. It was all over." The assistant director took particular satisfaction in narrating natural disasters. "They said in Sacramento people were rescued out of third-story hotel windows by river boats. Down here in the south—out in Colton, near Riverside—the whole town washed away. The only structure left standing was the church on the top of the hill. On the side of that church, which still exists today, you can see the high-water mark."

Denise was looking down, pointing both index fingers into her temples. "What I'm hearing you say is that Annie O'Rourke may be right. The kind of terrible flood she predicts is a possibility."

Parnell slipped a finger into his left ear, twisting it back and forth as he answered. "Well, we now have the Prado Dam, flood control channels and there's the Seven Oaks Dam, up near the source of the river. I believe all our preventive measures can handle anything but the worst case scenario."

"Worst case scenario?" The grasping hand paused in midair.

"Something like the flood of 1862. Or the one in 1825 that changed the course of the river. It used to empty into the ocean around Long Beach. Now it goes out at Huntington Beach, about fifteen miles to the south. And the silt that particular flood carried to sea created Newport Beach and the Balboa peninsula." The director rested both hands on his knees, sighed with relief at having completed his delivery of the bad news.

Denise paused, staring for a moment before returning to her notes and proceeding to the next question. "Do you believe the palm and veronica now in government custody have anything to do with this equation? I mean, with the United Nations General Assembly condemnation of their confiscation as a human rights violation, I guess we have to take this seriously."

Director Parnell held up his hands, as if to block any inquiry into his spiritual beliefs. "I was raised a Catholic, but as an engineer I really don't have much to say about such a connection."

Sweet Pea started to get up, then fell back and reached for the television remote. "Oh, boogers! What kind of Catholic are you? Why don't you just go out on a limb? We all know it's going to be the end of the world, just like the *Enquirer* said."

Her husband, Bruce, had nodded off in the far corner of the couch. The retired waitress lifted a slippered foot and kicked him in the thigh. "Hey, wake up! Maybe Annie will be on again, and maybe she'll say something about the Friday crew. Maybe she'll say something about me, you big lug!"

Bruce waved her off with one hand, trying to snuggle back into the arm of the couch. "OK, OK. Just tell me about it when it happens. Wake me then."

"I'll tell you about it, all right! But what do you care anyway? For instance, did you know that darn little nun, Sister Gianetta, insulted me yesterday at the meeting? I was looking around in the convent gift shop and said it would be a great place for my customized birdhouses. And she just ignored me, shined me on. That's what happened. Well, if you ask me, the cops are going to arrest Annie if she tries to go back and feed the men in the park again. I told her so, but she didn't listen. You see, nobody listens to me, not even you. Here I'm part of something important enough to be on TV and you won't even listen." Sweet Pea stepped on Bruce's left foot, leaned all of her weight against it.

"Hey, ouch! Damn it, what do you want me to do? I'm tired. Just let me alone. Oh hell, I know you won't do that. So tell me whatever you want. I'm listening." Bruce rubbed his face vigorously, but when he was finished, the wrinkles were still in exactly the same places.

~

"William, you must stop right here and take us down to the river." Annie was agitated as Navajo Bill steered his wife's minivan across the bridge that carried Imperial Highway over the Santa Ana River in Anaheim Hills. Since her faithful helper was ferrying her past the actual goal, she vibrated right to the verge of losing her temper.

Bill assumed his trademark bland smile, one that only occasionally slipped into a satirical twist at the corners of the mouth. "We can't park in the middle of a bridge, Annie. The cops will come along and give us a ticket."

The great nurse turned and inspected the passengers in the back of the minivan: Library Lady, the General, and the focus of the day's effort, Sally. Neither the General nor the *chi* master seemed to be paying much attention to the parking crisis. They were looking out opposite windows, the General at young ladies speeding along the river's bike path and Library Lady at a sign over the Anaheim Hills Best Western Motel. Sally, as usual, had eyes so thickly glazed with oblivion they were impossible to read.

Turning back, searching for a solution beyond the windshield, Annie fidgeted. "Well then, find a place to park and help get Sally down to the river. If this doesn't make her better, then none of the understandings that have been given me are right. And Lord save us, that can't be."

Bill made an illegal U-turn at La Palma, pulled into the parking lot of the strip mall that backed onto the river. As he held Annie by the elbow, shuffling along and offering support, the two of them led the therapeutic entourage across the bridge. Someone needed to find a way down. Although the bike path on the south side was beautifully paved and maintained, there had never been any thought of access to the river itself. The former Rockwell engineer surveyed the possibilities. Cobbled banks slanted at 45-degree angles down to the river, thirty or forty feet on both sides. "I don't think us old folks can make it, but the General might be able to get Sally down over in that riprap section."

Annie snapped her head around, glared at Bill. She had no idea what riprap was and hoped he wasn't trifling with her. She was in no mood for that. Just as the nurse prepared to press for an explanation, the General bellowed his first utterance of the trip. Uncharacteristically, he had neither sung nor chanted along the way. "Gonna take her to the *river*! Take her down, dunk her in, do the coffee thing. Yowsa! Do the special bath thing." He shook one leg to the side, then the other, demonstrating that his knee-high rubber wading boots made him ideally equipped for the expedition.

Library Lady was quick to offer her services as well. The cuffs of her black nylon warm-up jacket almost covering her hands, she hugged herself with enthusiasm. "Oh, I can get down there easy too. See? I came equipped. I've got my sneakers on. I can help the General, because he'll want a woman along to look after special needs."

Rather than inch his way down the riprap, as Annie and Bill expected, the huge warrior snorted assent, then charged down the embankment with great strides. His momentum carried him into the river, washing over his boots and up his thighs. He paused, a still object in the rushing current, looked toward midstream.

Annie was upset that things weren't happening as she'd planned. "Come back! Come back and help the two women down. William, tell him to come back!"

Navajo Bill, hands on slouching hips, grinning, enjoyed the General's outrageous independence and unpredictability. Since Annie had been badgering him all morning, he didn't entirely mind that the warrior was agitating her. "Oh, he'll be all right. Just give him a chance."

Looking over his shoulder, Bill noticed the dozen bicycle riders who had stopped on the path and were watching the proceedings, trying to decide if there was an emergency of some sort. One shouted to the engineer, signaled by raising a cell phone that he was ready to call for help. Bill smiled and waved him off.

In the meantime, the General had worked his way back up the embankment. Holding her shoulders as Library Lady steadied her feet, the two of them inched Sally down to the river, rock by rock. Library Lady brushed the Plague victim's hair out of her face and was attending to her clothes when the General snatched the sick woman up in his arms, carried her out into the swiftly moving river. There were yelps of shock from the bike path viewers as well as from Annie. She reached out her good arm with the idea she might somehow get down the riverbank and properly direct activities. Bill grasped her shoulder in restraint.

The General, now in water up to his chest, dropped his right arm, dunking Sally's head and shoulders into the river. After being pulled up above the surface again, blonde hair darkened and dripping from the water, she gave no response, no sign that she was in any way aware of what had happened to her. The General turned toward the south bank and his audience, began to sing "Wade in the Water" in his huge baritone voice. Library Lady clasped hands together in joy, joined on the chorus. Even Annie, although unfamiliar with the spiritual, tried to sing along. Turning back toward the middle of the river, the warrior immersed Sally once more, then walked out holding the woman like a waterlogged doll. As he reached the bank, water sloshed out of his boots. Singing all this while, he stepped back two strides, charged to the top of the riprap embankment with Sally still in his arms. He laid her gently at the great nurse's feet.

"My God, you are going to scare the poor girl to her death!"

The exhausted General looked especially ferocious. "It's my religion, woman! Underwater martial arts is what this is about. Allah protects me whatever I do. And don't you go tell me I'm backsliding."

Library Lady cleared the top of the embankment, scrambled to Sally's side. The Plague victim was still prone, soaked and breathing hard, with eyes tight shut. As the *chi* master touched them, the lids of the former Martha Stewart disciple sprang open. "My God! Look at them! They're clear!" Library Lady was right; the pupils had reconstituted themselves, unobscured by the thick glaze that had covered them for more than a month.

Annie waved her hand back and forth over Sally's eyes. They followed the hand, then looked up and returned the nurse's gaze. The aging teenager sat up, brushed her wet hair out of her face, and seemed to take notice of her surroundings. She thrust out her lips but was still unsure how to use them.

The great nurse crossed herself. "Merciful Mother Mary, thank you for helping this poor young girl!"

A man stood in the middle of the bridge, his car behind him still running, the driver's door swung open. There were other empty cars on the bridge and a crowd forming along the railing. In fact, as the Kitchen's therapy group looked up and took notice, they could see a traffic jam had developed on Imperial Highway in both directions.

The man on the bridge cupped hands around mouth and shouted. "My name is Mike Walters, I'm a reporter for the *Orange County Register*. What happened down there? Is the woman all right?"

Annie shouted back. "She's much better, thanks be to God. Before she went into the water, she was in such a sorry way. It was the Shadow Plague. Now she's so much better."

Leaning over the railing of the bridge, as if to get even closer to an unfolding news story, the reporter called back. "Are you telling me you cured her of the Cronkite syndrome by taking her into the river?"

After looking down at Sally, still sitting at her feet, and seeing her smile for the first time in over a month, it was hard for Annie to resist making sweeping claims. "Well, she may not be cured, young man, but she's so much better. I think today the Lord has showed the world how to survive this wicked disease."

Sally found her way to her feet unassisted. She waved at the witnesses along the bike path, now numbering in the dozens. Turning toward the bridge, she waved at the spectators who had gathered along the railing. A few people began to applaud, then more joined in. Whistles followed, and a collective cheering that lifted the Santa Ana River straight up out of its polluted bed.

A day later, after thousands of Shadow Plague victims had successfully taken the cure at the same location, the reporter who'd watched from the bridge was giving a personal account on a nationally televised special. He described the first known healing of the Cronkite syndrome. In the Los Angeles studio he was flanked by an epidemiologist on one side and by an anthropologist on the other. The latter was identified by the moderator as an expert on rivers, a man particularly knowledgeable in lore associated with the Ganges in India.

Grady and his wife, Marcia, listened to the UCLA professor's description of Benares: how Indians believed that the river washed away karma and that being born in its waters or dying in them constituted great good luck. Accompanying still shots of cremations on shore, people of all ages and castes streaming down stone ghats into the water, doing ritual obeisance in their sarongs and saris, floating bodies, flowers everywhere. The professor proclaimed the scene as brilliant and full of meaning as a Renaissance masque.

Grady registered disgust by blowing a raspberry. "What the hell does this guy know about Renaissance masques? Maybe once upon a time he went to the Pageant of the Masters in Laguna Beach. That's probably the kind of stuff he's thinking about."

With pursed lips, Marcia continued to twirl hair from her bangs around a finger. She kept eyes trained on the television set. "No, that would be a pageant, not a masque."

Feeling connubial chill coming on, the teacher-cook made an attempt to deflect the critique his wife was bound to offer. "By the way, would you please tell me how a bunch of painted people standing still in a goofy tableau constitutes a pageant?"

The darkness of Marcia's hair, eyes, and olive skin seemed exaggerated when she got angry. It was as if she drew night from the air and it congealed around her. "Pageant of the Masters. You see, if they call it a pageant, then it's a pageant. Anyhow, this guy obviously knows the difference between a masque and a pageant. That's why he's teaching at a prestigious university and is an expert on a TV show and you're sitting on the couch watching him."

"That's a pile of shit and you know it." Grady began to rise, ready to flee to the kitchen and the solace of a beer, but settled back, deciding to make a stand for just treatment. "Why do you always think everybody else in the world knows more than I do? Even when I'm right and someone else is wrong, you'd rather believe them. You're so unfair. It's like you enjoy cheapshoting me. I mean, what is it with you?"

Irritated by the disruption, Marcia turned her head, looked over the top of her glasses. "Only in your warped imagination are you the poor, picked-on intellectual, the unappreciated husband. I just get so damned sick and tired of talking to a victim, listening to all the whining. Do you remember when you used to have wild dreams and passionate ideas? What do you think made me fall in love with you in the first place? It may be hard to understand, but the reason I don't have any sympathy for you when you pull these routines is the same reason I hate Woody Allen movies."

Grady's conciliatory smile changed to a look of hurt. "But Woody Allen movies are funny."

Marcia was concentrating once again on the UCLA man, talking to her husband out the corner of her mouth. "Only if you're a narcissistic worm like him. Otherwise they're disgusting, irritating, and boring."

Having finished the argument, Marcia patted her husband's hand, then folded her arms. Grady was silent as long as he could manage, which wasn't long. Tension like this drove him crazy and inevitably to attempts at reconciliation. "OK, OK, you're right as usual. Let's not argue all night over this."

Turning to her husband, casting a glance that conveyed an odd amalgamation of affection, pity, and contempt, Marcia shook her head, refocused her attention on the television program.

"How about a foot massage? Skin cream and all, total reflexology, the whole works." Grady tried to lift his wife's left leg from the floor, but she resisted. He shifted to the middle of the couch, gently lifted the edge of the bathrobe and began to rub her calf and knee. Finally, without shifting her eyes from the TV screen, she allowed both legs to be lifted, her socks to be removed, and the foot therapy to begin. Grady used his thumb to stimulate various reflexology zones, particularly the heel, which controlled the genital area. After finishing with the sole of the foot, he massaged between the tendons and small bones on the top, then moved to the ankles, the calves (to stimulate muscle tissue and recirculate puddled blood), the thighs, and finally into the legs' point of intersection. Marcia was still complaining about Grady's unprofessional massage techniques as she removed her panties. Nonetheless, the massage ended, as Annie's Friday cook had planned, in the bedroom.

After the bumping and groaning had ceased and his wife's form lay still and spread-eagled over his sweating body, Grady thought back to their more romantic younger years. He remembered when palpable exchanges of energy took place as they held each other. Such powerful reverie brought to mind the latest update on Sally's remarkable story.

He twisted his head to try to look at his wife's face but then lay back on the pillow, not wanting to end the intimacy. "Did I tell you what happened to Sally after her river cure?"

Gathering in a deep breath and releasing it as a sigh, Marcia signaled in the negative.

"You know, back in her Martha Stewart days, before she came down with the Shadow Plague, Sally was so scared of the General, she didn't even dare come out to work on the serving line, for fear he'd actually say something to her. I'm sure she thought all Black guys were crazy about blondes. So she stayed in the cook shack and did dishes with Sister Claire. But when she came back from her sickness—or you might say came back like Lazarus from the dead—all she wanted to do was talk to him, hang out with him. She wanted to find wherever it was he lived on the street. Of course, Annie thought it was not a very good idea, especially since she was married and had children. But Sally insisted. She had all these important things she wanted to tell the General, things she found out when she was inside her sickness. So I guess she found him under a bridge, and apparently at least part of what she said was that she was madly in love with him and wanted to live with him for the rest of her life. Sally told him she had enough money for the two of them to be comfortable and happy. But the General would have nothing to do with it. He sent her back to her lawyer husband, and nobody has seen or heard from her since. What do you think about that?"

Having ended his narration, Grady became aware of the slow rising and falling of Marcia's chest, poised directly over his. As she inhaled, there was a slight rattle in her throat. Or, more precisely, a snore.

CHAPTER ELEVEN

BETTY TALKS
TO THE
BURNING PALM

The day Annie's Soup Kitchen was returned to the control of its visionary director, after great pressure had been exerted by forces both domestic and international, Betty Blankenship's first act was to walk around the back of the trailer and take a look at the liberated palm tree. Four holes created by federal tent poles were still clear in the hardpan, although footprints and other signs of activity appeared to have been brushed away. During the week the Kitchen was in government custody, Betty heard Annie agonize continuously over the veronica and the palm. At first the Friday lieutenant couldn't quite visualize the tree. That was no surprise, since she had always been skeptical about Annie's mystical hobbyhorses. What troubled Betty most, however, was that a clear image of the scruffy tree began to dominate both her dreams and her waking thoughts. Now that the palm was once more before her eyes, she recalled her former contempt for it. She'd always suspected that the cameraman had faked that infamous light show in an attempt to raise the ratings of his television network.

"Aaaahhh, Miz Betty. You going to give us some sugar, milk, and cups along with our coffee?"

Betty turned to see Perry thrusting glasses, nose, and moustache around the side of the trailer. She waved him off. "You go see Ethel about that. I'm busy right now."

Glancing over her shoulder to be sure she was alone once again, Betty stepped forward to inspect the palm more closely. She had an overwhelming desire to touch it, just to be sure her weeklong obsession was nothing more than a symptom of stress. As she reached out, a force she couldn't see took hold of her hand. A moment later, the tree burst into flame, engulfing her arm to the elbow. Betty struggled and attempted to cry out, but her voice would not pass through the gate of her throat. That was when the palm decided to speak instead.

"Your link with the fire before your eyes is a bond that cannot be sundered. The destiny of this tree and yours are one and the same. If it should die, you will die too. If it should live, you may be spared. But salvation will come only if you learn to speak the idiom of the tree. Spanish is the language of palms. You have two weeks to recall it and ask for mercy on your life."

As the pronouncement was completed, the fire vanished, Betty's hand was released, and she fell to the ground.

~

There are so many reasons to turn our backs on the improbable, to wear down childhood memories until we are fully convinced we never had the power of flight. Only the wise can fathom the depth of their ignorance. In fact, the pursuit of wisdom can be pretty confusing, beyond any talk of communication and information.

~

Perry had an idea. Why not memorialize Annie's epic struggle against and ultimate success over the forces of evil through street theater? It is difficult to ascertain exactly what the post-Babel linguist had in mind, but Roderigo was quick to add specific suggestions for the performance. When he said the pageant must be done in the tradition of Chicano Teatro Campesino, there were no objections. In fact, Perry said "*Viva la raza! Viva* César Chávez!" A stiff Santa Ana wind blew through the compound, snapping the plastic windscreen, creating the urgency of a whip as the group discussed the focus of their play. Phil said he didn't understand how there could be any debate. Three obvious messages needed to be conveyed, and each one would fit nicely into one act of the drama, resulting in a classic three-act play. There was the veronica, the fight with the feds, and the return of the Kitchen through world intervention. Roderigo objected to the use of the word "classic." He said Teatro Campesino came from the people and had nothing to do with classic European bullshit. Whiskey Ed also raised his hand in protest. He asked why they were excluding the feedings Annie did in the old days at the park, arguing those struggles and triumphs were every bit as heroic as more recent events.

Perry stared at his feet, pressed fist to forehead. "Aaaaahhhh, yeah, my man. I can see the fish in the water. What if I write down all these ideas and then read them back to you for your satisfaction? Annie, from beginning to end, amen. Yeah."

Turning on his heel and throwing up his chubby arms, Roderigo continued to take exception to Perry's plan. "No, no, *cabrón*. We're talking liberation street theater here, not fucking Shakespeare. You don't write stuff like that down, man, you just act it out."

Lucky, named for his brief association with the supermarket chain, was amused by the silver man's enthusiasm. "Hey, Roderigo, the only thing you know how to liberate is money out of people's pockets."

Roderigo began to pace, brushing imaginary dust off his pants. "Man, you don't know me. Don't talk like that out of your asshole. You don't know me good enough for that."

Phil got up from the table, walked over, and positioned himself between Lucky and the Kitchen's resident thug. "All you guys can do is argue, but you haven't even decided who the characters are going to be. For instance, are all of us going to be in this thing? Are we going play ourselves? What about the people in the shack, are we going to do any of them?"

"Aaaahhhh, yeah. I'm going to do Pastaman. I'm getting this Italian thing all lined up." Perry raised both arms, asking that his impersonation be given close scrutiny. "Bellatissima, baby!"

Now Whiskey Ed was caught up in the enthusiasm. "What about Annie? Who's going to play her?"

It was clear the electronics wizard had his eye on the part, but almost everyone else wanted to audition for it as well. Various of the men made brief attempts at an Irish accent, mimicking some of her characteristic gestures, but the more they tried, the less fun it became. There is always an uneasiness that comes when satirizing the holy, and the tryout for Annie's part ended in a long silence, each aspiring actor feeling guilty for his attempt to impersonate a saint.

Perry broke the somber mood. "Aaaahhhh, check this out. Forget Pastaman. That's too boring. I decided I'm going to do Betty. Bust-Your-Ass Betty. Just check this out." Perry adjusted his glasses, stalked back and forth with his hands on his hips, spread a mirthless smile across his face. Then came the characteristic abuse, the prayer that sounded like a satanic parody of Annie's, a curse more than a blessing. He shouted through his smile. "Hats off! Try to behave long enough to thank the Lord. Dear Lord, we thank all the kind people who have helped put this food on the table. We thank You as well for taking care of these scroungy, ungrateful, miserable people, as undeserving as they may be. May You soon get their lazy asses back to work, so they can take care of themselves and not bother us no more. Amen."

Perry was so caught up in his acting, he failed to notice the desperate cues for silence from his fellow actors, an attempt to warn him that Betty herself had walked up behind him and was observing the entire performance. They expected a human explosion, with such dire consequences Perry would be banished for life from the

Kitchen compound. On the contrary, the Friday lieutenant assumed a smile that looked like a parody of Perry's imitation.

"Well, I'm glad you're all out here having fun on this windy morning. I'm going to have to ask a small favor of you. Are there any Spanish speakers out here? If somebody would just step forward, I'll make it worth his while. I'll even cook rice and beans for lunch today. With nacho sauce on it."

The day laborers smiled and shook their heads, avoiding her glance, trying to slink away into the crowd.

"Come on, now. I just need a little help. Think of all we've done for you!"

Phil was the only one in the group who was not intimidated by the presence of authority. He leaned against a picnic table and folded his arms. "OK, Betty, we'll ask around. As soon as we find somebody, we'll send him right up to the door. You absolutely don't need to worry about this."

Betty scanned the crowd, heaved a great sigh as she realized no one but Phil would look her in the eye. As she walked away, Dracula whispered, "Man, Bust-Your-Ass Betty. Let's go dunk her in the river, guys. Give her the cure."

There was a great deal of gleeful cackling. However, DeLorean's face remained sober. "No, I don't think that would work. What she's got is even worse than the Shadow Plague. If you threw her in the river, all that would happen is she'd die from the pollution."

Phil waved both hands in energetic disagreement. "No way, man. She's too nasty to die from pollution. I bet the river would come off second best."

Hearing the outbursts of laughter, Betty had a hunch she might be the target but didn't want to let anyone guess she knew or cared. She walked to the washing machine area, began to bang washing machine lids, feign productive activity. After she was sure everyone's attention had drifted elsewhere, she slipped around to the back of the trailer to address the palm once more.

Betty stood before the tree, holding both hands tightly to her chest. "*Buenas dias, arbol.* I'm back."

The palm ignited but with a less showy flame than at her first encounter. And the voice seemed far less oracular. "Where's the Spanish? You're still speaking English."

Betty responded with a schoolgirl's pleading. "I bought a dictionary and a phrase book, and I'm working on getting a tutor."

"You've wasted a week. You only have one to go. The dictionary won't help you. This is not a question of learning; you have to *remember* your Spanish."

"Why do you keep saying that? I never knew any Spanish. I took two years of French in high school, but I don't remember a word of it." Betty summoned up her best imitation of Annie's brogue. "You've got to remember, I'm Irish, not Mexican."

"No, you're not Irish. And you have only seven days to remember the tree's language." With those words the flame went out.

~

When our ancestors emerged from underground armed with language, it turned out to be their best weapon against oblivion, the best way to remember that dark and powerful place from which they came. Special words allowed them to celebrate their link with the enchanted cave. Since the entrance to the aboriginal place was sealed, the only sure way to return is madness. For those unwilling to undertake that one-way trip, dreams and metaphor offer an alternative path. Betty Blankenship has forgotten that kind of invention. However, having heard and subconsciously recorded nearly two-thirds of the entire Spanish vocabulary, Betty already possesses everything she needs to speak and survive.

~

It was Tuesday and not her day to supervise, but she was there nonetheless. Betty stuck her smiling face through the cook shack door, said hello to the crew, and explained she had come back to take care of a couple of unfinished Friday chores. She proceeded to the bin that contained paper products and surplus bread, stepped briefly into it, then walked around the trailer to the palm tree. Betty glanced at one of the windows on the back, judged the angle, and for a moment considered the possibility she might be observed in her humiliating posture of supplication. But her mood was desperate; at this point pride was much less important than pleasing the tree.

On her knees before the palm, she waited for the voice to return and instruct her. The tree ignited into minimal flame, as if it were waiting to hear something significant before committing to its usual spectacular show.

Betty took a deep breath and began her oral report. "*Yo quiero un taquito. Viva la causa! Mole poblano. Cinco de mayo.*"

The palm tree vibrated and surged with an engulfing flame. "*Oh santo Dios! Es posible que tal haya en el mundo, y que tengan en el tanta fuerza los encantadores y encantamentos, que hayan trocado el buen juicio de mi señora en una tan disparatada locura? Oh señora, señora, por quien Dios es que vuesa merced mire por si, y vuelva por su honora, y no de crédito a esas vaciedades que le tienen menguado y descabalado el sentido!*"

Perry was peeking around the corner of the trailer again, silently watching Betty's responses. She spewed words at random, unintelligible as coherent discourse in any language, even to the expert on the Tower of Babel. Since he could not see the flaming presence Betty was addressing, her behavior seemed even more deranged than usual. Her voice, choked with fear, came in powerful bursts, each one more shrill than the last. Finally her voice lifted into an aria of anguish. Embarrassed by his secret witnessing of the madwoman's suffering and the discomfort heightened by knowing he'd publicly ridiculed her just a few days before, Perry retreated to the tabernacle.

Sitting with DeLorean at table six, the Kitchen's resident linguistics expert stared at the ramp that fronted the cook shack. "Aaaahhhh, my man, I can't convey to you how strange this place has gotten to be. Like, for instance, let me tell you what's going on around back." Glimpsing a flash of bright color out of the corner of his eye—to the right of the trailer, in the area of the laundry facilities behind the bathrooms—Perry stopped. He turned his head to take a long look but saw nothing. "I think this whole thing is getting to me, I mean because . . . "

Before Perry could finish the thought, the General emerged fresh from the laundry tub in a totally new outfit. He was wearing a huge yellow print dress, with long orange scarf thrown twice around his neck, all on top of his army fatigues. His garments, both over and under, were soaking wet. The General's head was covered, not by his usual Bedouin headgear, but by a large straw hat with curved brim, decorated with brightly dyed turkey feathers. His look was reminiscent, more than anything else, of a rakish pirate. As the huge man continued his dramatic strut back and forth in front of the tabernacle, still wearing knee-high rubber boots spilling sudsy water, DeLorean observed that the General had struck a perfect balance between Annie's characteristically colorful dress and that of the protagonist from a flamboyant production of Verdi's *Otello*.

The huge warrior demonstrated the prophetic powers of the retired auto maker by bursting into song. The fragment of a much longer libretto, one that snaked through the enchanted cave of his mind, went something like this: "Annie O'Rourke, O'Rourke, O'Rourke, I am the feeder of Lemon City, the savior of all Orange County!" After intoning a long chorus of snorts and drones, the warrior once again took up his theme. "Against the monsters of this city, gorgons and harpies, I fought to victory. I held to my honor and prevailed! I feed the worthy poor, give them chicken and mashed potatoes, spaghetti and green salad, gumbo, yams, and fried zucchini! Pies, cakes, and bagels. Corn on the cob, beans, and strawberries in cream! The feeder, the savior, full deliverance from our enemies!"

There was no doubt the General had attempted through diction to elevate Annie's activities to grand opera heroic style. Each time he

hit a word and note he wished to emphasize, such as "harpies,"
"pies," and "beans," he raised a clenched fist.

The ancient nurse emerged like Juliet onto the balcony, in this
case the ramp in front of the trailer. Not shy about being in the
wrong opera, she exclaimed at the General's outlandish aria. She
wondered aloud to the volunteers who surrounded her if the General hadn't somehow raided her clothes bin. After an assistant ran to
the holiest of holies and returned to verify that the padlock was still
in place, she calmed herself. It was now possible to watch the huge
drag queen warrior, enjoy his impersonation of her with the awe the
experience properly inspired.

On the other side of the trailer, Betty was still on her knees,
pleading with the tree. "*Si, si, si! Me gustan las palmas!*" Crying and
keening, she set up a powerful counterpoint to the cross-dressed
baritone with the larger audience.

Whiskey Ed was the first to pick up the soprano. Searching for
its source, he looked up to the roof of the trailer and spotted the
Mysterious Stranger. He nudged Perry in the side. "Look, man! Look
who's up there conducting!"

Perry raised his eyebrows in disbelief, then exclaimed. "It's the
bearded dude, waving his arms like Leonard Bernstein!" The entire
audience observed the scarecrow figure directing, first the General,
then the voice that rose from behind the trailer. Unable to wait for
the performance to end, the linguist cowboy shouted his approval.
"Bravo, maestro! Bellatissimo!"

Noticing all eyes in the tabernacle had switched from the oper-
atic warrior to the roof, Annie shaded her eyes with her hand and
looked up. "Goodness, it's that poor man again. What on earth is he
doing up there? He can't be in his right wits. How will we get him
down now? And who is that shrieking around back by the railroad
tracks? Or is it one of those terrible cleaning cars again?"

Annie turned to the Tuesday crew, who were still in shock over
the unexpected entertainment. The Kitchen director smiled and

touched fingertips to cheeks. It was a familiar signal that she was about to tell an amusing story. "You know, when he first came here to the Kitchen, with his old man's beard . . ." Annie paused for a grimace. "I had never seen the like. Filthy clothes, all stiff with dirt. Well, I took him to the bin and said, 'I want you to take off all your clothes. I'll look away.' You see, I had already laid out a shirt, a pair of pants, and the underthings. Well, he had the biggest smile. I don't suppose he could have been very particular, being dressed that way, but he loved the new things ever so much. He walked so stiff. And I said, 'Love, do the pants not fit you?' He said everything was lovely. And his feet were so black! I don't believe he'd ever worn shoes. So I cleaned and dressed the poor feet and gave him shoes." Clapping her hands together, Annie let her spirit take flight, far beyond the ongoing opera and its audience—clients, volunteers, and press.

Seeing the cameramen shoot the General's performance through the fence inspired Phil and Roderigo to approach the media gallery regarding their own upcoming event. They sauntered to the gate, engaged several reporters in conversation. Roderigo waved off the warrior's aria with a gesture of disgust. "Man, you think this is something? This is nothing. The real show coming up day after tomorrow. You guys sure want to get down on it for national TV."

The cameramen snickered as they kept taping the General, and the reporters joined them. This scornful reception thoroughly offended the silver-haired thug, and he was preparing to kick the fence to teach them a lesson. Phil caught Coyote Man by the elbow, pulled him away before he could do damage either to personnel or equipment. "Easy, Roderigo. Let me talk to these nice people. I'm sure they're not going to want to miss it. This play's going to be big time. Guaranteed. Teatro Campesino, revolutionary theater kind of stuff. You television guys just might find yourselves in the play, you never know. I made up some tickets here." Phil held up a fan of red paper strips. "Make sure you get one, you won't regret it. Take more than one if you like, feel free to pass them around to whoever."

As Annie's men tried to seduce the media, a sudden shower of stroboscopic light fell over the negotiations of the little group by the gate. Everyone looked up, catching the swirling ellipses of the hawks just overhead. Straight from the dream caves in the canyons of east Orange County, the birds air danced in loops between the sun and the onlookers, dizzying everyone who stood below. When their motion slowed, solidified into flakes of light that fell like manna from heaven, all rapt viewers were overwhelmed by a strange satisfaction.

Intersecting feathered rings pushed west to the Santa Ana River, turned south-southwest to follow the modified channel left by the Army Corps of Engineers. The hawks flew a course between Disney-land and the Arrowhead Pond, home of the Mighty Ducks, over the Orange Crush, the intersection of the 5, 57, and 22 freeways, past a Las Vegas–style mall called the Block, past the Bowers Museum, Santa Ana College, Centennial Regional Park, Orange Coast College, and finally flew directly down the middle of the river, the invisible boundary between Costa Mesa and Huntington Beach. As the lumi-nescent red-tails flew past the beach and over the basin of a thou-sand watersheds we call the Pacific, they felt its power. They touched the air with the tips of their feathers, trying to sense those secret currents, sometimes warm and sometimes cold, that create weather and determine the future of the world.

CHAPTER TWELVE

BENT VECTORS

Annie O'Rourke made her volunteers laugh when she declared they'd all be receiving 100 percent raises. "The checks are in the mail," she'd always say. But when the magnificent nurse joked about work in the Kitchen giving them absolution, an odd nervousness always fluttered over their eyes. They may have laughed in response to her jibe, but they all hoped that exactly such a reward awaited them.

Embarrassed even by the Kitchen director's formulaic intimacy, Grady took a long drink of Gatorade, then shouted out. "Does that mean we get plenary absolution, Annie?"

Wanda raised both hands and shook her head. "No, no, that won't do. It's plenary indulgence. Full absolution and plenary indulgence. They're not the same thing."

Smiling her mischievous smile after witnessing the professor's rebuke, the nurse of the sad and joyous countenance let her eyes drift through the doorway. Not the one that led to the ramp outside the cook shack but the doorway in the air no one else could see.

The last time the Friday crew worked at Annie's Soup Kitchen was Halloween, the day before the rain began. There had been no warning of impending disaster—other than Annie's apocalyptic predictions, which were not calendar-specific—so none of them knew it would be the last day they'd see each other or anything dry in Southern California for a very long time.

Mary Jo had replaced Sally just after the middle-aged teenager slipped into the darkness of the Shadow Plague. And the newcomer stayed on, even after Sally's miraculous river cure, because the Martha Stewart disciple soon abandoned Annie's cook shack. Mary Jo, a good ten years younger than Sally, was well-accepted by everyone except Grady, who found her cheap blonde dye job, double ponytails, and Mary Jane dresses a horrific parody of Sally. Although unstated, he had always felt a great fondness for the stricken lover of good things.

Today Mary Jo brought in cookies with orange icing, decorated as jack-o-lanterns. Distributing them to the various volunteers—all but Betty, who was absent without leave—she shared her latest life adventures and strategies for success. First, the announcement that she'd entered her twelve-year-old daughter in another beauty contest. There was no way, Mary Jo declared, she'd allow the child to grow up to the hard life she had. With all the style and composure little Susie would learn in competition, the solicitous mother was sure no door would ever be closed to her. Regarding her own current difficulties in the area of personal finance, the new volunteer expressed confidence they'd be resolved by adhering to two basic principles. First, never buy a lotto ticket unless the jackpot is over twenty million dollars. Lesser amounts, if won, would merely serve to distract, since they would be insufficient to support the lifestyle she planned on achieving. Second, sue for large sums whenever the chance presents itself. Although none of her lawsuits had worked out as yet, she argued that they were necessary to keep her busy while she awaited an appropriate lotto jackpot.

Distancing himself from Mary Jo's lecture on finance and social class, Grady dove into the containers of castoff vegetables and fruits. Lifting a box filled with overripe bananas, he spotted another filled with hazelnuts. He stood astonished, staring down at the unusual find, trying to decide how they might be used.

"Oh, nigger toes! I haven't seen those since I left the farm."

He looked up. It was Sweet Pea, who could easily read the shock in his eyes. She laughed and did a little Shirley Temple dance. "Sorry, Grady, guess we don't call them that anymore."

Turning on his heel and retreating to the other end of the trailer, where Wanda was constructing peanut butter and jelly sandwiches, he caught a snatch of her conversation with one of the clients. The man, who often shared insights on political conspiracies with Wanda, leaned through the door, speaking in low tones.

"When the oil runs out and they blow all the main electrical lines, that's when they'll pull the string on the trap. But as long as we still have our guns, I know we can beat 'em."

Grady could not resist. "Beat who? Who are we going to shoot now?"

Wanda pulled herself straight. Although capable of a ferocious stare, she directed a look of tender sadness at the teacher-cook. She cared enough about him to grieve that he would have to succumb along with all the other ignorant liberals. "We're talking about Russians and the United Nations plot. You know Gorbachev has his headquarters in San Francisco, don't you? He's in charge of all our military base closings."

Grady liked Wanda and wanted to be polite, but he couldn't suppress a snicker. "The Russians are coming on fishing trawlers to take over the United States?"

Wanda had returned her attention to the double row of bread slices laid out before her on the counter. "Grady, whether you want to believe it or not, the Russians are still our enemies."

Moving through the doorway, the teacher-cook paused, even though he knew it would be better to keep moving. "OK, OK, but I want you to know that I still like Gorbachev. And I think Yeltsin was a pig. Talk about ingratitude, Gorbachev dismantled the Soviet Union, provided his people a chance for democracy, and liberated the entire world from cold war, and everybody says he's a bum. I don't get it."

He was out on the ramp now, trying to resist the argument that still awaited inside. Scanning the tabernacle from right to left, it was the usual chatting, jiving donut and coffee crew. Nothing out of the ordinary until his eyes fell on Skulford Elephant, who had grabbed the cyclone fence with both hands and was shaking it with a vigor that seemed beyond his nature. After sending shock waves down the fence in both directions, he withdrew his hands, paced back and forth along the barrier, then grabbed it and shook it again. Grady was fascinated. Although he'd heard the little man say odd things and had always observed a disconcerting strangeness in his eyes and demeanor, he'd never before seen any signs of violence. Whiskey Ed strolled over to the fence and began to talk with the agitated card maker. Perry and Library Lady followed. Finally, Roderigo joined the group. Set up at his usual picnic table, the General glared with disapproval at the Magnificent Seven minus two.

Grady was trying to guess what was transpiring with this unusual gathering of clients when Annie stepped out the far door with telephone receiver in hand. "Is there a Wayne here? Is there anyone named Wayne?"

A number of voices called out in unison. "He's in the bathroom!"

Annie shouted back, without a pause. "Well, it's high time he was out of there!"

〜

Gray whale migration routes along the Pacific coast are charted by the earth's magnetic lay lines. A result of crushed together tectonic plates, deep fault lines etch into California north and south. These tattoos on her lovely skin are also magnetically charged. When wind-driven wildfires wash down canyons like flash floods, they also leave their characteristic traces and demarcations. Earth, wind, and fire have narrated California's watersheds, carved her story down the adobe tablet that is the coast. Each stroke, each incised letter makes the obscure queen named California more vulnerable to catastrophic flood.

～

On Saturday, November 1, the rain began. It was early in the morning and a fog of sleep protected the inhabitants of Troll City. The General was still wrapped in the space age sleeping bag Annie had given him, wedged up under one end of the bridge. Less than a minute after beginning as a light shower, the rain increased to a torrent, fell so hard and fast the General looked out and imagined he was lying on the ledge behind Niagara Falls. He could see nothing beyond the wall of water dropping over the edge. Other trolls groaned and pulled their bedding tighter around them, but the great warrior pulled himself out of his bag, walked down the stone and cement incline, strode out into the storm. He tilted his head back and opened his mouth, tasted the rain. Rolling tongue over lips, he savored the complexities and nuances of the liquid, pronounced his considered opinion. "Tasted rain from all over the world, in wars and good times too, but this stuff is different. Tastes like blood and darkness."

Knowing that great danger demands heroic response, he packed up his kit and began to strategize, identifying the best locations to take a stand in the early phases of this battle.

～

The first stage in the development of the flood was marked by nonstop heavy rain. There were stories about ruined shoes and leather jackets, the usual rain in L.A. banter on Southern California talk shows. Local news anchors gave solemn warning that everyone should drive with great care on the freeways. None of this was new. Even the feature stories on the rescue of three dogs and a horse from concrete-lined river channels were familiar. When the normally jovial weathermen showed visible concern over the huge system "parked" on the coast, sweeping their arms over the green screens that allowed the television audience to witness the size of the monster, some might have taken heed. And yet in a land where chronic amnesia can pass almost unnoticed, the genuinely new can be extremely hard to identify. As houses began to slide into canyons, most Southern Californians went on with their routines with little more than a sense of nuisance. In fact, young devotees of extreme sports used the mud slides as an opportunity to put their snowboards to use out of season. A double fatality that resulted from this new sport simply joined the daily list of traffic accidents and shootings.

For a time there were still heroes: the men who saved the dogs and horse, a fireman in Laguna Beach who grabbed a tree branch as a hillside gave way beneath him and reached down and plucked a baby out of the torrent of mud. Although the mother and father were lost, this tiny survivor was dubbed a "miracle baby," and television stations solicited contributions for the child's education fund.

A day later one of the local stations did a feature on an Azusa man named David Santini. He had adapted a pickup camper shell to fit on the small fishing boat he kept in his driveway. This action was a result of what he called his "Noah vision," a dream that had come to him on the first night of the rain. He had provisioned the ark for a long voyage. During the first day, he and his family kept watch on the storm, but that evening they boarded the ark and decided to stay there for the duration of the flood. The reporter interviewed David and his wife through the camper's open window. Having done the best he could for his family, the man projected a surprising amount of confidence in the face of catastrophe. His only regret was that he had room just for his family. He expressed the hope that someone who had a larger boat would be able to take animals on board as well. After the feature was aired, there was a jocular exchange between the news readers, the weatherman, and the sports announcer. They laughed as they vowed a follow-up to the story of David Santini and his family. In his monologue the next day, Jay Leno had two prime jokes on the modern-day Noah.

During the fourth night, two power stations were knocked out by mud slides within minutes of each other, and the resultant power failures created a cascade effect. When the dominoes had stopped tumbling, there was no power anywhere in California south of San Luis Obispo. By the morning of the fifth day, there wasn't a passable road in the southern half of the state. Those who had not had the foresight to evacuate, and that was very few, were stuck where they were. The lower floors of most hospitals were flooded and most by this time had lost their auxiliary power. Governmental services and infrastructure were in a state of total collapse. By the time the governor called in the National Guard that evening, the only access to Los Angeles and Orange County was by helicopter. Even that was problematical, because so few helipads atop large buildings could accommodate army transport helicopters. Hilltops didn't help much, because most were waterlogged and unstable. Even if a helicopter could be landed, it was difficult to navigate from there to the people who desperately awaited rescue.

The break in the rain on the sixth day, for a little over four hours, seemed like a particularly cruel deception. When it started again, the rain came down even harder than before. Those who had prayed for mercy and divine intervention began to despair. People around the world who watched the catastrophe unfold, with hourly updates throughout the day, wondered if this indeed were a sign of the promised end. Of course, Southern Californians, who had developed self-regard into a high art, could not see themselves at all. Even if their televisions had not washed away, the lack of electrical power made them useless.

The flood's second stage began on the eleventh day of rain when the Prado dam, near Yorba Linda, collapsed and tore away thousands of tract homes that zigzagged up the gently sloping floodplain toward the hills. As the water cascaded toward the sea, it took out most of the flood channels that had been built by the Army Corps of Engineers, destroyed all roads and bridges within a mile of the Santa Ana River. National Guard troops were as surprised by this turn of events as civilians. Surviving soldiers tried to maneuver their rubber rafts to safer high ground, abandoning a good deal of the equipment they had set up on the lower areas. Now it was the Coast Guard's turn to take charge of rescuing those who remained. They commandeered every seaworthy vessel in the yacht harbor of Dana Point, but that armada was not enough to take care of the hundreds of thousands who were stranded. The boats from Newport harbor might have helped, but those that hadn't been taken out to sea were lost in the tsunami produced by the collapse of the Prado dam. The river itself had changed course and now embraced the Pacific fifteen miles to the south of its previous entry point. In the process of that change, it had slashed through the villas of Newport Beach, silting up the back bay and harbor beyond recognition. Desperate people had lashed themselves to makeshift rafts and floats, but there was no navigating the raging currents, and most were washed out to sea, to drown or die from hypothermia.

On day seventeen there were few who imagined the scenario could worsen, but when the Seven Oaks dam collapsed, up in the mountains near the source of the river, they had to rethink. Such an enormous amount of water and mud was released from that catastrophic event, total devastation was complete. Rain fell intermittently over the next eight days, beat on the hillsides, bringing down remaining houses and continuing to fill the reservoir that had once been greater metropolitan Los Angeles.

On the twenty-fifth day there was a spectacular sunrise. The rain had ceased and overflying helicopters surveyed a seascape of gleaming muddy water whirling toward the ocean. It was only when the debris carried by the water was scanned with binoculars that observers could make out the thousands of human and animal bodies spreading to the horizon. Many saltwater fish were attracted to the carrion as it passed over an imaginary line of demarcation into the Pacific, but the scavengers suffocated in the mud-clogged freshwater that floated above the saline and added their floating bodies to the masque of death. The day before Thanksgiving was the first time since the beginning of the month anyone had seen the sun, and the first time it was possible to make a clear assessment of what had taken place.

~

Things that no longer exist in Orange County: televangelists, malls, Disneyland and Knott's Berry Farm, express delivery, smog, cappuccino parlors, backyard koi ponds, inflated gorillas affixed to the roofs of car dealerships, the Duck Pond (which, like the rest of the county, is in fact underwater), sports utility vehicles, Thai restaurants, sushi bars, real estate sign dancers, juice bars, time shares, toll roads and freeway diamond lanes, pumps cranking up oil from beneath the beach, supermarkets with club cards, gated communities, yacht brokers, three-wheeled baby joggers, jacuzzis, landfill developments, John Wayne airport.

~

The thirty-five-foot yawl was showing no sail, chugging along at a modest pace on the power of a diesel engine. It was navigating through heavy debris to the east of the remains of Edison Field, the stadium that once housed the Anaheim Angels. Colossal supports having been undermined by fast-moving water, the north side of the park had crumbled. What was left suggested the wings of a titanic submerged bird, maybe an eagle or a hawk, about to launch its body out of the water. The yawl was manned by the Magnificent Seven, minus the heroic nurse and the General. The five were cruising within a mile of the former temporary location of Annie's Soup Kitchen, but they hadn't come for the purpose of salvage. Annie's trailer had been destroyed and washed away the day the Prado dam collapsed.

A nervous Perry, scanning clumps of debris in the distance, hoped he wouldn't sight a Coast Guard launch. "Aaaahhhh, man, I wish we had the General on board. Our butts are just hanging out here, waiting to be kicked. You know, like a shot fired across the bow, and the next one hits us."

Hugging her sides and sobbing, Library Lady could not be consoled for the losses the land had suffered. She didn't care that she might be mistaken for a looter. No life situation could be worse than floating over a mass grave, of people, animals, everything she had ever known. It occurred to her that the USS *Arizona*, at the bottom of Pearl Harbor, might be considered a pleasant place compared to this. Whiskey Ed wrapped his arm around her shoulders, hugged her, still keeping an eye on his low-end oscilloscope. He'd picked up a warning signal. "I don't know what it is, but I've got something here. Due north. If it's the Coast Guard, we'd better be looking for a place to put in and hide."

Letting go of the wheel, Skulford stepped around Roderigo, who was lounging in the stern, arms behind head. The card maker jumped from one foot to the other, shifting into the manic mode that always inspired anxiety in his colleagues. "Think the General is the only one who can handle stealth? How the hell do you think I got this boat? You people with your Shadow Plague memories, what a bunch of fucking zombies. Nobody's going to see us or bother us. The Coast Guard is the least of our worries."

Roderigo began to laugh in the back of the boat. "Hey, did you see that goat just floated by? Man, I love to eat goat, when somebody knows how to fix it. Like me. But that goat didn't look too good."

Watching the silver man giggle at his own joke, rap his heels on the deck, and do a reclining punk dance, Whiskey Ed wondered how the man could stay warm in a sleeveless T-shirt. However, finding the giggle contagious, he escalated it into a guffaw. This would be an excellent time, Ed thought, to lighten things up. "OK, listen people. I've got a question to ask. You need to help me out on this one." Roderigo stopped laughing and sat up. Perry, Library Lady, and Skulford turned and gave Whiskey Ed their attention. "They make olive oil by pressing olives, right?"

"Aaaaahhhhh, yeah. Bellatissima, my man. That's how the Italians do it, last I heard."

The frizz-haloed wizard swept his hands through the damp air. "OK, then, do they make baby oil by squeezing babies?"

$\sim$

The great flood had one unforeseen benefit. In the refugee camps scattered across the interior of the state and into Arizona, victims of the Shadow Plague spontaneously regained their mental faculties. Even without the famous river cure, thousands of zombies experienced miraculous transformation. As this phenomenon was reported by the media, practitioners of alternative medicine hypothesized that the flood itself was a mass cure in the same way that individuals experienced personal reclamation bathing in the Santa Ana River. Depending on the spiritual beliefs of the theorizer, the phenomenon was called either water therapy or baptism. One media skeptic argued that although the precise vectors of the Cronkite syndrome had never been established, it was clear those disease vectors were now bent, perhaps permanently turned back upon themselves. But at what cost, he added, to the general population? At what cost to the environment?

$\sim$

The General, dressed in camouflage fatigues that had deteriorated beyond recognition, waded through chest-high water. The liquid filth in this area was without currents or undertow, so he was making steady progress toward the hill before him. "All these wet days I been thinking about the changes, how this music's finally going to play. Me and the water. Last one standing. Sho-do-ben-do-be-do. I declare myself Governor of these Islands of California. Government and movie stars and the snakes of all uncleanness slide us into a world of hurt and sorrow. Hmmm. Agh. Hmmm. I accept this distinction because I finally graduated into being something for a change. Yowsa! Unlike the rest of you sorry-assed Californians, I got no fear of water. It's my combat training, and night flying too. When you sleep in high-grade rubber boots, got my skills in under-water martial arts, nothing in the world you ain't ready for. Got to make a count: all the islands in my empire. I think there's more than Hawaii, maybe more than the Philippines. Then we start looking at all these dead people. They keep floating and bloating and stinking, along with balloon cows and pigs and cats and dogs and a lot more little animals. We got to take care of business with all this deadness. 'Chill of the Night' kind of stuff. Knick knack paddy wack kind of stuff. The long march home. Governor's got to see the future, so I got to get the water down low enough to find that dream garden."

The General finally made his way up to Santiago, the southern-most and highest of the twin peaks of Saddleback Mountain. On November 25, after twenty-five days of nonstop rain had come to an end, he surveyed the ruins of what had been the richest subur-ban county in the United States. More precisely, he swept his eyes over the water that covered virtually all of it. Other than the scat-tering of natural high points and the upper stories of tall buildings thrusting up through the water, there wasn't much to see. Of course, there were the boats on patrol around anything that was deemed to still have value. And there was the single National Guard helicopter flying in low from the north.

Flat on his back, the General let the mountainside lift and hold him. The whites of his eyes were yellow, but that certainly didn't come from staring at the sun. "Been thinking about scat boogies, playing the changes. There are three sides to my new state, so nobody can see out the box but me. Heroes always work that kind of gig. Straight ahead and out of sight. Some of them swimmers out there got powers, and you know who I'm talking about, but they bailed on me. Don't need the General no more. So I got to handle this water by myself. Going back to the World, going home, and strictly solo. Noodling, bedoodling all over the map. Old Annie's Soup Kitchen is my Ithaca, and the Santa Ana my Penelope. Got to get my honey river back." The General lifted his right leg, poked a rubber-booted foot at a cloudless sky. He was bebopping in midair. "Rolling, rolling, rolling on the river . . . Boom, shicka-licka-licka. Boom, shicka-licka-licka."

When the National Guard helicopter landed and Annie was helped out of the cargo door onto Modjeska, the northernmost of the twin peaks of Saddleback, she stood in silence on her new Mount Ararat. As the nurse of the sad and joyous countenance looked into the valley and surveyed destruction of biblical proportion, reporters, cameramen, and still photographers deployed around her, looking for the right angle. Each one wanted an image as compelling as the Marines raising the flag on the peak at Iwo Jima. The whirring and clicking around Annie made her wave at the air around one ear, as if the sounds came from mosquitoes rather than machines. In fact, a combination of water, mud, and carrion had bred a plague of flies and mosquitoes, but those pests were concentrated mainly in the lower areas. And yet swirling above the scene the nurse surveyed was a reminder of the scourge: a cloud of turkey vultures, thick as swarming insects.

After a time even the media people took their eyes from the ancient prophet and began to look around them. Although the water that had spread across the land was beginning to recede, the panorama more resembled an inland sea than the county where people once considered a BMW to be a sensible second car. As the press stared in astonishment at the metamorphosis, Annie was getting down to business. She asked one of the guardsmen to help her kneel so she could offer a prayer of penance and acceptance.

Crossing herself in broad gestures, she clasped hands together in prayer, shut her eyes tight. "In the name of the Father, and of the Son, and of the Holy Spirit. Amen. Bless us, O Lord, the ones You've let live through the storm, and thank You for Your bountiful gift of life, for letting us see the sun and moon one more day. We know we have deserved this terrible punishment and we will try harder to bring more pleasure to Your eyes than anger. Help us to be wise in the ways we go about putting Your world back together, and cleaning it up. Give us the strength to do a proper job of taking care of all the marvelous things You have given us. In the name of the Father, and of the Son, and of the Holy Spirit. Amen."

There was a murmur among the reporters, and one stepped toward the kneeling old woman to get in the first question. But she had not yet opened her eyes. After taking a deep breath, she was ready to continue her supplication. "Eternal rest grant to the souls in purgatory, to all the many, many souls who have suffered and passed away in this disaster. May the eternal light shine upon them, may they find proper burial, and may they rest in peace. Amen. I ask God in His mercy to bless each one of us, to help us and guide us, and grant with God's help we'll soon be able to once again take care of ourselves. We know we must never poison Your world. I have talked to Uriel and have promised him I'll do my best to keep it from happening again."

The National Guardsmen maintained bowed heads before the healing power of Annie's prayer, except for the sergeant who stood erect by the helicopter, training binoculars on the other Saddleback peak. He was about to shout out that he'd spotted a uniformed comrade on Santiago but paused when he realized Annie had still not finished her prayer. She crossed herself again.

"Most Sacred Heart of Jesus, we place our trust in You. We thank You, Father, for this day, and for the sunshine that warms us, and the air we breathe, and the earth we hope to see again, and, yes, even the water we now have too much of. In the name of the Father, and of the Son, and of the Holy Spirit. Amen. God bless us all."

The great nurse's optimism soared with her public acknowledgment of humanity's new covenant with God, but the news that there was a living soul to be saved nearby made her equally ecstatic.

After everyone was loaded into the cargo helicopter and it quickly covered the mile between the two peaks, she was astonished to find that the stranded soldier was the General, emaciated with dysentery from drinking foul water for days, and probable hepatitis, but still alive. The great nurse wanted to get down on her knees with him and give thanks to a merciful heaven, but the warrior was insistent on first explaining his theory of the dream garden. Unwilling to wait until the waters receded, he said that if he had a scuba tank he could take her on a tour of its marvels that very day. He added that due to his own prowess in underwater martial arts, he did not himself require any special equipment.

As Annie listened carefully, nodded her head in agreement, the word *garden* flashed in her mind's eye. She had the sudden realization that the first and most difficult obstacle to the repopulation and reconstruction of Orange County was a lack of food. Since all crops had been destroyed and there was nothing usable to be salvaged from supermarkets or warehouses, when the people returned, how would they be fed? And where would they stay? It had finally occurred to her that it wasn't a limited number of street people needing special attention but all of Southern California that was now homeless. As two guardsmen helped her back into the helicopter, followed by the shaky figure of the General, she muttered another prayer for divine guidance.

$\sim$

Nineteenth-century whalers called the California gray whale "devilfish," because it was dangerous and not easily taken. Females were known to attack harpooning skiffs, even ships, if they felt their calves were threatened. In modern times the same whales—brought back from the brink of extinction—often beach themselves to die. Towed out to sea, they will beach themselves again and again. Authorities argue over the cause of this behavior. Some say the mammals have contracted a disorienting disease from polluted waters, others that it is nothing more than depression. But how depressive can a whale be if it loves to surf, as does the California gray, especially in the waters off Todos Santos in the Baja, its winter breeding grounds? The only bottom-feeding whale, it prefers shallow water, where it rolls to the right, often deeply scarring its hide on rocks as it sucks in plankton and other microorganisms. Along the coast the human inhabitants of California are sometimes privileged by the sight of breaching, flukes, and spume during their migrations between the Arctic and the Sea of Cortez. Scrawled over their sides, scars and barnacle clusters narrate the stories of these travelers, the farthest-ranging mammals in the world.

CHAPTER THIRTEEN

COMMUNAL IMMUNITY

If you want to carry the purgatorial load on your back, struggling up the mountain, OK. That kind of self-indulgence keeps therapists and the publishers of self-help books in business. But what happens when you emerge from an actual hell and mud is everywhere? There is joy, because now everything can be made new, from scratch. But there is sorrow, because the stuff of this new world is the death rot of the old and almost everything it contained. Is there a religion we could convert to that would help us accommodate the fullness of this experience? There is no biblical text that tells what to do after the apocalypse has come and gone. We stand here alive and panting, the dazed survivors.

~

Colonel Stevens threw open the tent flap and strode back in, right to the edge of the table. Arms crossed over chest, he unloaded three days of anger. "I don't think you're listening to me. Food and shelter is exactly why I'm here. That's the job of the National Guard, not civilians. Ms. O'Rourke, we've done what we could for you. I'd like to remind you that California is in a state of emergency. Your presence here is a danger to you and potentially to the personnel under my command."

As her haloed hair began to vibrate at a higher frequency, Annie raised her eyes from her bowl of mashed potatoes to the red face, and the glare of her high temper caught the commanding officer off guard. "Well, you know I am so grateful to you for flying me back to California in the helicopter. You are very good to do that, Major. But I can tell you that the Lord knows exactly where to find me when He's ready to take me. Whether it's here or anyplace else, I'll be passing on all the same. In the meantime I am going to stay and help. And when the authorities start to put it all to rights in Orange County, I want to be sure they do a good job. I hope you'll let me stay as your guest. If you won't, then it will be as your prisoner. But stay I will."

Colonel Stevens raised his leg, slammed down a combat boot on the chair next to Annie's. "Don't think this holier than thou stuff is going to work on me. I'm no fool, and I'm not part of your do-gooder fan club. I don't think you're a saint and I sure don't think you're a prophet. This business about predicting the flood—all it means is that you're a lucky guesser."

The nurse sat back in the chair, raised her chin, and inspected the source of condemnation. Eyes wide open and mouth parted slightly, it was as if she were trying to judge the danger of a rabid animal. But he hadn't finished yet.

"It's bad enough being forced to escort all these damned press people around. I know you have friends in high places, but that doesn't give you a right to be here. If I wasn't a rational man, I might start thinking you knew all about this flood because you started it yourself. Some kind of pact with the devil. It seems like all you have to do nowadays is have communist ideas and feed a few people and you're a goddamned saint. You think you're Mother Teresa? Well, I want you to know not everybody is convinced that even she was that great. So what if she got a Nobel Prize? Look at all the communists they gave that damned prize to. People have lost the common sense they were born with. That's all I've got to say. If you stay, just don't expect me to fly you around and be your chauffeur. Here on out, you're on your own."

From the interplatoon basketball game outside the tent came the sound of a slam dunk, then a tremendous cheer. After the Colonel made his exit, Annie fidgeted over her potatoes for some minutes, contemplating the depths of folly and mean-spiritedness to which a human can fall.

Grasping the seat of her chair with one hand and the edge of the table with the other, Annie began the troublesome process of getting to her feet. She hadn't gotten far when she noticed a dark-haired young woman standing next to her, dressed in military fatigues. The nurse eased back down to the chair and turned her head to give full attention to the new arrival. "You know, young lady, if that man sent you to try and take me away, I'm afraid you're just wasting your time. It won't do. It won't do."

The woman laughed and held up her empty hands. "Don't you recognize me, Annie? Gabriela Vargas from KXON-TV. I did the interview with you over at your soup kitchen in Lemon City."

After staring for some moments, her gray and blonde hair vibrating, the great nurse's face broke into a smile. "Oh yes, my dear, I do remember you. I'm so glad you're here." She reached up and grasped Gabriela's hand and asked for assistance. "But you know the Soup Kitchen is gone now, completely gone. Except for the wonderful palm tree that is putting out another leaf. Bless us all, but the Lord has washed everything clean, and I'll have to start over again."

Once she'd hoisted the Saint of Lemon City to her feet, Gabriela stood back and gave her a once over. "You're looking wonderful, considering all you've been through. We've all been through, I should say. Am I wrong, or have you gotten slimmer?"

Annie smiled, looked down as she smoothed her matching green sweater and dress. "Oh, there are so many men here. And you know I love to be with the men. I'll be getting married soon, and I'll ask you to be the bridesmaid. Or the flower girl."

Gabriela Vargas paused a moment, but after catching the gleam in Annie's eye, she knew she had permission to indulge in a hearty laugh. The women were still hugging when the cameraman—his equipment shouldered and ready to shoot—pushed open the flap, walked through the tent's door.

~

It is often said that change comes slowly, if it ever comes at all. If you accept this conventional wisdom, it's so easy to give up on the idea of political reform, or the dream of living in a place so clean you no longer think about the air, land, and water. After all, an individual has only one lifetime, and how much of that can be devoted to difficult, even impossible tasks? And yet great changes result from revolution, not evolution. When people are infected by the virus of hope, the disease of irresistible joy can spread with the speed of plague, as it has done so many times through human history. Each time it appears, the power of hope dissolves stone in the citadels of power, and we are given one more chance to get it right.

~

Since there were few buildings fit for habitation and the returnees to devastated Orange County still numbered less than ten thousand, the complete lack of Christmas cheer wasn't hard to understand. Not that there weren't legions of souls inhabiting the place. Hungry ghosts searched for human husks to inspirit, incubi of pure greed from five hundred years of dissatisfaction gathered to reinforce the curse of this earthly paradise. Before the flood, Orange County inhabitants trusted concrete and light to insulate them from such dark powers. Driving on the freeway, bathing in sunshine beside the dazzling Pacific, it was easy to forget that alkaline adobe clay defined the land. All desert life, including humans, existed on a dangerous edge. Now the pretense was gone; the aqueduct's collapse had returned Southern California to its natural arid state. As the desert queen lay on her back, deeply melancholy, her myriad creatures struggled over her body. In a sudden conversion, as she shifted the spine that defined a coast, light broke into her heart and laughter rose up through her skin.

Under skies choked with carrion birds and clouds of voracious green flies, the closest thing to a holiday festivity this season was the convocation called by the governor of California at the Santa Ana Civic Center. Parts of some of the buildings there had been cleaned, and noisy repairs continued throughout the complex. The lower floors of the Ronald Reagan Courthouse, made serviceable by a blitz of National Guard labor, were now the headquarters for the Orange County Restoration Project. But even before that crucial cleanup was completed, the Guard had restored the jail and filled its cells, largely with looters. The reassembled Sheriff's Department had built a huge temporary animal pound, featuring stacks of cages, that took up most of the Civic Center's public parking lots. Dogs and cats lucky enough to outrun rising water and reach the hills, along with surviving coyotes—the distinction between wild and tame now being academic—had returned to scavenge through the mud. These marauders were a danger to refugees who'd returned to scratch through the ruins of their homes, assess the possibility of rebuilding. For the feral creatures, anything that moved looked like a meal. At first National Guardsmen systemically shot these animals, but popular outrage at video footage of extermination made the expanded pound a number one public relations priority.

Since the redemptive efforts of the suburban county had already shown some progress, while those in Los Angeles had shown almost none, the governor chose the plaza of the Civic Center for what he billed as a crucial announcement, coupled with the unveiling of the blueprint for the state's future.

The Magnificent Seven, minus Annie, were among the churning crowd that had gathered at the Civic Center plaza. In the midst of fortune hunters, scam artists, mercenaries, thugs, and extortionists, the conjurers decided to split up and reconnoiter individually, then return to a prearranged spot and exchange intel, as Perry put it. They needed to get the lay of this new land. Whiskey Ed had always been suspicious of government authority. Even when emergency conditions prevailed, he was pretty sure military or paramilitary organizations did more harm than good. Sniffing out agents of such legalized thuggery was his primary goal today. As he activated the usual combination of computerized intellect and castoff electronic equipment, the wizard attempted to map the multilayered structure of Big Brother's information-gathering network. He suspected they were there in the plaza, but just where he wasn't sure. Men dressed in jackets and ties, looking like they'd watched too many TV shows and bad spy movies, immediately set off his internal alarm system. However, other than the hefty guys with wires trailing from one ear, part of the governor's advance security team, there were few of those types at the gathering.

An urge, a palpable desire for some kind of satisfaction, moved through the assembled citizens. When they found the holiday gift bags—the promise of which had drawn them to the plaza—contained only an apple, an orange, and an energy bar, the crowd became even more restless. Among construction workers and tradesmen, honest homeless and scoundrels, there was shoving and grabbing, a coming together and a pushing away. The young man, who'd pressed something edible into a woman's hand, stretched out on a nearby bench. She lifted her Pendleton, slipped down filthy jeans just enough, and sat on his face. Under the flannel, denim, and army olive that covered the crowd, the different organs of the body politic pursued their urges more discreetly. The kind of guys who once staked out freeway onramps, holding pieces of cardboard scrawled with pleas for help, came together with carpenters, plumbers, cement workers, and electricians. On this new frontier, redefining fashion and cultural edge for the whole country, everything was up for grabs. Breasts, bags full of testicles or loot, necks to be nuzzled, kissed, or bitten, ears to be tenderly licked or popped by a blow to the head. There were slipping hands, tongues, cocks, and knives, each in search of a pocket to pick. Whiskey Ed needed no special equipment to sense the sweaty energy that surged around him. He felt the urge as well. But as he scooted through the crowd, checking the scope he'd wrapped in his jacket, Ed was astonished at how little electromagnetic activity he monitored, especially at low-end frequencies. Other than his gifted colleagues of the Seven, there was nothing much out of the ordinary here.

Library Lady stepped with great care through the crowd, practicing a combination of visual recon and mental tai chi. Her sensitivity to the play of free energy on human surfaces made the crowd a different quilt for her. She picked up a preponderance of reds, oranges, and muddied colors, not surprising if you considered the environmental difficulties people had to cope with. Corpses of every species remained scattered over the landscape, only slowly being retrieved and incinerated in huge pyres by National Guardsmen. Predators that had eluded the same Guardsmen ranged for live prey in the valley of the shadow of death, and the grim music of that place was sung by plagues of frogs, mosquitoes, and flies that seemed to have generated directly from the mud after the floodwaters receded. As she continued to scan the crowd, her attention was attracted by a spike of light purple. She moved closer, then recognized Sister Claire and Sister Gianetta.

The sisters of the cloth took up positions in front of the podium, waiting for something else to happen. They both wore the same outfit: white blouse, blue skirt, and sweater. As they stood side by side with crossed arms, Sister Gianetta looked like a slightly demonic doll-size miniature of Sister Claire. Having returned from the Colorado convent in which they had taken refuge and having discovered that California authorities had no use for their expertise, both were frustrated. Not in the way of the quilted crowd, but enough to put a slight edge on their usual compassion.

"I tell you, these guys must have been out of circulation too long. Do you see the one in the red logging jacket over there, the one with a nice head of hair?"

Standing on tiptoe, Sister Gianetta tried to locate the object of her lanky colleague's interest. "No, I don't see anything red. Are you talking about the sign on that building?"

By turning shoulders, Sister Claire directed the birdlike head's line of sight. "That one over there. See, he's staring at us now. Would you believe it? He asked me out for dinner. And I said, where could a person go around here nowadays? Are we talking about a campfire and a can of beans? That'd suit him fine, he said. Well, main course aside, I said, what on earth would you do with a poor old nun like me? I guess that would be up to you, he said."

As Sister Gianetta looked up at the liberation theologian, a thought crossed her mind. "Do you think many of the people at Annie's Kitchen died in the flood?"

Sister Claire sighed deeply, turned away, then stopped as her eye was drawn by a commotion on the other side of the plaza. Men were shoving one another, scrambling for something that had fallen to the pavement. She saw a bald head bob up and down, then focused on its halo of frizzed white hair. "Is that Whiskey Ed?" She knew it had to be when she saw Perry pulling him by the arm. There was a tall Black man standing close by, who looked like the General, except that his face and head were shaven and the old fatigues were replaced by jeans and a denim jacket.

Sister Gianetta stood on her tiptoes. "Who is it? Is it anybody we know?"

The haircutting nun waved both hands to attract the attention of her old Soup Kitchen clients, but the crowd closed around the scuffle and the men disappeared. As she tried to decide whether to plow through in pursuit or put off the reunion to another time, someone behind her violently grasped her arms. A silver-haired woman with crazed eyes and a ragged shawl thrown over her shoulders moaned and shook the nun, cried out and shook her again. "*¡Sor Clara! ¡Sor Clara! ¡Mi prima, mi cara prima!*"

The lanky nun wrenched the grasping arms from her chest, skipped away from the clinch. Ready to defend herself, she threw up her fists. But as she pieced together the features of the distorted face, the nun recognized Betty Blankenship. "What's happened to you, cuz?" As she tried to fix on the eyes, they darted away from her gaze. "Oh Lord, you're gone, aren't you, my dear? You poor thing you, you're totally gone."

Betty wrapped herself more tightly in her shawl, throwing weight from one foot to another. "*Viendo yo esto no quise dejar de probar la suerte, y así como llegue a ponerme debajo de la cana.*"

"Impressive you learned Spanish so fast. But why are you trying it out on us? I sure don't know much, other than what I learned working clinic down in Ensenada, and I don't think Sister Gianetta knows Spanish either. Well, hallelujah, you're still alive! I had no idea whether you and Ozzie made it out or not. Just how did you end up this way, dear? Tell me in English."

Betty stared at her cousin with a look of total incomprehension. Already frantic when the encounter began, the jerky motion of her body showed a rising anxiety level.

"*Y puesto que a mi y a mi camaradas nos había parecido mejor lo de enviar por la barca a Mallorca.*"

The lanky nun grasped her cousin by the arms, as much in self-defense as from compassion, but the distraught woman gnashed her teeth, rolled her eyes, generally contorted her face, then bolted into the crowd. Sister Claire felt as if she'd been sucker punched. Breathless, she dropped hands to knees, turned head sideways to her tiny companion. "What the devil is going on here?"

Holding her chin in one hand, furrowing her forehead, Sister Claire's sidekick had a suggestion. "Maybe this is a new disease. It's a little bit like the Shadow Plague, but instead of losing your mind, you just become Mexican."

When the governor finally arrived at the podium, he was modestly welcomed by an audience otherwise occupied. His hands were still outstretched above his head when the applause died out. A long harsh note of feedback screeched as he greeted his fellow Californians, assured them he was proud to be numbered among them, and declared them pioneers of a new state. Announcing that he'd now entered the valley of light where Annie, who was seated among the notables on a folding chair, had always dwelt, he proclaimed a new covenant between the people of California, the Great Almighty, and Mother Nature. In the document he'd authored, there was a solemn promise never again to allow sins against Nature to be committed in California, so that never again, he hoped, would the punishment of a devastating flood be visited upon them.

Gesturing toward the gallery of notables, he pointed out an Indian man and woman dressed in powwow fancy dance buckskins and thanked them for their spiritual guidance in drafting the document. Then, after raising hands heavenward, the converted politician read his vision aloud. As he got to the part describing his new, redemptive love for Mother Nature, a melee broke out in front of the podium.

"Get your hands off me, motherfucker!" A man and a leather-clad woman, looking much tougher than he, scuffled, as Sister Claire, standing nearby, sized up the happy couple. The governor cleared his throat until he found his place on the page.

"With our new reverence for Mother Nature, we will no longer be a disease, and we will possess communal immunity against diseases like the Shadow Plague. We swear to preserve this legacy for all generations to come. Let these sacred promises be upheld as long as grass grows and the rivers run."

The leader paused and bowed his head as a light scattering of applause ran through the audience. It was hard to hear because the hum of the audience's conversation was significantly louder. In a back corner of the plaza, behind the podium on the courthouse side, Perry clapped hands over ears, began to gag. "Aaahhhh, this is ecoporn, my man. That's like crossing your fucking fingers when you make a promise. When the government said that shit to Indians in the old days, they'd already broken the treaty the poor suckers just signed."

Shaking his halo of frizzed hair emphatically, Whiskey Ed tried to whisper his colleague into silence. "Tell me something new. The governor's full of it, but do you think Annie would let him get away with conning us like that? If these promises are lies, she'll make mincemeat of him."

Meanwhile Library Lady affectionately massaged the bulge under her black nylon jacket. When the world's attention needed to be redirected toward matters of justice, she was ready to take action. Glancing back at the former Soup Kitchen director for spiritual comfort, she made a discovery. "Hey guys, look! Isn't that DeLorean sitting behind Annie?"

Perry craned his neck. "Aaaahhhh, don't see him, Evelyn. Hey, did I tell you I ran into Bust-Your-Ass Betty? Man, is she talking some primo but strange Spanish. Don't know how she learned it. I think maybe she's turned into a prophet."

Standing next to the *chi* master and linguist cowboy, done up in his new denim clothes and clean head look, the General appeared to be on another page. He stared straight into a clear sky, humming "I've Got to Admit It's Getting Better."

Roderigo removed a pack of cigarettes from his trademark half-buttoned shirt, pulled one out and lit it. Perry made a grab for the pack, but the coyote man turned a shoulder, slipped it back into his pocket, and smiled.

"Aaaahhhh, man, where did you get the smokes? Those babies are hard to come by nowadays. Can you spare one for the dude?"

The silver-haired thug blew smoke into Perry's face, then placed the cigarette between his teeth, raised his chin in a dare, and cackled.

Skulford Elephant, who had attentively watched the governor's presentation, took a seat on the pavement and folded his legs into a lotus position. Wondering what he was up to, the people around him took several steps back. That was when the croaking began to be heard above the conversational rasp of the crowd. Heads in the audience bobbed as people skipped, danced, and yelped trying to avoid the moist hopping creatures. Skulford, still in the lotus, had not moved.

There was a gleam of delight in Library Lady's eyes as the frogs broke through the ever-widening circle of legs. She scrutinized the talented card maker, trying to understand his connection to the phenomenon. "What's Skulford doing?"

Perry knew. "Aaahhhh, he's calling frogs."

The resident electronics wizard was searching for a scientific explanation. "But how can he be calling? I can't hear a thing."

"Aaahhh, my man's operating above the range of human hearing. It's a lost art."

Thousands of frogs, croaking in low-frequency pulses like a gathering of chanting monks, silenced the governor at the podium. Behind the ring of frogs, the retreating crowd watched the creatures serenade the politician in a language more fitting his new ecological sensitivity. When silence finally fell, the figure behind the great seal of the Governor of California stood isolated and alone. Still seated in his lotus, at the edge of the ring of green sentries, Skulford spoke up for the watershed, delivering his most telling critique: a thunderous belch.

$\sim$

It was another talking heads television program: a panel of smug liberals and smugger conservatives sitting around a table ready to hash out their expert opinions on the latest hot item, the speech delivered by the governor in Santa Ana and the document now being called the California Covenant. But death and funerals always stimulate sexual desire, and the abundance of both in California had created an active subtext under the round table.

"My question is this: Is the California Covenant a sign of the future, a whole new movement, or just a momentary aberration?"

As the moderator—or more aptly, provocateur—ran through the guest list, it appeared this was the conservatives' day to be angry.

A white-haired man, droopy eyes masked in darkness, led off. "First of all, let me just say I think it's outrageous for the governor to imply that business and industry have caused the Great California Flood and now they somehow need to be punished for it." Appearing to search the ceiling for inspiration, he added a concluding thought. "The man must be suffering from posttraumatic stress syndrome."

Raising her pencil, the perky woman in red protested. "Not so fast. Every last thing Annie O'Rourke has commented on or predicted so far, like the cause and cure of the Cronkite syndrome, has been right on the money. I personally would not exclude the possibility that she is correct, that the hand of the Almighty can be felt in all this. Bob, I'm surprised you would, considering how much you usually press religion and morality." Beneath the table she pushed away the hand squeezing her knee.

Raising his brows did little to dispel the darkness of the eyes entombed beneath. "Let's keep religion out of this." His hand slipped up her thigh. "Bashing business is politics, plain and simple. Where did the governor's silly stuff come from, a nervous breakdown? I mean, considering the delays in the state's emergency reaction and the great loss of life on his watch, I fully understand why he feels guilty. Just how does he think the new California will be employing people without a healthy business sector? Cleanup jobs will be great for a while, and give the homeless something to do, but what about real jobs? Where will they come from? This guy has spent too much time out there on the coast with tree-huggers, eating the wrong kind of mushrooms."

The young man dressed like a lawyer laughed at the joke but offered a quick retort. "Excuse me, but as far as I can see, everybody in Southern California right now can be considered homeless. And that's going to be true until they rebuild."

Noting that comments were getting less lively, the moderator feared the fickleness of channel surfers and shifted direction. "And what do you all think about John DeLorean resurfacing in the Golden State, running an 800 number out of Denver? Take a look at this photo. He was sitting right there in the audience when the governor gave his speech." The grainy enlargement showed the dapper ex-trucker in a windbreaker, his silver hair swept back over his temples like a yachtsman.

Dark Eyes flipped his above-table hand in a gesture of dismissal. "Now there's a name to conjure with when you're looking for moral guidance. I suppose the governor has been consulting with him too. Great stuff. Buying these poor people out for 10 percent of assessed value."

The perky woman jerked in her chair, seemed confused. "Can't they just rebuild, like after the fires and earthquakes?"

Pursing his lips in disapproval, the lawyerly man took this one. "Regular home insurance doesn't cover flood damage. You need flood insurance for that, and almost none of them have it. What I want to know is, how does DeLorean's offer square with the back-to-nature California Covenant? Sounds like a reverse Robin Hood scam: stealing from the devastated and giving to the rich. Himself, in this case."

The dark-eyed man's smile of pleasure, tugging up the corners of his mouth, belied his expression of disapproval. "He makes Donald Trump's New York bankruptcy land grab look like peanuts. Flying out from New York to California in the middle of this mess, and taking brilliant advantage of human tragedy. On a staggering scale."

Now the moderator himself had vital information to add. "Let me jump in here. I actually talked to him briefly on the phone. He swears he's been in California for years, as a regular at Annie O'Rourke's soup kitchen."

"And I'm his fairy godmother."

Turning to the young man in the pinstriped suit, an ostensible expert on business law, the moderator sought insightful analysis. "Do you think this scheme has any chance of succeeding?"

"A very good chance. What choice do people have? The biggest question is, where is DeLorean getting the money to leverage it?"

~

As the General walked north from the Civic Center—on muddy tracks that were once streets, past ruined buildings and gutted houses—his destination was never in doubt. The bridge that once sheltered Troll City had been destroyed in the flood, but even in its ruined state, for him it was still home. However, this nexus of lives and energy, la Ciudad de los Duendes, was home to him alone. Annie had procured a government issue sleeping bag for the warrior, and he'd scavenged enough plastic sheeting and wooden debris to construct an exclusive penthouse apartment in the twisted metal and concrete at the top of a buttress. The survivors among the former citizens of Troll City had found shelter elsewhere, in the more attractive wreckage of houses, shops, and industrial parks.

The warrior lay in the sun, hands behind his head, on the shattered thrust of an angled concrete support. Surveying his territory, he thought about the future. Although weak from hepatitis, he was ready to embrace the obligations of high office, restore the welfare and happiness of the world. In his capacity as the new Governor of the Islands of California, he snorted and droned, snorted and droned, then choked and broke off into a snicker.

"Who was that sorry-assed never-been-in-the-army clown back at the Civic Center? Governor of what? Flies and frogs, the little drugs they put in your water, sandbags and backward half-tracks. How you gonna impress actresses with shit like that? They ask for an autograph and he's got to go looking for his hand."

After sliding butt-first down the penthouse ramp to the ground, this undaunted seeker pulled a number of concrete chunks out of the hardened adobe. He balanced them atop a tepee configuration

of broken drift. Dancing around to the rear of his impromptu
podium, he was ready to meet the press.

"Been through war, flames, plague, and dying. After it was over,
actresses took me home for cocktails. But I'm still on patrol. You all
need a governor with martial arts. Who else is going to keep these
Islands of California from cracking into each other? I kissed Penelope and she knew who I was. Wanted me to be in her next movie.
Dog Man Unchained. And I'm going to get back to her on that. Allah
defends the righteous. He lays down water and mud, then covers it
up for a little rest. Going to be carnivals every weekend. This is no
time to be talking to experts."

Gesticulating fists and flattened palms brushed a concrete edge,
collapsing his podium. He leaped back, assumed his familiar martial arts stance. "Nobody move! There's darkness on the dream garden, all across the face of the earth. You think this is a technical difficulty, but the network I'm on hits every universe, all kinds of folks
you'll never see. But take off your shoes, let your feet grow a little.
Wash them every day. That's when you start to feel the ground. It's
growing too, and all the Islands of California. When it's done, you're
never gonna have to ask a stupid question again."

~

Don Quixote's mind wanders. He is planning the journey ahead,
knowing that to proceed he must travel in all directions at once and
through all dimensions of time. He thinks of his beloved Dulcinea
del Toboso and of the beautiful young convert from Algiers. Con-
cocting a master plan, he has memorized its main ingredients: faith
in the beauty of the country never seen, sudden conversions that
propel us toward its shores, an endless supply of ransom money to
buy our passage there, and the passionate madness that makes us
insist on telling and revising all our stories until we arrive at a recog-
nizable home.

CHAPTER FOURTEEN

AS LONG AS
RIVERS RUN

Phil Tabangbang and Dracula cleared brush on the muddy flats where a development in its infancy had completely washed away. Phil whistled "Honky Tonk Woman" and Dracula, whose lack of uppers precluded that kind of musicality, hummed along. After having done this kind of stooping and dragging for a couple of days, the ladies' man of Annie's Soup Kitchen weaved his long black hair into a single braid, so it would stay out of his face as he worked. Shirtless torso glistening in the morning sun, Phil could have been mistaken for one of the muscular Chinese workers who built the intercontinental railroad from California to Utah. Both partners took a break from their work and stretched. Gazing north, their eyes rested on the ruins of the old Tustin Marketplace, where three white towers rose like minarets out of a desert oasis. After several close calls with the National Guard convinced them it was better to homestead in the time-honored fashion than be shot as looters, the two Kitchen alumni had agreed to become partners. Proceeds from sales of salvage, to the numerous fences who had quickly materialized, had allowed them to put together a decent grubstake. Dracula envisioned a chicken farm the size of a rancho, pointing out that startup was cheap, the birds took care of themselves, and profits were significant. Phil leaned more toward an orange grove. He had powerful nostalgia for the time before developers uprooted and burned the citrus trees that had blanketed the area. Using a hatchet he'd obtained from a young guardsman in exchange for a crystal vase, Phil trimmed tree branches into stakes and Dracula drove them into caked earth with a stone. After pounding stakes for three days, defining the boundaries of their estate, Dracula was reconciled to Phil's more modest goal.

They'd made a good start on a house, erecting walls on all sides about two feet high. A homemade flagpole flew a banner fabricated from the back of a plaid flannel shirt. Sleeping inside the meager protection of that foundation, they dreamed each night that the walls had risen magically in the moonlight. Cricket song fastened posts and beams. Their imagined fortress against a cruel and unjust world covered itself first with adobe, then whitewash. Beside the hacienda rose a watchtower, suspended in midair by the labor of a hundred doves, each grasping a terra-cotta roof tile and beating its wings.

As they pursued their labor and dreams, days were days, and it was hard to differentiate one from another. But Phil and Dracula knew what was up when they saw the band of men approaching along the dry wash that tore its way down through the flats. Dracula had expressed concern about building too close to the low area, but Phil countered that the recent disaster had been declared a millennial event, and what was going to happen to the homestead a thousand years down the line didn't worry him at all.

Earlier that morning the two had hiked over to the ruins of the Marketplace to see what they could buy or barter. They were also curious about the explosion they'd heard just before dawn. Squatters who lived in the ruins explained that the authorities—which particular branch they weren't sure—had dynamited one of the partially collapsed sections of the mall, hoping to drive them off. Former street people, who now claimed legitimate residence, were gleeful about the helplessness of the very forces of order that had once leaned so hard on them. Dracula heightened their amusement with a demonstration of his frightening grin. After beginning negotiations with one of the squatters for an iron skillet, the homesteaders noticed the man had a boom box as well. More important, he had the batteries to run it. But news was about all there was to hear, since most of the commercial stations had not as yet returned to the airwaves. The announcement that Annie O'Rourke and six other people were wanted by the FBI, for having carried out two acts of domestic terrorism, seemed like an odd kind of joke to Phil and Dracula. But when they heard the names of the others listed in the indictment—Edward Blatsky, Evelyn Stubbs, Roderigo Vasquez, Perry Winston, Robert McCarthy, and a man they said could only be identified by his assumed name, Skulford Elephant—the two of them knew it was serious.

They were clearing brush back on the northwest section of their claim as the band of men approached. Noticing that all of them carried rifles or shotguns slung over their shoulders, Dracula let his anxiety be known.

"Hey man, look at the hardware they're toting. What do we got to match it? A couple of sticks and the hatchet."

Phil smiled, projected his usual cool. "Don't worry about it. They're probably just going to pass right on through. If they try to roust us, we'll just leave and come back later. No big deal."

There were eleven men in the group, and as they approached their appearance became no less threatening. Each wore a nasty look on his face, along with a belt of shotgun shells or rifle cartridges slung diagonally across the chest. Phil stepped forward to the gray-bearded man who seemed to be the leader, tipped him a casual salute. Smiling, hands on hips, the Kitchen alumnus was his usual supremely confident self. "Hey, what are you guys doing way out here in the boonies? Going hunting for quail?"

They all laughed, looking toward their leader for an answer. He gazed northward, toward the ruins of the Marketplace, then turned his head, fixing Phil with his stare. "Could be. Or could be we're clearing vermin off this land."

Dracula stood behind Phil, unable to control the physical signs of his fear. But he got up enough courage to step slightly to one side and address the band's leader. "We been here a while and haven't seen no vermin. Maybe a couple of wild dogs and coyotes, but that's not vermin."

One of the recently arrived men unshouldered his shotgun, holding it only slightly below dead level. "Well, well, a chinaman and a toothless wonder. Hey Jack, do you think they still have bounties for this kind of trash?"

Phil, while still smiling, was beginning to glance around for routes of escape. "OK, enough with the comedy. Just what do you guys have in mind?"

The gray-bearded leader had a ready answer. "I don't know what the hell you think you're doing, but somebody owns this land and they're not happy about you being here."

"Who? Are you talking about the developer jerks that got washed away in the flood?" Phil laughed, then returned to an aggressive smile. "Why don't you tell them to come on over and have a chat with us themselves?"

Even as he shook, and his words came in pulses, Dracula was also ready to protest. "Yeah. Possession is nine-tenths of the law. This homestead is ours now."

The leader leaned forward and laid a globule of brown spit at Phil's feet. "Well, I got news for you. Somebody bought it from that company. Anyway, it's none of your damn business. They asked us to keep vermin off the land. And that means you, so you're going to have to vacate these premises pronto."

Phil kicked loose dirt over the insult. "By what authority are you going around carrying guns, threatening people? Are you sheriff's deputies or something?"

The leader took a step forward and sneered. "That's right. We're deputies."

Still looking around, evaluating various scenarios, Phil only pretended to pay attention to the conversation. "Why don't you show me the badge then?"

"He wants to see the badges, guys." As the leader raised his right arm, all of his men swung their rifles and shotguns to the ready. "How's that for badges?"

Unwilling to call their bluff and fearing he was about to wet his pants, Dracula ran for the hacienda. Phil was looking over his shoulder, watching the retreat of his partner, when he was stunned by an enormous explosion at his ear. Simultaneously, Dracula jerked forward and landed on his face. In another moment, Phil's view of the electric blue California sky blew out like a candle at midnight.

～

Sally was greeted by John DeLorean outside the Ronald Reagan Courthouse at the Santa Ana Civic Center. Still undergoing repair and restoration, dust from sandblasters blew in their faces as he held the front door for her. Guiding the red-hot real estate genius and her people to a small meeting room on the second floor, DeLorean chatted about his new friendship with the governor. Entering the room, the former Martha Stewart aficionado saw the Mysterious Stranger sitting on the other side of the table. He had a stuffed rattlesnake at one elbow and a stack of old legal codexes at the other.

As the principals reestablished connections, Sally's two bodyguards jumped on chairs in various parts of the room to check lights and fixtures for security cameras and listening devices. DeLorean locked his fingers behind his head, leaned back in his seat, and laughed.

DeLorean's offer to the resurrected Shadow Plague victim to join him on his Rancho DeLorean project was met with derision.

"Rancho DeLorean? And you're talking about teaming with me? I don't think so. My nonprofit foundation is all about green space, letting the watershed return to its original beauty."

"We're really close on this. I was thinking cattle. You know, going back to the days before statehood. Not even sure I'd put in any later additions like oranges. Do you see what I mean? It'd be like going back to the golden age."

"I don't think we're that close."

The Mysterious Stranger leaned forward. "How about 'Rancho California,' would that be better?"

Sally stared at the skinny man for a moment, then giggled. "Sure. You can check out any time you want, but you can never leave."

The silver-haired smooth talker wanted to get back to business. "Look, I admire your angle: tax write-offs from charitable donations to your foundation. I'm sure you know that with the evaluations you're getting on property and salvage, your offer is netting out above my 10 percent of last assessment."

"So create a foundation yourself." Sally stood up and her bodyguards quickly book-ended her. "Look, we don't have much to talk about here, John. I do have one proposition for you, though. Even if I can't stand what you're doing, we can still help each other by trading parcels to consolidate our respective blocks. I'll send my people to work it out with yours."

Out the door before DeLorean and the Mysterious Stranger could get out of their chairs, Sally had closed the meeting. The entrepreneur turned to his partner, who was looking similarly glum.

"I just can't tell you how much it hurts. Even after all of these years, people just expect the worst of me. After all, who wouldn't want a Southern California without developments and malls, just like the old days?"

~

You can buy a will-writing kit for $29.95. If you get past queasiness over making a last testament, the belief held by many that it is something like a premonition of imminent death, you're sure to rest easier when it's done. Having taken care of your heirs, you know that if they squander or misuse what you've left them, it's their fault, not yours. But what of your acts and thoughts, your spiritual legacy? A Korean proverb says, "When a tiger dies, it leaves its skin." Great men and women are sure to produce a legacy of honorable fame. A tiger skin: orange slashed with elegant black calligraphy, and the whole composition edged with purest white. A natural work of art like that, in all its fearful asymmetry, could last a lifetime, maybe two, but must someday succumb to mildew and moths. At that point the only memory of the fearsome tiger is in the mind of God.

~

In Los Angeles City Hall, electricians, advance people, and general gofers were setting up for a press conference. Behind the podium, the high-water mark halfway up the wall was still clearly visible. This was a different crowd from the mellow Santa Ana group that listened to the first public reading of the California Covenant. They were mostly media people, restless and hungry. The hunched-over man who only days before had proclaimed himself the environmental governor, leaned toward the microphone and began to speak, this time in a humbler tone.

"I have a brief statement I'd like to read. After that, I'll take your questions.

"It is important for me to clarify some of the ideas I put forward in what is now known as the California Covenant. What I outlined in that document was meant to set the spiritual tone for rebuilding California, and it should not be taken too literally. Obviously some people who heard what I said have made gross misinterpretations, because they have charged me with being antibusiness. Nothing could be farther from the truth. Now, more than ever before, business and industry in this great state are the foundation of our lives and happiness. As we make progress in our efforts to restore the manufacturing and service sectors, we will be working very closely with our colleagues in the business world.

"It's hard to believe, but there are people who have interpreted my remarks in Santa Ana as a green light to squatters and so-called homesteaders. Hear me loud and clear. In spite of our continuing emergency, the protection of property in this state is our highest priority. Trespassing will be prosecuted to the full extent of the law, just as it was before the Great Flood."

The governor looked up from his text to assess its reception. Seeing a larger than usual jury, sitting sternly in judgment, he dropped his eyes, cleared his throat, and began the hardest sell.

"Finally, and I come to this part with great sorrow: the arrest of Annie O'Rourke and her associates. As much as we admire the woman for her service to others, she has been charged with very serious crimes. The rule of law must be maintained, no matter how much we personally care for those who have violated it. If we make exceptions, then our society will surely degenerate into anarchy and chaos.

"And now I'll take your questions."

The reporters smirked as they watched the governor eat crow over his momentary, aberrant burst of idealism a few days before. But what was really on the media's collective mind was the arrest of Annie O'Rourke. A woman who had achieved sainthood in the eyes of most of the world's citizenry was now behind bars, and there was a lot of anger in the streets.

A reporter, hair swept over his bald spot and glued in place, threw up an arm. "Governor, it has been suggested that the severity with which Annie O'Rourke has been treated is political payback for her role in helping you write the California Covenant. Is there any truth to that?"

Holding fast to both sides of the podium, the governor cleared his throat. "How can I answer such an outrageous allegation? Suffice it to say that she is being treated just as any other citizen charged

with such crimes would be treated. After all, we're not talking about a parking ticket here. Her arrest is the result of having perpetrated terrorist attacks."

Sister Claire, who had slipped past security through the back door, jumped out of her seat in the right rear corner of the room. "You hypocrite! The only terror I can see is you being afraid of the powerful people you offended. You spoke some pretty words and got slapped down. Now you're trying to make them all happy by putting her in jail. Shame on you, and shame on them!"

Two security guards seized the lanky nun by the arms, but she was not going to be led away easily. After struggling for a few moments, she slumped into the limp posture of passive resistance. The reporters, who had turned around in their chairs to watch the dramatic protest unfold, gasped as she fell out of sight. Several shouted to the guards to leave her alone. Others screamed "First Amendment!" The governor, who had his lips frozen into the same meaningless smile throughout the melee, timidly mumbled the word *unauthorized* into the microphone.

After the guards stood back from their quarry, the determined nun was back on her feet, shouting quotations from Gustavo Gutierrez, the country priest who fathered liberation theology. The governor drew his finger across his throat, signaling that cameras and sound people should cut off the broadcast. Sister Claire, interpreting this gesture as a threat against her life, began to shout Hail Marys at the top of her voice, pausing briefly to call on the Lord to help those blinded by greed to see the wickedness of their ways. In the midst of her prayer, the press corps surrounded her, escorted her past the grasping guards and into the street, where their questioning continued.

～

"Shackled hand and foot? This is a bit much." Rubbing his left wrist, chaffed after the removal of an overly tight cuff, Whiskey Ed's face flushed red with mortification.

A manic Roderigo snorted and wiped his nose with the back of his hand. "No, man. They were smart to do that. Had to. Otherwise I run away, and you know something, they never gonna catch me. Pssssuumm!" The shape shifter cut through the air with a projectile shaped like his hand, suggesting the speedy movement of a cartoon character.

"Aaahhhh, Miz Annie, Lord knows I never argue with you about anything. Because you're the boss. Everybody agrees on that." Perry turned on his heel, indicating not only his colleagues of the Magnificent Seven, but also other prisoners throughout the holding cell. "But tell me again why we gave ourselves up to the cops. I mean, I thought we were doing just fine on that underground railroad thing. The heat was never going to nail us as long as we kept moving. People were nice, and you know I liked having my picture on TV. Yeah, beaming right into *America's Most Wanted*."

In the contiguous holding cell for women, the visionary nurse reached out a hand to Library Lady, who helped her to her feet. Walking up to the bars of the cell and gripping them firmly, she was vibrating at a slightly higher frequency than usual. As if explaining something to a child for the third or fourth time, Annie lectured the linguist cowboy.

"Young man, we must not allow them to say to all the world we're criminals. Put trust in the Lord. He is a God of mercy, and He will defend and deliver us. What we must do now is tell the truth and shame the devil."

A couple of the looters who'd gathered next to Perry and Ed in the men's cell guffawed. The nurse snapped her head around and glared at them. "God loves every one of you, no matter what you've done. You should be happy in knowing it, that is so, though I can't believe mockery to be good laughter."

The tall woman with bloated T-shirt and jeans joined Annie and Library Lady against the bars on the women's side, wanted to accentuate the nurse's statement. "Yeah, shut your fucking mouths over

there. Have a little respect. This is Annie O'Rourke. She's like a fuck-ing saint or something. Keep talking bad to her and you suckers are going to hell for sure."

More guffaws from the men's side. A lean and wasted man, with tattoos of barbed wire encircling both biceps, jumped like a monkey halfway up the bars and stuck there. "Sure, sweetheart. I'll shut my mouth if you open yours. I can feel a big boner coming up, and it's going to be long enough to reach all the way over and cream you good."

Annie's defender held up her little finger. "Does this remind you of something? Or am I giving you too much credit?"

Catcalls from the men's side. It was beginning to get rowdy. The men's benches cleared as everyone pressed against the bars, looking for entertainment, something to break the monotony. On the other side, the benches emptied as well, and a chorus of tough women tore into the men with imaginative insults to their masculinity. During this square off, Library Lady led Annie back to a seat and helped her ease down onto it. The great nurse's normally shining face was colored by sadness and disappointment and showed a sub-tle distancing from the embroiled humans around her. For the trained eye, these were warning signals. But as she sat on the bench, motionless except for her palsy, her eyes glazed over. This symptom was impossible to ignore. She was having another hypoglycemia attack. Although there wasn't enough sugar in her reserve to rise to her usual range of visionary babble, she began to mumble desolately. "William is in Seattle and he refuses to come home. He says he never will. I don't know how the Kitchen will do without him."

After using pinkies to stretch both corners of his mouth, Perry delivered a long, ear-shattering whistle. "Hold it! That's enough already! Have some respect, will you? Do you know what's happen-ing next week? It's Annie's ninety-sixth birthday. No more trash talk-ing. I mean, have some respect. Aaaahhhh, sorry Annie for lipping at you. It's all my fault this stuff happened. I started it."

Whiskey Ed seemed fascinated by his own feet shuffling on the water-stained concrete floor. "Yeah, Annie. If you can take being in jail, then I guess we can too. Sorry about what I said."

On the other side, the great nurse accepted the apologies with the kind of detachment that would lead you to believe she'd never seen the Magnificent Seven before. But then the General, who'd been sitting quietly on the floor in a corner of the cell, left strictly alone by any potential bullies, began to chant. When she heard his droning, Annie perked up, rising out of hypoglycemic stupor. Her eyes drifted to the left, where she saw Roderigo stretched out on a bench. He was asleep, dreaming of fur, claws, and fangs, racing through sage scrub at top speed. A huge, self-satisfied grin spread across his snout from ear to pointed ear. After staring for a long moment at the shape shifter, gradual recognition illuminated Annie's eyes, and her own mischievous trickster smile returned.

Library Lady was studying Annie and the jagged aura that floated around her. In spite of the recovery, she'd never before seen the great nurse fall so precipitously toward blood sugar blackout. The *chi* master sensed that the leader of the Magnificent Seven might be in more trouble than usual. "Hey you guys, I think Annie needs something to eat or drink. We haven't had anything for quite a while. Somebody call a guard. Or maybe a doctor."

As if she'd conjured him, a guard came down the corridor, leading a man in a navy blue blazer, maroon tie, and loafers with little leather tassels. The uniform was unmistakable; he was a lawyer. "OK, listen up." The guard showed no signs of enjoying this kind of errand. "Mr. Marshall wants to talk to Annie O'Rourke."

Library Lady stepped toward Annie, put a protective hand on her shoulder. "Who wants to talk to her?"

Mr. Marshall stepped forward, unleashed a smile of deliverance. "I'm representing John DeLorean. If I can get some information from the seven of you, we'll post your bail and have you out of here in no time."

Annie struggled to her feet, in spite of her colleague's attempt to keep her seated. "You can tell that man we want nothing of his money. It's terribly dirty, a sin and a shame. He's been taking property from poor people who lost everything in the flood. It's a sin! The Lord knows that, if no one else does."

Waving his arms in a vain attempt to stop Annie's tirade, Whiskey Ed finally had an opportunity to object when she slowed to take a breath. "Come on now, Annie, if this guy wants to get us out, the rest of us are all for it. Maybe that 800 number thing isn't so bad. You know Sally's got one too."

The great nurse paused, held her chin. "She doesn't have the money, dear. I won't believe it until I hear it from her own lips. But Mr. DeLorean has done a very bad thing. We fed and clothed him all these years, and he turns and takes money from the helpless and unfortunate." She wagged her finger at the lawyer. "Go back and tell him what I said. I'll have none of his money. It would make us worse than church robbers."

Perry and Whiskey Ed let their heads fall against the bars of the holding cell but beyond that made no attempt to express their exasperation, other than retreating to a bench and moping. The lawyer left, the General lowered his chanting to a low hum, and the two cells settled into a quieter pattern. Some inmates dozed, others conversed quietly in twos and threes. Skulford squatted next to Roderigo and for the first time offered Coyote Man his perspective on their dilemma.

"Ever see my cards on Mulholland and Chandler? The history of Los Angeles and the valleys around it has always been about stealing water. They turned a desert into paradise and made millions of bucks. Now, after getting way too much water, the same kind of guys are stealing all the land again." The enigmatic card maker raised his misfingered hand, then withdrew the glowing digits and stuffed them in his pocket.

After the yelling and raucous laughter of their brief verbal exercise period, the two holding cells settled into sleep. Detainees, who had

been wrangling only an hour before, leaned against one another to avoid stretching out on the cold cement floor. Sleep moved the Magnificent Seven and more common criminals into a free zone, a long curvaceous Pacific beach without barriers. In that place anything could be negotiated. There was so much territory everyone could homestead, and the sun, that golden fruit of dreams on an unfettered horizon, was within the daily reach of even the poorest citizen.

The next morning, a chastised Mr. Marshall was back in the Santa Ana jail again, sent by his irritated boss to finish the job he'd been assigned. DeLorean had convinced him that his future employment prospects were contingent upon the success of the second try. A different guard led him down the corridor, this one more friendly, chatting about the recent stock market turnaround. As they arrived at the holding cells, both were confounded. The guard released a warbling shriek. He ran to the wall and punched the alarm button. While the rapid beat of the horn kept time, the distraught jailer danced back and forth in front of the bars, as if some unseen dimension of the material world might reappear and put things to right. The lawyer was still and silent, as he rocked back on the heels of his tasseled shoes, holding himself tight with both arms.

In the women's cell were two dogs, and in the men's four dogs and a coyote. Among the sleeping human prisoners, the animals seemed calm, as they sneezed, yawned, shook their ears, or scratched. But Annie O'Rourke and her confederates were gone. Nothing of the Magnificent Seven remained but their clothes, in seven piles scattered around the two cells.

CHAPTER FIFTEEN

THE MAGNIFICENT SEVEN LEAVE HISTORY TO ITSELF

As word spread about the Magnificent Seven's escape from the Santa Ana jail, the political hammer came down. Outrage in high places at the mockery of it was even greater than anger over the loss of the prisoners. For the terrorists to slip away, then leave dogs in their place, was unforgivably arrogant. Worse still, the media and general public seemed to relish the humiliation of the authorities. During subsequent interrogations of those under suspicion for assisting the breakout, the words *traitor, conspirator,* and *collaborator* were frequently used. People on all rungs of the political ladder, including the top one, received threats of career-ending disaster if the matter weren't satisfactorily resolved. The jail guards on duty the night of the escape proclaimed their innocence, and even the holding cell detainees insisted they heard nothing, saw nothing, and simply woke up to the dogs. An inspection of security camera tapes offered no evidence to contradict those stories. After being held briefly as evidence, the dogs themselves, and the lone

silver-haired coyote, were transferred to one of the cage complexes in a Civic Center parking lot.

~

Grady Roberts, tucked away in a Lemon City tent encampment, had a tantalizing dream during that infamous night of the dogs. He saw the Mysterious Stranger walking down an alley in Laguna Beach, barely lit by the unreal Pacific twilight. He was hesitant to follow the man with a beard covering most of his chest, but his forerunner kept turning and beckoning him on. Still yards ahead of the cook, the man went to one knee, retrieved a cluster of feathers from the pavement. As Grady approached, the Stranger swung around and thrust out his arm. Perched on the end of it was the foundling, a taut-muscled red-tailed hawk.

Although normally he was not very imaginative, the frustrated writer awoke the next morning and remembered his dream in all its details and knew furthermore that it carried an important message. After scrambled eggs and sausage from the mess line, he wandered around the Lemon City encampment trying to interpret the image of the fierce hawk. Metaphor had always failed him, but he knew he was close on this one. There was fog that morning, and as he looked up to estimate the time it would take to burn off, he saw a swirl of red-tails. One of them separated from its feathered community and flew south, and he too began to move in that direction. A little over an hour later, having arrived at the Santa Ana Civic Center, Grady sat down on a bench and waited. Not long afterward, the Mysterious Stranger strode vigorously around the corner of the Ronald Reagan Courthouse. Wearing his uniform—greasy stocking cap, undersized windbreaker, shorts, dusty bare feet—and holding a small paper bag in one hand and a green garbage bag in the other, he tipped a salute to the cook. Grady rose to meet the dream messenger, ready to ask for instructions, but the man had anticipated his inquiry.

"This one's clothes. The other has money, to get the dogs out of the pound and pay the captain. You need to find a boat moored at Dana Point harbor called the *Todos Santos*. You've got to get all of them out there by tomorrow at noon." The Stranger turned, without waiting for a reply, twirled his umbrella, and proceeded in an awkward strut until he was out of sight.

Holding the two bags as if they were potentially dangerous, the cook returned to the bench and sat down. In his mind's eye he tried to balance a flurry of winged forms, spinning blurs of light. It was as if he himself had taken to the sky, like a red-tail in one of those mad swirling aerial dances. Grady was alone now. His wife, Marcia, had kept moving eastward after being removed to a refugee camp in Arizona. She had joined her sister in Vermont. When Grady contacted her there, Marcia explained that it was time for both of them to restart their lives—separately. Since that traumatic moment, fragmented images from his life had continued to whirl in Grady's mind. After receiving his mission from the Mysterious Stranger, those fragments began to assemble themselves into a brilliant mosaic. He was too close to the work of art to make out the pattern, the larger picture. Knowing that he'd have to wait for such a vision, he was still confident that a powerful revelation was at hand. In this case, waiting didn't bother him. The moment was all that mattered. His adrenaline response to the Stranger's request was a joy in itself. As a man who shunned conflict, challenge, and stimulation, he knew his cheerful acceptance of the errand was entirely out of character. And that delighted him.

Checking a number of parking lots, the cook finally found the location of the dogs and the coyote that had been retrieved from jail. By the time he'd paid for their release into his custody and begun to move them down the street like a small flock of sheep, it was already past 10:00 A.M.

As the freed dogs pranced, nipped one another, and barked at everything that moved, Grady pushed toward the wreckage of the

5 freeway. With no experience as a shepherd, he found it difficult to keep up with the coyote and yellow Labrador that led the pack. At the same time, he had to prod the struggling basset hound along. It always lagged behind the pack, marking each felled telephone pole with a few drops of urine. When he arrived at the freeway, Grady turned south, continued his trek with the dogs over fractured concrete. Working through the interchange of the 5 and 55, he marveled at the beauty of the high-speed exchanges when they no longer serve any practical purpose. The concrete, washed down to steel foundations in some areas and in others caked with hardening adobe, was as grandiose as the Roman Colosseum. Grady the pilgrim pondered the astonishing collaboration of nature and humanity.

As the teacher-cook moved south, the dogs and coyote spread farther apart, unnerving him as they dashed out of sight to sniff through ruins, bark and howl, nip at one another and race away, disappearing down sinkholes. As the cook worried over his responsibility, he imagined how useful a bird's-eye view would be for keeping track of his charges. He lifted his right arm, then the left. Seeing corresponding movements in an imagined aerial point of view, he made several more tests. Only minutes later, he came to the astonishing conclusion that his new vision was not a daydream but an out-of-body experience that existed in real time. For the first time in his life he was in two places at once. Seeing only from an aerial view at this moment, rather than ground level, an awkward navigation system for an uninitiated hiker, Grady tripped over the rubble of a collapsed retaining wall. Shins badly bruised, the Kitchen volunteer lay prone, exhausted, and in pain.

In that position of helplessness, as he felt electric current pulse through his arms, legs, and hands, the shower of images began. Beasts and humans, of all descriptions, disintegrated and reassembled in different configurations. The bimorphic creatures howled and sang, whirled and danced in the direction of a figure standing at the hub

of their circle atop a small conductor's pedestal. Grady tried to get a better vantage point in order to see the face of the conductor but could never see more than shoulders, neck, and the back of a head covered with silver hair. It was hard for the cook to judge how long he lay at the first station of his pilgrimage, the first inn of rest on his way to Dana Point. But when he got to his feet, the dogs were there, tongues lolling, drooling jowls folded back into crazed smiles, waiting for him to move on.

Although short stretches of the freeway were in almost pristine condition, there were so many breaks in the road it was impassable to any vehicle, even a Hum Vee. As the man and his dog companions worked their way past the ruins of the Tustin Marketplace, they saw smoke rising from within the complex. Remembering the bands of armed vigilantes they'd already dodged along the way, they picked up their pace. The shepherd and his flock passed into Irvine, unidentifiable if it weren't for the large number of military freight and personnel helicopters going in and out of what was left of the old El Toro Marine Air Base. For a moment Grady fantasized about the ease with which Dana Point would be reached if he could only hitch a ride on one of them. But when he considered the manhunt that was on for anyone connected with the Magnificent Seven, he decided to avoid presenting an easy target, even from the air. That was when his aerial vision lifted him from ground level once again, and he watched the dogs and himself become invisible to air traffic.

Impassable though it may have been to vehicles, the Golden State Freeway offered a reliable guide to anyone proceeding on foot. The ruins delivered the teacher-cook and the dogs to Laguna Hills by sunset, and they made good progress up the Crown Valley Parkway by nightfall. He kept pushing through darkness and exhaustion until finally deciding to stop for a rest. It was cold, and having left his tent that morning unprepared for what he would eventually undertake, Grady was badly underdressed and underequipped. Shivering as he squatted at the edge of the parkway's broken margins, the dogs he was shepherding edged in close, insulated him from the damp night air. All of these animals—two-legged and four-legged—cuddled and shared warmth. All except the coyote, who continued to crash through nearby brush.

When he awoke from the second station of his pilgrimage, Grady rose to continue his journey. He'd decided during his dream, a lucid one, that it can never be too late to begin a new life. However, remembering Skulford Elephant's odd warning back at Annie's Soup Kitchen, he also concluded that personal choice had little to do with it. The dream this time was brief. A human face pressed against a filmy wall that resembled opaque cellophane. The physiognomy was familiar, but Grady could not place it. After repeatedly pushing into the filmy barrier and passing through a number of exaggerated expressions, the face opened its mouth and tore through with its teeth. He knew the face immediately. It was the squat and surly man who had always insulted his food at the Kitchen, habitually snarling in response to polite treatment. The man who'd been banished time after time, the one he'd often seen suffer the wrath of Annie's hand. It was Roderigo.

Groggy and stiff, Grady had no idea how long he'd been down but was increasingly confident he could beat the Mysterious Stranger's deadline. The dogs and coyote were still frisky, and they set a brisk pace westward over rolling hills to the Pacific Coast Highway. Having arrived at Highway 1, they moved quickly over its remains to Dana Point harbor. The guide walked the rough-planked docks searching for the *Todos Santos*, then paused to glance over his shoulder at the hills to the east. They were silhouetting themselves against the first glimmers of dawn.

The captain's name was Scott, first or last he didn't specify. He accepted the paper bag without inspecting its contents. Bundled up in a hooded gray sweatshirt, he was as hard to read as the face behind the cellophane. What the cinched hood did reveal—washed-out blue eyes and a stubble that seemed to cover his face from forehead to

chin—was about as personable as a hedgehog. Uninterested in listening to any of Grady's explanatory comments, the captain returned to his business below deck. It was as if the man had read the script long before the acting out of it had begun. After the dogs were on board and began to settle down to sneezing, stretching, and sniffing the decks and gear, the captain moved to the wheel and made final preparations to get under way.

In spite of the captain's unwillingness to chat, the cook had a number of serious questions to ask. What was the destination of the *Todos Santos*? What were his instructions now? Was he required to accompany the animals on the voyage, or was going along even an option? As he sat in the stern of the cruiser, the animals perked their ears, whined and whimpered, then smiled again, dropping a shower of saliva drops on the deck. Grady briefly considered disembarking, with the object of trying to find his way back to some remnant of his former life, but only briefly. After Scott cast off, and the *Todos Santos* chugged quietly through the harbor and past the breakwater, the former cook turned northwest toward the cliff Richard Henry Dana described in *Two Years Before the Mast*. This was where tanned hides from Mission San Juan Capistrano, processed by the slave labor of Juaneño Indians, were tossed down one hundred feet to the Yankee traders anchored below.

As the cruiser picked up speed and moved out to sea, taking a west-southwest bearing, Grady saw the pink and gold of the dawn reach out to him from behind the hills. Watching the boat's wake, he heard moans and low guttural noises at his back. It was the dogs again. He turned and observed them as they lay panting in various positions on the deck. There was an odd turning in their eyes as their snouts, ears, and paws oozed in fluid distortions. The clawed protrusions on the terrier were growing longer, rounder, evolving toward something that more closely resembled human digits. Hair was receding on some parts of the canine bodies and at the same time filling out on others. The bodies themselves were becoming larger and longer. As Grady's heartbeat increased, he remembered that the Mysterious Stranger had told him to be prepared for anything on this pilgrimage. And yet there was no fear. For the first time in his life, he was convinced that he was in precisely the right place and time. This was the kind of mission that had always eluded him. As Grady dreamily counted the animals, he came up with six instead of seven, and a flash of panic seized him. The silver coyote was missing. Glancing overboard, he could see nothing but waves and wake. Then he heard it: Roderigo's obnoxious, yipping laughter rising from within the cabin.

~

California has always revealed itself according to migratory patterns: opening and closing, moving and standing still. Its truest native sons and daughters, the gray whales, have cruised north and south in their seasons, often within clear sight of shore, for millions of years. The coast itself has changed, its rocky shoreline migrating, sometimes revolting violently, and then lapsing into years of slow, imperceptible evolution. The *Todos Santos* and its passengers were on their way to the joyous breeding and surfing grounds of those same gray whales. The Golden State would be lonesome for its heroes. But the promise of that lovely woman called California, snug and sassy inside her irresistible skin, would also inevitably draw the conjurers back again. Regardless of the spirit expended in dream work and all of those crushing hangovers that follow it, regardless of the success or failure of imagined cities, both visible and invisible, along the coast, that woman—the keeper of the feathered hope we call the hawk—will always be well worth the trip.